Regard for the Living
by Timothy M. Savage

© Copyright 2025 Timothy M. Savage

ISBN 979-8-88824-688-7

All rights reserved. No part of this publication may be reproduced, stored in a retrieval system, or transmitted in any form or by any means—electronic, mechanical, photocopy, recording, or any other—except for brief quotations in printed reviews, without the prior written permission of the author.

This is a work of fiction. All the characters in this book are fictitious, and any resemblance to actual persons, living or dead, is purely coincidental. The names, incidents, dialogue, and opinions expressed are products of the author's imagination and are not to be construed as real.

Edited by Becky Hilliker
Cover design by Catherine Herold

Published by

köehlerbooks™

3705 Shore Drive
Virginia Beach, VA 23455
800-435-4811
ww.koehlerbooks.com

REGARD FOR THE LIVING

TIMOTHY M. SAVAGE

VIRGINIA BEACH
CAPE CHARLES

In memory of my brother,
the first US Navy Hospital Corpsman I ever met.

Scott Joseph Savage
1964–2024

1

Saturday, September 22

8:29 p.m.

A BLACKED-OUT HYUNDAI GENESIS sports car wove in and out of traffic on East Girard Avenue. It skidded to a stop in the right lane at the Frankford Avenue traffic light. When the light changed, the engine revved and its tires squealed, leaving a puff of smoke as the car accelerated westbound. At the end of the block, the car was much faster than the traffic flow as it shot around a right curve and drifted away from the sidewalk, fishtailing as the tires slipped on the embedded trolley tracks in the left lane. Approaching a knot of slower cars in the left lane at North Second Street, it swerved into the right lane and blew by them, kicking up road dust and loose gravel. With no traffic ahead, the car's engine screamed even louder as it recklessly passed pedestrians and trolley boarding platforms.

The Hyundai was unimpeded for a dozen blocks, until it encountered stopped vehicles obstructing both sides of the street. Braking hard, the tires squealed and smoked, but the Hyundai was still too fast to stop. The front wheels pivoted right and left, pulling the nose of the car up onto the sidewalk. The rear wheels bounced and skidded over the curb and the right rear fender dragged along the wall of a condemned apartment building. In a cloud of burnt rubber smoke, the car came to a stop against the building.

Behind the car's damaged body panels, the engine was silent, but soon ground back to life, roaring through the tailpipes. The tires spun for a moment before regaining purchase on the pavement and backing the car off the sidewalk. Stopping in the street, the left door popped open, and the silhouette of the driver's head extended above the roofline of the car. Against the wall of the building lay the mangled and bloody shape of a pedestrian, an old woman and her crushed handcart of belongings.

The driver yelled back into the car, "You see that, Busta? I think she's dead!" and disappeared back into the car. The door slammed shut, and in the next moment, the car left a patch of rubber on the road as it roared in reverse to the next intersection then disappeared into the darkness of an unlit side street.

2

Saturday, September 29

7:10 a.m.

KEVIN MALONEY'S EYES flicked open at the mechanical sound of the front door deadbolt unlocking. He raised his head off the couch, where he was sleeping, and scanned the nearly black basement apartment. The only discernible shapes were the two windows, where morning light leaked around the edges of the shades. The familiar creaking of hinges punctuated the gray arc of light swinging across the room as the front door opened. Silhouetted in the entryway was a sizable man holding a duffle bag and a plastic grocery sack. Kevin grunted in recognition of his older brother and mumbled, "Hey, Brian."

"Sorry bro. I was trying to be quiet," Brian replied.

Kevin said, "You were, but there's nothing you can do about the fact that Philly's seventy decibels of ambient noise isn't enough to mask the sounds of a well-lubricated lock."

"I suppose you're right about that." Dropping his work bag on the floor, Brian closed the door and sidestepped to the kitchenette, where he turned on the light over the sink. He laid out the contents of the sack and asked, "Want breakfast? I got firehouse leftovers."

Kevin rolled upright on the couch and rubbed his eyes. After a protracted yawn he agreed. "Yeah, sure." Dressed in a dark blue T-shirt and matching shorts, both emblazoned with yellow block letters that spelled NAVY, Kevin stood up and stretched, bumping his knuckles on the low ceiling. He then ran his hands over his close-cut copper hair and freckled face, and asked, "Since when does your crew have leftovers?"

Brian chuckled as he turned a knob on the control panel of the little oven. "When the rookies are running the kitchen."

Kevin grunted as he shuffled toward the kitchenette.

Brian continued. "They either don't know how to cook, or how much to cook." After laying some plastic-wrapped items on the counter, he continued. "In this case, they cook well, but the portion size was way off." Brian unwrapped the four English muffin breakfast sandwiches and placed them on a cookie sheet. He slid them into the oven and set the timer dial on the control panel. Turning back to his younger brother, Brian asked, "So, anything from your new mentor, the mysterious deacon?"

Kevin replied, "It's protodeacon."

"Oh, right. Protodeacon," Brian redoubled. "What's the Proto part mean, anyway?"

Kevin said, "It means his bishop picked him to be the highest-ranking guy in a group of deacons. I'm going to meet him Monday, after he gets back from Saint Sophia."

Brian asked, "Saint Sophia?"

Kevin replied, "That's his Ukrainian Orthodox Seminary in Jersey." Brian grunted in response and Kevin continued. "And Uncle Matt says our archdiocese is working out the kinks on my new position. He said I'll probably start after the end of the current pay period."

"Very nice. And how was your outing with Detective Johnston? You get to see her backup piece again?"

Kevin snickered before saying, "It was fine, and no, there was no gunplay . . . or any other kind of play."

Brian said, "I figured that night with the unconscious cat guy in the stairwell was an anomaly. Well, maybe next time, eh? That is, if there is a next time. Will there be a next time?"

Kevin broke into a short laugh, then said, "Listen to you stammering along."

Brian asked, "Is there, or is there not going to be more of Detective Della Johnston?"

Kevin's face turned serious, and he asked Brian, "So, if a female says they are dating a guy, does that make them boyfriend and girlfriend? Or is that another kind of level?"

Brian smiled as he turned away and said, "Ah, the work of the older brother is never done." Looking back at Kevin from the door to his bedroom, Brian added, "We will discuss this, and other relationship topics after I take a quick shower. In the meantime, don't let breakfast burn."

3

Monday, October 17

1:10 p.m.

THE SOARING WINDOWS of the Ukrainian Catholic Cathedral of the Immaculate Conception bathed the vast, sky-blue interior of the building in shades of yellow sunbeams. Far above the main floor, the bear-like Protodeacon Stepan Micevych stood at the front rail of the choir balcony. A deep black cassock, with a hood draping down the back, covered his bulk from collar to floor. Stepan's equally black eyes were surrounded by wrinkles. His scalp was devoid of hair, and a full, graying beard obscured the lower half of his face. Despite the aging appearance, his physique was still animated with purpose and strength. Kevin, emerging from the stairwell, came to a stop next to Stepan and said, "This is amazing."

Withdrawing a hand from under the wide sleeve of his cassock, Stepan gestured across the octagonal-shaped sanctuary. On the opposite side, the altar was isolated from the rest of the space by an ornate gold screen. In a low-pitched rumble, he said, "You see the figures on the iconostasis?"

Kevin nodded.

"Those are paintings of the four evangelists, Matthew, Mark, Luke, and John. And on the doors leading into the altar? That depicts the Angel Gabriel, announcing to Mary that she will be the Mother of God." When the echo of the statement dissipated, Stepan added, "This whole place, this institution, is full of stories from which we are to learn."

Kevin's gaze followed the layers of arches up to the gold-trimmed dome and the image of Jesus holding an open book upon which the Greek letters Alpha and Omega were written. He then asked, "Just out of curiosity, why do the Orthodox churches have these crazy domes?"

Stepan grunted slightly and replied, "You see, there is another story. They are inspired by the Hagia Sophia, in Constantinople. It was built by Romans before the fall of their empire, and you know how they were with the arches and domes, yes? Anyway, it was once the largest church in all of Christendom. Then the Ottomans turned it into the largest mosque." After a pause he added, "The Ottomans. You know about them?"

Kevin said, "Not really. Aren't they the guys with the scimitars and hookahs?"

Stepan grunted again. "It is a shame nobody takes them seriously anymore." Then looking up, as if speaking to the image of Christ, he said, "Always we are teaching . . . yes, I know." Turning his attention back to Kevin, he said, "You see, the Ottomans were a great military power for more than five hundred years. They controlled the eastern Mediterranean and much of the Arab lands, but like all empires, when the collapse came in the last century, it left behind complicated problems. Many fights over territory in what your comrades called 'the sandbox' came from the Allied partitioning of the Ottoman Empire at the end of the Great War."

Kevin waited until the echoes of Stepan's voice died away before asking, "You mean World War I?"

Stepan nodded before saying, "British and French negotiators with a map and a pen divided up the Middle East, ignoring cultures and tribes, and always saving the best parts for themselves."

"That helps explain why I never understood what we were doing when I was over in that part of the world." Then changing subjects, Kevin said, "Speaking of complications, I'm not sure how I am supposed to fill your shoes."

"You will do fine." Stepan paused to stroke his beard a moment and then continued. "You will have difficulties; I cannot say you won't. Maybe less with the cat and more with institutions."

Kevin's eyes squinted as he asked, "I'm not sure I follow."

Shaking his head, Stepan continued. "People prefer habit and routine over problems. Only when problems like the cat get big do the people make a fuss."

Kevin tilted his head in response.

Stepan continued. "But how do we spread the word about the cat problem without too much noise? You see, if a cardinal, or the pope," he said, gesturing with both hands toward the ornate icons at the far end of the sanctuary, "or even a venerated saint tried to explain the nature of our problem in public, they would be mocked. The various factions in the Church would use it as a chance to diminish them."

Kevin asked, "Politics inside the church are really that cutthroat?"

Stepan answered, "There is always infighting, even in the name of God."

"I guess I need to keep my eyes and ears open," Kevin observed.

Stepan agreed, "You will always be under examination by the factions that see this institution as a business."

After a pause, Kevin said, "Then I guess we continue to work this problem on the down-low."

"Down-low is street slang? Like secret?" Stepan asked.

"Not exactly like a secret. We only tell the people who need to know. If the cat problem gets bigger than we can handle, we can always ask for help later. For now"—Kevin held his forefinger before his lips and whispered—"hush-hush."

"Yes, hush-hush," agreed Stepan before changing the subject. "What do you think of the cathedral?"

"Pretty fantastic. I grew up within a few miles of here and didn't know it existed. The altar screen is remarkable," Kevin offered. He then asked, "Why don't we share more about our faith traditions? We're really on the same team."

"It is a mystery to me, but I think there are reasons my community keeps to itself, staying on the down-low," Stepan replied.

"You are a fast learner, aren't you?" Kevin chuckled.

"In the old country there was always persecution from the government or the Russian Church. Many times, my people had to go into hiding. Entire monasteries and convents went underground."

"I guess the Communists weren't big supporters?" Kevin asked.

"In Poland we had a hidden convent for seventy years. The Party could never find it. If they did, it would have been bad, very bad for the sisters," Stepan said while drawing a finger across his throat. "But enough of the cathedral. Let us go see your uncle."

"I'm sure he's excited to get this going," Kevin agreed as he followed the protodeacon to the stairs.

On the main level, they passed through several doors and a choir storage room until they emerged into the dome-ceilinged apse. Pausing before the entry doors, Stepan turned toward Kevin. Extending a hand from under his cassock, he gripped Kevin's shoulder and said, "Remember, my church has a long history of the hush-hush. If you need sanctuary or a guardian angel, you will find it here."

Kevin looked directly into Stepan's eyes and nodded in silence. Stepan grinned, then briskly headed for the door, saying, "Come, I have a driver waiting for us."

Kevin followed the protodeacon down the stone front steps to North Franklin Street. A spotless black Lincoln sedan with heavily tinted windows was parked against the curb. The driver, dressed in a black suit and tie and wearing Wayfarer sunglasses, was leaning against the right rear fender conversing on a cell phone. Seeing them approach, the driver flipped the phone closed and hustled to the rear door. He opened it for Stepan.

Stepan nodded and said, "Thank you, Borys," as he ducked into the car. Kevin instinctively rounded the car to the left side and entered the rear door. When the driver was seated behind the wheel, Stepan said, "The seminary, please."

Kevin looked over the interior of the car and then commented, "Not exactly on the down-low in this car."

"The rector insisted. He said it was faster and safer to have Borys drive. Because I don't know the city so well, I agreed."

Kevin smiled at the explanation and observed, "Well, it is more comfortable than my Jeep."

The sedan traveled west on Fairmont Avenue at a leisurely clip. Impatient drivers passed when they could. As often as not, the passing cars were stopped at the next traffic light when the Town Car closed the distance again. Several hundred feet from the traffic light, when he should have begun braking, the red traffic light switched to green and Borys motored through the intersection at speed.

After observing this pattern for a dozen traffic lights, Kevin said, "I can see why the rector said it would be faster and safer. Either Borys is super lucky with the traffic lights, or he has a system. How is it we never get stopped?"

"You are most observant, but I don't know the answer," Stepan said. "Maybe you should ask Borys."

Kevin leaned forward in the seat and scanned the dashboard. He pointed toward a black plastic box attached to the sun visor.

"Hey Borys, what's that gizmo?"

"Emergency vehicle preemption—makes green light on command," Borys grunted.

"Well, that's handy, but it can't be legal," Kevin declared.

"For you, no. For me? Special exemption."

4

Monday, October 17

2:29 p.m.

BRIGHT SUNLIGHT GLINTED off the black Lincoln sedan as it rolled through the iron gates at the street entrance of the St. Charles Seminary. Slowing to a stop at the guard booth, a uniformed man waved in recognition and raised the barricade. Borys drove ahead and circled to the right behind the massive seminary complex. He halted the car on the west side of the building, and Borys hustled out of the driver seat to open the right rear door. Stepan stepped out at the same time Kevin emerged from the other side.

"Thank you," Stepan said. Borys nodded silently and closed the door. Kevin circled behind the car and joined the other two men standing at the right rear of the car. "Please lead the way." Stepan gestured to Kevin and then said to the driver, "We'll be a while."

The Lincoln silently motored away as they made their way to

Father Matthew O'Conner's faculty office. The old priest met them in the hall outside his door. "I'm so glad you are here, and perfect timing too. Come," invited the priest. "We're going to meet some people who will explain the arrangements."

Turning corners and passing through doorways, the trio moved farther into the massive complex at Father Matthew's shuffling speed. "Kevin, I think you will find the accommodations to your liking," he huffed, as they passed occasional faculty members and seminarians in the long passageway. The corridor finally dead-ended at an elevator and stairway. Father Matthew pressed the call button and the doors opened immediately. They entered the car, and the doors closed.

"Three, if you would, please," the priest said.

"Going up." Kevin grinned as he pressed the button.

Arriving at the third floor, the elevator door opened into a tile-floored hallway. It was lined with tall, vertical windows on the left, and dark wood doors on the right. The doors were marked only with black number tags at the top of the frame. The ceiling was lined with fluorescent light fixtures along its full length, but they were off, leaving the linear space illuminated only by the indirect sunlight of the early fall day. The windows gave a view of the main gate and the residential neighborhood across the street. Beyond the trees and roofs, the buildings of downtown Philadelphia peaked above the horizon.

Father Matthew led the way down the hall. After passing several doors, he stopped at the one labeled 319 and said, "Here we are." The door opened into a conference room. An elliptical table was oriented parallel to the hallway and surrounded by eight chairs. Windows, like those in the hall, formed the opposite wall. The blinds were partially drawn, making bars of bright sun and shadow across the dark wood furnishings.

Seated across from the door, a middle-aged man in the black attire of a priest looked up from a notebook and a small stack of papers. "Enter and have a seat," he said in a monotone voice while gesturing to the chairs on the door side of the table. "Kevin, it is so good to meet you. I'm Father John Tucker."

Kevin extended a hand across the table, but the priest was already looking back at his papers. "Nice to meet you," he said, his voice trailing off as he sank into the middle chair. Stepan and Father Matthew sat on either side of Kevin.

"I'm the archbishop's vice chancellor," Father Tucker declared. "I will be your point of contact with the Church. Your assignments will come from my office. If you have any questions or problems, they should be addressed only to me." Handing a business card across the table, he continued. "This is the number you should call if you need anything. When the switchboard answers, use no names. Just ask for room 319. The call will be routed to me no matter where I am. Understand?"

"I think so," Kevin replied.

"Good," Father Tucker affirmed. Folding his notebook closed on the stacks of papers, he announced, "I'm going to leave now, but I want you to stay put. Representatives of the relevant departments will come into the room and explain the details of your engagement."

Kevin nodded as the priest departed the room. When the door closed behind him, he turned to Father Matthew and said, "I thought you said I was going to like the arrangements."

"Rest easy," he chuckled. "The archbishop's staff always take themselves too seriously."

Stepan chimed in, whispering in Kevin's ear, "This Tucker is what spies call a cutout. Like a circuit breaker between you and the important people. If this program goes poorly, the damage to the institution might consume him, but it will go no farther."

Just as Kevin let out the long breath he was holding, the door clicked open behind him. A small elderly woman in the dark blue habit of some unidentified order of sisters shuffled into the room. She carried an overstuffed folder and circled around the table. She held out a hand to each of the men. They shook hands and she smiled with a warm glow in her cheeks and a soft reflection in her eyes. "I'm Sister Elizabeth from the finance and accounting office. All my friends call me Betty."

"It's nice to meet you, Sister," Kevin said in a relaxed voice.

"I'm here to complete your employment documents and set up your banking privileges."

"Okay," Kevin replied.

"We'll start with the usual W-4, I-9, and direct deposit authorization." Betty slid the forms and a pen across the table to Kevin. "I think you will find all the information is pretyped on the forms. Don't worry about the supporting documents; we have copies of everything we need. Just double-check the information and sign in the appropriate block."

Kevin reviewed the forms in silence while Father Matthew studied the woman. Finally, Mathew asked, "You don't have a pin or device from your order? Are you a Sister of Saints Francis and Clare?"

"No," she said before quickly turning to the folder and extracting another pack of papers. "This is your new employee packet." She addressed Kevin as he continued glancing at the forms. "It contains all the particulars about your compensation and benefits package, health and dental plan, and so on." Kevin nodded as she continued. "Read them over when you get home. It should be very straightforward. We get paid every other week. Your first deposit will be on the twenty-eighth. Also, inside the folder is your company credit card, medical card, and your department identification card."

Kevin signed the payroll forms and slid them back across the table. He pulled the packet open and fished the three cards from an envelope. The first was a white plastic medical card with his full name and the current date. The next was a green and white ID badge that listed his name as *K. Maloney*. Under a recent photo the title *Assistant Facilities Manager* was printed. The third was an

American Express Card embossed with his name.

"The badge has a magnetic strip for the door and after-hours access. The AmEx is for all expenses related to your work. Supplies, travel, and so on." Betty stood up, collected the papers back into her folder and started around the table saying in a quick clip, "Any questions? No? Then I'll be on my way. It was a real pleasure." A moment later the door clicked shut again.

The three men sat in silence for a long while before Stepan spoke, saying, "Betty might be somebody's sister, but I don't think she's a real sister."

Just then the door opened again. This time a burly man dressed in a dark-green work uniform and brown boots came through the door. He had wispy blond hair combed over a balding head. His face was round and jolly, and his hands were thick and calloused. The sweet scent of freshly mown grass wafted in his wake. He circled the table and parked himself in the recently vacated chair on the far side. Reaching across the table and gripping Kevin's hand in his thick fingers, he said, "I'm Earl Warren." Turning, he said, "Hello Father O'Conner," and shook hands with the old priest and then shook hands with Stepan. Stepan nodded with a slight grin as Earl continued. "I guess I'm going to be your supervisor—for pay purposes. They tell me not to expect you around much, because you'll be working off campus most of the time."

"So, it seems," Kevin agreed.

"My office is next to the vehicle shed on the northwest corner of the campus. Stop in when you get a chance. We'll get you set up with a uniform account and a locker. Suppose I can get you out on a mower once in a while? We can't cut grass fast enough around here."

"Sure thing," Kevin agreed with a smile. "By the way, I might need some tools for my job. Can I get them through you?"

"Yeah. We can order whatever you need. I got accounts and catalogs from all over. I also understand you'll be moving into the old farmhouse at the end of the lane. You'll need these," Earl said, while fishing a key ring from his shirt pocket and sliding it across the table. "Nobody's lived in there for a while, so let me know if you need anything fixed."

"Good to know." Kevin nodded in surprise.

"Well, I guess that's it; that's everybody you're supposed to meet," Earl said as he hefted himself out of the chair and made his way to the door.

"Just a sec," Kevin interrupted. "Is there any reason my brother Brian couldn't bunk with me in the farmhouse?"

Earl paused for a moment, scratched his ear, and grunted. Resuming his progress, he said, "I guess that's up to you." Opening the door, he added, "If there's nothing else, I'll see you around."

When the door clicked behind him, Kevin looked back and forth between Father Matthew and Protodeacon Stepan and said, "That's it?"

"I believe it is," Father Matthew shrugged. "Welcome aboard!"

5

Monday, October 1

9:36 p.m.

KEVIN SLOUCHED ON the brown corduroy couch, his head resting on the back cushion. His eyes were focused on the ancient tube television positioned against the wall. On the other end of the couch, Brian sat upright, slightly leaning forward, attentively following the NFL Monday Night Football game between the Bears and Cowboys. An empty pizza box lay on the floor between them. At a commercial break, Brian looked at his brother, and asked, "You going to fill me in on your meeting today?"

"I was going to say something at the next commercial break," Kevin mumbled.

On the screen the football game cut away to an advertisement for Old Spice Deodorant. Brian looked at Kevin and asked, "Well?"

"Fine, but first, I was wondering, are you real attached to this apartment?"

"Are you kidding me? You think I like living in a subterranean shoebox?"

"I guess that's a no." Kevin grinned and pushed himself into a more upright position on the couch. "One of the benefits of the job is a house on the grounds of the seminary. I'm going to move out there, and I was thinking I could pay you back, you know, by giving you free room. There's plenty of space, and I'll probably be gone a lot. What do you think?"

"Nah, I can't do that," Brian scoffed. "You need your own place."

"Really, I don't think it will be a problem. It's an old farmhouse with four bedrooms. Way bigger than one single guy needs."

"We'll look at it before we make any decisions," Brian compromised as the television image returned to the football game.

"They got me all set up. I feel like a secret agent. I'm undercover as an assistant facilities manager." Brian nodded and grinned as Kevin continued his description. "I'll be getting paid every two weeks, I have a company credit card, a full benefits package, and no rent."

"Wow, that's huge. With all that, who needs the fire department?"

"Yeah, no kidding," Kevin agreed.

Brian asked, "What's the detective got to say about it?"

"I haven't told her," Kevin said in a declining voice.

"About the job, the farmhouse, or asking me to be your roomie?" Brian asked.

"She knows I'm taking the job, but I haven't told her about anything else. We haven't had a chance to talk," Kevin shrugged. "And maybe I'm a little worried. I don't want to freak her out about my living at the seminary."

"To be honest, I'm a little uneasy about the idea myself. You know, all the priests and everything watching our every move."

"It's not like they are going to be in the house with us. Nobody's going to judge you every time you cuss. It'll be fine. Besides, the farmhouse is like a half mile from the nearest campus building.

Nobody will know we're there."

"If I move in, somebody's going to know when I come and go. It will get awkward," Brian countered. "I don't like that, and the seminarians might not like it either."

"I might have a solution for that, but first you've got to come out and look at the place."

"All right, fine," Brian relented. "We'll go take a look tomorrow morning."

6

Tuesday, October 2

10:12 a.m.

KEVIN COASTED HIS white Jeep Wrangler to a stop at the barricaded entrance to the seminary. He set the parking brake and put the shift lever in neutral while Brian waved at the mirrored window of the gate house on the right side of the drive. A uniformed man appeared from behind the structure and stepped up to the passenger side of the Jeep. He leaned against the windshield frame and addressed Kevin through the open window. "Mr. Maloney, how are you this morning?"

"Good, but Tony, you can call me Kevin. I'm just a worker bee like you."

"Okay, but it doesn't feel right. You roll with some bigwigs."

"Really, it's fine. Anyway, Tony, this is my brother Brian. He'll be here a lot. Can we get him a permanent pass or something?"

"Aw, he doesn't need that. I'll pass it along to the other shifts.

Hang on." The guard ducked back into the booth and returned with a little notebook and pen. Turning to Brian, the guard said, "What kind of car do you drive, Brian?"

"A red Jeep Cherokee."

"And the license tag number?"

Brian recited slowly. "A-N-D-two-one-two-four."

"Got it," the guard declared. "Anything else Mr. Maloney? I mean, Kevin and Brian?"

Brian chimed in again, "Do you keep a log of the vehicles that come and go?"

"We're supposed to, but to tell you the truth, we really only record the tags of the cars turning around in the driveway or the ones we turn away."

"Thanks, Tony," Brian said with a wave as Kevin shifted gears.

"Okay, fellas. Have a good day."

After the guard raised the barricade, the Jeep revved slightly and eased past the guard booth. Turning right, Kevin steered along a lane that led into the western portion of the sprawling complex. Passing apartment buildings and a chapel, the ground rose slightly to a crest, then the lane turned left and sloped down toward the southwest corner of the property. To the left spread a sea of neat lawn and hedges, to the right a fence line was overgrown with shrubs and trees. Ahead, the high-ground view revealed a hospital and roof tops all the way into the neighboring Delaware County.

"That's some buena vista there, Kevin," Brian commented as Kevin slowed the Jeep with a downshift. At the low corner of the property along East Lancaster Avenue, an outcropping of trees and shrubs concealed a white two-story house. It was square in shape, with symmetrically placed windows and doors and two small brick chimneys in the center of the roof.

Kevin turned into the shady drive that curved behind the house and braked to a stop at the back door. "This is the place," he announced.

"I thought you said it was a half mile from the nearest building.

It looks more like a couple hundred yards to me," Brian observed.

"It's far enough, okay?" Kevin replied as he exited the Jeep. "Come on, I want to show you something before we head inside."

"I'm coming," Brian grunted and followed Kevin around to the front of the house.

Standing near the end of the driveway and the lane coming down from the main complex, Kevin pointed to the overgrown fence along Lancaster Avenue. "See that gap down there? That's a back gate. If I can get Mr. Warren's approval, we'll get an automatic opener on that, and we'll have our own driveway."

"Boy-o, that's some good thinking. Skip the front gate all together."

"Not bad, eh?" Kevin turned back toward the house and said, "Come on. Let's see what I've signed up for."

Leading the way up the stone steps, Kevin pulled open a screen door and inserted a hand-worn brass key into the deadbolt. The lock clicked open easily, and Kevin pushed the door inward. He stepped into the spacious kitchen and moved aside for Brian to follow him in. The brothers stood at the entry, surveying the harvest-gold appliances and faded yellow-striped wallpaper running down to a pale-yellow faux brick linoleum floor.

"Well, the kitchen hasn't been updated since 1976, but it's functional," Kevin observed. "Mr. Warren said he'd fix anything that didn't work, so we got that."

Brian twitched his nose and said, "Little musty, but not life-threatening," then walked to the sink and rotated a knob next to the faucet. When nothing came out, he said, "I think the water's been turned off. Need that checked."

Kevin crossed to a yellow wall-mounted phone with a coiled cord that hung all the way to the floor. He held the handset to his ear. "Dial tone. Probably on the seminary phone system." Pressing the 0 button, he said, "Let's see what happens." Kevin listened and then said, "Hi, Kevin Maloney here. Just checking to see if the line works." He listened a little longer, then said, "Okay, thanks."

Turning to Brian, Kevin said, "Yep, seminary phone. Dial 9 to get an outside line."

"No phone bill then. I guess that's a plus," Brian shrugged. He then pointed to a pegboard on the wall behind the door. "Nothing says home like a place to hang your coat and keys."

"I guess you're right. Come on, let's see what else there is," Kevin encouraged as he moved through a dark-stained wood-framed doorway. In the next room, the shades were drawn over the windows, casting the living room in a dim yellow light. The walls were covered with a flower-patterned paper, and the floor was wide wood planks stained almost black. A staircase on the far wall disappeared into the upper floor.

Brian stepped in behind him and said, "The brown corduroy couch will fit in here really well. Like they were made for each other." He then worked around the perimeter of the room, pointing to the outlets. "Still has ungrounded outlets." Looking up to the glass globe fixture in the center of the ceiling, he said, "Try flipping on the light."

Kevin looked at the area near the doorframe, but there was no switch. "Where is it?" he asked.

Passing an exterior door, Brian said, "Nothing over by the front door either. This place was probably built before electricity, so the switch could be anywhere. Try back in the kitchen."

Kevin ducked back into the previous room and a moment later there was an audible click and the glass globe lit up.

"That's it," Brian called out. "At least the power is on."

"Several push-button switches on the other side of the wall," Kevin stated as he walked back into the room.

"Hey look, there is a co-ax wall plate." Brian pointed to a spot low on the exterior wall. "You know what that means, right?"

"Cable TV!" Kevin declared with a grin. "I wonder if that's included in the package?"

"It would go a long way toward getting your brother to move in with you."

"All right, let's see what else there is," Kevin encouraged while Brian investigated another door on the far side of the stairs.

Swinging the door open, Brian said, "Bathroom wedged in when the house was modified for indoor plumbing. Original porcelain fixtures, and a free-standing fiberglass shower stall added somewhere down the line."

"That's promising. Have you seen any HVAC controls?"

Brian pointed to the center wall and said, "Here's the thermostat. There are also old-school cast iron grates to allow hot air to pass to the upper rooms." He gestured toward the ceiling.

Kevin scanned the floor and pointed to a modern register. "Here we go. Somebody put in ducting, so the furnace is probably in the cellar. No sign of a washer or dryer, but they might be down there too." Continuing to the base of the stairs, he said, "What wonders will we find up here?"

Brian replied, "I'm suspicious already."

At the top of the stairs, a landing opened into four doorways. Each door led to a small, empty bedroom. Kevin quickly scanned the rooms and returned to the landing while Brian surveyed them carefully. "They're all about the same. Two windows and no closet, except that one. The chimney cuts into it."

"I should have guessed there'd be no plumbing up here."

"It's not like we aren't sharing a bathroom now," Kevin observed.

"True, but it's only a two-step from where I lay my head."

"It won't hurt you to climb some stairs. Seen enough? Which room do you want?" Kevin asked.

"Who says I've decided to move in?"

"Whatever, but I'm taking this little room, if that's okay with you."

"It's your house, amigo," Brian agreed as he finished examining the third room before coming to the one Kevin had just claimed. Stepping through the doorway and turning around, Brian belted out, "Hey! You snookered me!"

Kevin laughed out loud and said, "For once—I get the fireplace and closet!"

7

Sunday, October 7

12:54 p.m.

THE BASEMENT APARTMENT was approaching maximum capacity. Kevin and Brian slouched outward on opposite ends of the corduroy couch like a matched set. Detective Johnston, her hair tied back under a green and white Eagles bandana, sank into a large pillow on the floor between the brothers. Mark Francini, dressed head to toe in a green Eagles track suit, reclined in a bean-bag chair at the end of the couch. All eyes were on the picture tube of the dusty wood-grained television set. The screen flashed info about each football team and players' statistics.

"I feel like this might be the end of an era," Mark declared.

"What do you mean?" inquired Brian after sipping from a bottle of beer.

"You know how things can come together? It's revolutionary or amazing for a while, then it just peters out. And if you try to recreate that sensation, it just never feels the same," Mark explained.

"For real?" Brian inquired, looking over at Mark with a distorted grin.

"Yeah, I mean, it's only been a month, but it feels like this was something really important, and now it's going away."

"Yo, Mark. I know the Eagles aren't real strong right now, and they're probably going to get mauled by the Steelers, but it's just football, man." Then gesturing toward Mark with his beer, Brian said, "As a sports reporter, you should be a little more dispassionate."

"Oh, I wasn't talking about the game. The Eagles kinda suck right now; everybody knows that. I was talking about here, this place. You know? Watching games in this apartment, just our little gang," Mark tried to explain.

"Did you start drinking before you got here?" Kevin asked with a laugh.

"Hey, pizon," Brian chuffed. "Nobody wants to hang out in a little crap hole like this forever, watching the game on a twenty-year-old set with marginal reception. After all, this isn't an episode of your favorite Thursday night sitcom."

"You guys lay off," Johnston interjected. "I know what you mean, Mark. This place, this time, it's a unique period tied to this apartment."

"Well, if you wanna move in on November first, I'll see what I can do," Brian said with a laugh. "I, for one, won't miss hunting for a parking space, or knocking my head on the low doorframes."

"And the cat? Remember, Uncle Matthew is sure there's more of them out there," Kevin lamented. "The fun and games are just getting started. In fact, I'm surprised another body hasn't turned up already. By my calendar, we're overdue."

"All right, enough," Brian asserted. "I'm watching a football game here, even if the Eagles are going to lose. We can talk about cats and touchy-feely stuff later."

"Thank you, bro," Kevin agreed, and silence overtook the room while the game got underway.

From the television, the announcer called out the players' names. "The Steelers' Shaun Suisham will kick, and Brandon Boykin is back for the catch..."

After the kickoff, the game gave way to a round of commercials and the conversation resumed.

"So, when is move-in day, again?" Mark asked.

"This Tuesday. You want to help?" Brian asked.

"Working, sorry," Mark replied.

"I'll be in Jersey," Johnston chimed in.

"It's better to wait until we've got some stuff in there anyway," Kevin mumbled, before perking up, and saying, "Oh, by the way, Mr. Warren said he's got window air-conditioning units for the house. He didn't put them in this year because nobody was living there."

"That will save you a couple bucks. He should have put one in anyway. It would have cut down on the mustiness. But we'll get it straightened out," Brian replied, then added, "How about the water?"

"He's got the plumber on it. And get this, there's a storeroom full of furniture too." Kevin added, "We can have our pick."

"Really?" Brian's voice sparked with enthusiasm. "We should check it out before we haul any of this broken-down junk out there."

"I can go over and have a look," Kevin said.

"Too bad I'm working. You should take Johnston along. She's bound to have better taste than you."

"Thanks, bro," Kevin chuckled.

"Yeah, thank you Brian." Johnston laughed. Pointing over her shoulder at Kevin, she said, "He thinks everything should be gray, green, or camouflage."

"What's wrong with that?" Kevin replied.

"If the only company you want is retired Marines, it's just fine," Johnston explained, "but if you want to attract anyone with more sense of taste than what's on their tongue, you'll need to do a little better."

Kevin rolled his eyes and shook his head. Mark and Brian

laughed and high-fived Johnston. "Tough crowd," Johnston said with a chuckle, then patted Kevin's leg.

"Good work, gang. And we'll meet at the new place for the next game?" Mark asked.

"Not unless Mr. Warren has a better TV than this. Otherwise, it's at your house," Brian declared. "Now everybody shush."

8

Monday, October 8

10:20 a.m.

DETECTIVE JOHNSTON GUIDED the blue unmarked police car northwest on Lancaster Avenue. In the right seat, Kevin examined the interior of the Chevrolet Impala and then looked directly at Johnston. "By the way, thanks for the ride."

"No problem. Kind of goes along with being in a you-and-me thing."

"Like dating?" Kevin suggested.

"Yeah. That," Johnston replied.

"Does that mean you'll take any excuse to hang out with me? Or will there generally be some kind of tit-for-tat favor thing?"

"Maybe both," Johnston replied with a slight grin.

Kevin made a quiet "hmmph," and then directed his attention to the radio equipment installed between the seats. Pointing to the hand microphone, he said, "Can I try it?"

"No," Johnston responded with a dead-serious expression.

"I'm very experienced with comm gear."

"Who are you going to call, and what would you say?" Johnston asked.

"I don't know. Maybe something from a cop TV show. Like, 'One Adam Twelve, calling all units! There is a ten seven twenty west bound on Lancaster!'"

"Very funny. I don't even think you should be in this car, let alone touching the equipment."

"Aw come on, touching your equipment is kind of my thing," Kevin teased, reaching across the seat toward her knee.

Smacking his hand away, Johnston mocked, "That's it, sailor. Just keep your hands to yourself and be quiet until we get to St. Charles. All right?"

Kevin folded his hands and sat up straight. "Yes, ma'am."

"That's better. And there is no such thing as a seven twenty in the Philly ten codes."

"I made it up," Kevin replied. "Want to know what it is?"

Johnston said, "Absolutely not. Just sit there quietly."

After a few minutes of silence where Kevin watched the passing scenery, he turned again to Johnston and asked, "You're not freaked out by this, are you?"

"What are you talking about?" she replied.

"I mean, we're not going too fast, are we?"

Johnston glanced over at Kevin for a moment before answering, "Too fast? Are you kidding me? We're not moving in together, and we're not getting married. No. I'm just going to look at some secondhand furniture and check out an old house."

"Okay, that's kind of what I thought."

Johnston glanced again, and said, "Are you okay with our relationship?"

Kevin answered, "It's fine. I mean, I haven't even been to your place. We're fine. Slow and steady wins the race."

"Good. This is serious business. We've only known each other for a couple months, and we don't want to do something we'll regret."

"Right," Kevin agreed. "So, about your place. How come I've never been invited over? I don't even know where it is."

Johnston looked from the road to Kevin and held his gaze for a moment. "It's not time yet."

Kevin turned his eyes back to the passenger window and sighed, "Okay. No problem. I'm sure you'll tell me when it's time."

As Johnston opened her mouth to speak again, she was cut off by the sound of digital chimes. "Hang on a second," she said as she fished in her purse and withdrew a flip-phone. Flicking it open, she held it to her ear and said, "Johnston." She listened for a moment and then said, "Got it." Snapping it shut, she dropped the phone back into her purse and turned the car into the next side street.

"What's up?" Kevin asked.

"You're back in the game," Johnston said as she maneuvered around the block. "The boss told me to get you over to the Eastern State Penitentiary Museum entrance as soon as possible."

"As in Senior Detective Caporaso?" Kevin questioned.

Johnston nodded. "The same."

"How did he know we're together?"

Johnston replied, "He doesn't. He probably figured I'd know how to find you, since you don't have a reliable form of communication."

"Smart guy. Did he say anything else?" Kevin enquired.

"Nope. Just where to go."

"Then I guess that's what we'll do."

Johnston turned northeast on 52nd Street into Fairmount Park and crossed the Schuylkill River on the Girard Bridge. As they ascended from the river, the trees and lawns gave way to crowded city streets. On eastbound Fairmount Avenue, traffic ground to a standstill at each stoplight, and Johnston began muttering under her breath with each halt. At each pause, Kevin examined the towering apartment buildings with shrubbery and waist-high decorative fences dominating the south side of the busy street. Then he turned his attention to the other side, where three-story row houses crowded the north sidewalk.

"You need an emergency vehicle preemption device," Kevin commented.

"Yeah, that'd be nice," she remarked. "What do you know about those?"

"I just heard about them from Stepan's driver. He's got one."

Johnston swore, "What the hell?"

Kevin smiled, "Said he had a 'special exemption.'"

"Of course—because there's so many life-or-death church emergencies. Sounds totally legitimate. Anyway, we're almost there. Just a little farther."

Two blocks ahead, the massive stone towers and walls of the penitentiary rose above the row houses and trees. Johnston slowed the car and began scanning the right side of the street, saying, "Tell me if you see a parking space."

Pointing ahead, Kevin said, "Directly in front of Jack's Firehouse."

"Yeah, got it," Johnston replied. She steered into the empty space in front of the century-old brick firehouse that had been converted into a restaurant. "You know, if we were going to Jack's, we'd have to park four blocks away."

"I've never been there. Maybe we should get a bite after we're done here," Kevin suggested. "Since this just became a business trip, I can try out my company card."

"You know we're going to look at a corpse, right? There might be all kinds of gore and guts, and you're thinking of lunch?" Johnston asked.

"You're right, it's a little early. Call it brunch."

Johnston rolled her eyes and switched off the car's engine, saying, "Oh brother. Let's go see what they found."

9

Monday, October 8

11:03 a.m.

THE EASTERN STATE Penitentiary's massive stone walls stretched two blocks and towered over Kevin and Johnston as they approached the main entrance. "I did a paper about this place in college. Well, not really about the place. More like the philosophy behind it."

"Oh yeah?" Kevin replied. "I just knew it was here. It always featured in the neighborhood ghost stories. I guess I should come back for a tour some time."

"You should. It's a very interesting facility. When it was built in the early 1800s, the city fathers wanted it to be a deterrent to crime. That's why it looks so imposing. A neo-gothic combination of giant fortress and cathedral that takes up four city blocks. At the time, it was the most expensive and largest public project in the country."

"Should be enough to scare most people," Kevin agreed, as they walked to the center of the south wall.

Entering the squat stone portico, Johnston said, "But that's the thing. Real criminals aren't like most people. They aren't built the same as you and me, so they don't see this as a deterrent. They know what's coming if they get caught, but they don't really think about getting caught. The future is as far away as the moon."

At the entryway, a young woman wearing a maroon shirt with an embroidered museum logo and a name tag spelling out *Molly* in multicolored letters greeted them from inside the door. "Welcome to Eastern State Penitentiary."

Flashing her badge, Johnston returned the greeting. "Hi, Molly, I'm Detective Johnston. Can you point us to the other police officers?"

"Oh sure," she said. "Go straight ahead through those gates, then turn right out the door. Follow the paved path inside the wall all the way around to the back of the yard. They are on the far side of the cellblocks. You can't miss them."

"That's a long way. Isn't there a shorter route?" Johnston asked.

"There probably is, but I don't know it for sure," Molly replied. "Much of the penitentiary is closed to the public. It's easy to get lost in here, so I recommend the long way around."

Johnston said, "Thanks," and led Kevin through the passage. Exiting into the daylight of the interior yard, she resumed her monologue. "You know why it's called a *penitentiary*, not a *prison*, right? That was a very deliberate distinction. This place was intended to give each inmate some alone time to contemplate his relationship with God. After doing some penance, they could rejoin the world as a reformed and productive member of society."

"Did it work?" Kevin asked. "I mean, they still use the term penitentiary, so it must have been a little bit successful."

"Not really. In my opinion, it could never work. A lot of criminals are just hell-bent on breaking the law, and no amount of reprogramming will fix 'em. But they tried. Each inmate went into an isolation cell. No human contact at all. Not with the staff, not with the other inmates, sometimes for years."

"That's harsh," Kevin observed.

"It is. And it mostly made people go crazy. But if they were docile and compliant, they called it a success. But the solitary confinement plan didn't last long. People are clever, especially natural rule breakers. They figured out how to tap codes, pass messages, bribe the staff, and before you know it, the solitude-with-God part was gone, and the place devolved into a big prison. The penitentiary part was doomed to fail even before they finished building the place."

Reaching the southeast corner of the yard, Johnston and Kevin turned around the end of Cellblock 1 and continued along the east wall. Passing the remains of a greenhouse, Kevin said, "I don't get the layout of the buildings."

"It's a wagon wheel. We're looking at the spokes. Each block has a long hall that leads to a hub in the center," Johnston explained. "This building is kind of the exception," she said, pointing to a structure that didn't match the surroundings. "It's Cellblock 15. The maximum-security unit. Of course, they called it Death Row, but nobody was executed here."

Another left turn around the end of Cellblock 3 in the northeast corner took them west along the wall. Ahead, across the facility's baseball diamond, Johnston nodded toward a small cluster of police personnel near the kitchen building. "I think that's where we're going."

Johnston and Kevin approached the group, waving to the uniformed officer who stepped toward them. The officer nodded and said, "Top o' the morning, detective. That was quick."

"I was in the neighborhood," Johnston replied, her jaw visibly tensing.

Canting his head toward Kevin, the officer said, "So this guy's supposed to be our expert consultant for mutilated and disfigured bodies?"

"Yeah," Johnston replied. Then looking back at Kevin, she said, "Kevin Maloney, meet Officer Hertz." Turning back to Hertz, she said, "Old Hertzy here is our lead public relations jackass, on account of his smooth and reassuring style." The other officers chuckled at Johnston's remark while Hertz rolled his eyes.

"Give me a break, Johnston. You know I was the best partner you ever had."

Johnston grumbled, "You wish."

"Let's see what you've got, Officer Hertz," responded Kevin in a quick monotone. "I got other things to do today."

"Okay, I can respect a man who's all business," Hertz recovered. "Right this way, Mr. Maloney."

Hertz led him up the steps to a double door. He paused in the doorway and said, "Watch yourself in here. The floor tiles are loose, and paint is peeling off the walls everywhere. It's probably all full of asbestos and lead, so try not to breathe too much."

"Good to know," Kevin replied as they passed through the receiving and stock rooms and entered the main kitchen.

Tall windows lined the left and right walls of the kitchen. Worktables occupied the center of the room, covered in paint chips and dust. Ancient commercial cooking equipment stood abandoned, rusted in place. Linoleum tiles crushed and cracked with each step.

"I can see why the public isn't allowed in here," Kevin remarked. "Any idea who the victim is?"

"They haven't accounted for all the staff, yet. So, it'll be a while," Hertz answered.

"Have you seen any cats around since you got here?"

"Uh, the museum's got these white life-size statues of cats around the place, but not live ones. Why?" Hertz asked.

"Just a thing. They like dead bodies, and this looks like a place they might hang out," Kevin explained. Then, pivoting in place, looking all around, he asked, "So where's the body?"

"Over here," Hertz said, pointing out the windows on the right.

Beyond the dusty glass, inside a tall fence, were the modern electrical transformers and switching equipment that supplied the penitentiary. A high voltage sign was posted on every side of the enclosure. The nearest transformer was stenciled in bright orange *Danger! 440 Volts*. At its base, lying in a pile of ash on the ground, were the remains of what appeared to be human long bones, connective tissue, and a scorched skull.

"I guess I was expecting something with more blood and guts," Kevin explained.

"You need to get closer, Mr. Expert? 'Cause we're still waiting for the electric to be shut off from the street."

"No. I'm afraid I can't help you. It doesn't look like anything I could recognize."

Kevin turned and walked back the way he came, tailed by Hertz. At the door, Kevin saw Johnston look up from her conversation with the other officers. Her eyebrows twitched up.

Kevin descended the steps back to ground level and said to her quietly, "Impossible to tell. I'll ask Molly about feline residents on the way out, but this is a dead end."

Johnston said to the uniformed officers, "I'm sure the duty detective will be along shortly. Stay safe."

Hertz chuckled and said, "Some expert you got there. See you next time, Johnston."

Johnston growled, "Yeah, see you next time, Hertz," as she turned her back and walked away with Kevin trailing her.

10

Monday, October 8

11:57 a.m.

DODGING BETWEEN CARS, Kevin and Johnston trotted across Fairmount Avenue in the middle of the block. Reaching the opposite sidewalk, Kevin asked, "So, what's up with you and Hertz? He seems like a real jerk. I mean, I hope he's better at the rest of the job, because he sucks at the interpersonal relationship part."

Johnston turned west toward her unmarked police car. Walking briskly ahead of Kevin, she huffed, "Yep, he's all that." After a few more steps, she added, "He's like my personal antagonist. My kryptonite. He can piss me off in ten seconds flat. I want to say he's a chauvinist pig, or he's sexist, and he's a bully, but no single description captures the true essence of Hertz."

Reaching the car, Johnston unlocked the doors and abruptly dropped into the driver's seat, slamming the door behind her. Kevin slid in the opposite side, closed the door, then looked over at

Johnston. "I take it we're not going to Jack's."

"No. I seem to have lost my appetite."

"Yeah, me too," Kevin agreed.

Jaw set and eyes glaring straight ahead, Johnston started the car and eased out into traffic.

After a pause, Kevin asked, "You worked with him when you were a patrol officer?"

"Yes, and I still come across him from time to time. He gets under my skin, and he just takes shot after shot. But it's not just me." Johnston made a left turn on Corinthian Avenue before continuing her thought. "As you saw, nobody's safe from his random disregard for humanity."

"I know the type. We had one of those guys in H and S Company. They called him 'Bull,'" Kevin recalled. "He had a way of just saying my name that got me going. He knew how to get right to the edge, you know?"

"Yeah. Never quite crossing the line. That's Hertz. Then something asinine will happen where he turns out to be the hero and the lieutenant will sing his praises and tell the rest of us we should be like Hertz!" Johnston exclaimed, shaking her fist in the air. After she exhaled, her voice returned to a more relaxed tone. "I've really got to let it go. It's him, not me."

"You're right. Now, let's do something fun, like picking out secondhand furnishings."

"Anything will be better than Hertz," Johnston murmured.

"See? There you go. Chin up. Look to the future," Kevin encouraged.

After several minutes of silence, Johnston commanded in her usual voice, "Since I didn't want to get closer to Hertz than necessary, tell me what you observed at the scene."

"There wasn't much," Kevin offered. "There was some kind of very hot fire and all that was left were some bones and ash. The only thing recognizable was the blackened remains of what appeared to be a human skull."

Johnston brought the car to a stop at a traffic light. Turning to Kevin, she said, "Doesn't sound like one of the cats."

"Maybe not. Since Molly didn't know about any cats hanging out in the area, I'm not going out on a limb for this one. The body is just too messed up. If the medical examiner can't get a DNA match, then we'll call it a possible victim. In the meantime, I'll hang on for the next call."

11

Monday, October 8

3:45 p.m.

KEVIN AND JOHNSTON stood outside of Father Matthew O'Conner's locked office. Looking up and down the hallway, Kevin remarked, "I've never seen his door closed before. I would have pegged him for an 'always open' kind of guy."

Turning their attention to the door, Johnston said, "Did it occur to you that he might be in there? Maybe he's trying to get some work done? Or taking a nap? Why don't you knock?"

Kevin shrugged in response and presented his knuckles to the door. "Sure, but I doubt he's in there."

"Just knock!" Johnston ordered, and Kevin let loose three raps on the wooden door.

When there was no response, he repeated the knocks and said, "Uncle Matt, are you in there?"

"Why no, I'm right here," Father Matthew replied from behind them. Johnston pivoted quickly and dropped her hand to her right hip. Kevin stood bolt upright, and the sole of his shoe made a slight squeak on the floor as he pivoted to the voice.

"You scared the devil out of me!" Kevin declared as he turned around to face his uncle.

"I know I really shouldn't sneak up on you like that, but it was too easy to pass up." Matthew chuckled as he opened the office and gestured for them to enter. "So, what brings you two around? Some kind of adventure, I'm sure."

"Well, we were in the neighborhood, and thought we'd stop in before Detective Johnston has to get back to work," Kevin said.

"I suppose I shouldn't be surprised," the old priest said as he maneuvered into his desk chair. "We're practically neighbors now. How is the move coming?"

"We were just working on that. We did the grand tour of the house, then we went rummaging through the big storage room for some furnishings."

"That sounds productive," grinned Matthew in response.

"You won't believe this leather sofa we snagged. I'm telling you, it's crazy. That little old house will be a showplace of modernity in no time at all," Kevin declared.

"I'm anxious to see it." Matthew redirected his attention and asked, "How about you, Detective, what have you been up to these days?"

"The usual," Johnston said in a lilting voice. "Victim here, bad guy there. You know how it is."

"I'm glad to report that I'm not familiar with the life of a detective beyond what I see on television," Matthew chuckled.

"So, enough about us, what are you up to?" Kevin inquired. "You seem to have a little extra bounce in your step today."

"It shows, eh? Well, I have some good news. I probably shouldn't share it just yet, but since it involves you, Kevin, I guess I can spill a few beans."

Kevin's eyes lit up as he said, "Yeah? I'm getting an assistant cat exterminator?"

"Well, not exactly," Matthew smiled. "I just came back from visiting our travel coordinator. Stepan and I are going to Rome to research the mysterious visitor."

"That's great. I'll take whatever intel I can get," Kevin replied.

"When do you go?" Johnston asked.

"Not for a couple weeks."

"Have you ever been to Rome?" Johnston asked. "I mean, I assume you have, because I guess all priests go to Rome at some time in their career," she added.

"Indeed, I have, but no, not all priests go to the Vatican." Uncle Matt's eyes took on a glassy cast as he described his previous trips. "I was there twice. When I was in college, then a decade or so after I was ordained. Did you know Rome is called the Eternal City? Really, it is an amazing place. All of Italy is amazing. The food is so good! They have the best tomatoes. So much better than our generic beefsteak tomatoes. They say it is the volcanic soil that makes them so delicious. I don't know if that's true, but I . . . never mind. I'm rambling, aren't I?"

"I'd ramble, too, if the department was sending me on a trip somewhere," Johnston said.

"Maybe we can have a bon voyage party at the new digs before you go?" Kevin offered.

"That might be fun," Johnston agreed.

"Fine idea. Will you invite your mother out? I'd love to see her."

"Yeah, we'll get the whole gang out here. There's plenty of room, and hopefully we'll have some furniture in a few days," Kevin agreed. "In the meantime, if you need anything for your trip, let me know. I'll be right down the road."

"I haven't even thought about packing up. It's been some time since I traveled anywhere. Gosh, what an adventure this will be," Matthew declared.

12

Tuesday, October 9

7:30 a.m.

THE SUN WASN'T far above the eastern treetops when the white Jeep stopped at the seminary's front gate. A uniformed guard stepped out of the small building next to the driveway and approached the open window of the vehicle. From behind the steering wheel, Kevin asked in a cheerful voice, "How you doing, Tony?"

"All right. Are you moving in today?" Tony asked, pointing at the back seat stacked with green military seabags.

"Indeed, I am," Kevin grinned. "My brother is following with another load."

"I'll be looking for him," Tony said and waved Kevin into the compound.

The Jeep revved slightly as it rolled forward and then turned right onto the road leading to the old farmhouse. Turning past the maintenance buildings, Kevin shifted out of gear and coasted down the slight hill until he came to a stop beside the house. Reaching up to turn off the ignition, Kevin paused and said, "Check engine light. Alternator light. Great. I guess I'll add that to the list." Clicking off the key, the engine went quiet.

Kevin sat still for a moment, then engaged the ignition again. The engine turned over once but failed to start, then fell completely silent. "Figures!" he mumbled to himself. "At least my stuff is here." Climbing out of the seat, he crossed the drive to the kitchen door and propped it open. He returned to the Jeep, collected two seabags, and walked into the house. A minute later, Kevin emerged from the door just in time to see a large red Toro bat-wing lawn mower descending the road from the maintenance buildings. It buzzed to a stop at the parking area and Mr. Warren stepped down from the cab of the idling machine.

"Hey, Kevin. Excited about move-in day?"

"Yes sir. Is the furniture delivery still on for later?" Kevin asked.

"You bet. The window units are installed, and the water should be running clear now. Anything else you need before I get after some of this grass?"

"I don't want to bother you now, but I think I need a new battery in the Jeep. Is there somebody up at the office that can give me a jump if I need to go out?"

"Yeah, no problem. Any of the guys can help you. If that don't work, grab a set of keys by my office door and take one of the work vehicles."

"That's great. You sure?" Kevin asked.

"You're one of my guys now," Mr. Warren shrugged. "I gotta trust you with all kinds of expensive equipment. An old pickup ain't nothing."

"Sounds good." Looking at the Toro, Kevin commented, "That's a really sweet machine. All I've ever used was an old push mower with a temperamental Briggs and Stratton."

"Yep, this is one of my babies," Mr. Warren grinned, revealing a patch of chewing tobacco sandwiched between his lip and his lower teeth.

"I'll let you get back to it. Thanks again!" Kevin said as Mr. Warren returned to the cab of the mower.

After he released the parking break and pushed another lever, the wings of the cutting deck lowered to the ground. Another control engaged the cutting blades, throwing a green cloud of dust along the driveway as the blades spun up to a steady high-speed hum. With a jaunty wave, Mr. Warren accelerated the mower out onto the wide expanse of dew-covered grass between the house and seminary buildings. Kevin watched with a grin as the mower cut a wide swath across the lawn. "What a job. I think I could be happy doing that one day," Kevin said to himself as he returned to the Jeep for more seabags.

13

Tuesday, October 9

6:52 p.m.

KEVIN AND BRIAN sat on the front steps of the farmhouse in the cool evening air. They were both dressed in dirt smeared shorts and T-shirts. Brian took a sip from a can of beer, his eyes following the sun's descent toward the west horizon from under a sweat-stained fire department ball cap. Shifting his elbows to the top step and settling back, Brian observed, "I might come to like this sunset view."

"It's not too bad. A lot more visible sky outside the city," Kevin agreed. After a long moment of silence, he added, "That secondhand bed is looking pretty good compared to the old brown corduroy couch."

"I'll bet it does, little brother," Brian agreed, offering a closed fist between them that Kevin promptly bumped with his own. "We should go grab a bite to eat and drop off the trailer. What do you say?" Brian asked.

"Right. I think I'll find a clean shirt. This one's got a full load of stink already."

"Don't bother. It'll just get dirty moving the trailer around. Besides, we're just going to get some cheesesteaks. Not like it's a date with Detective Johnston."

"You're right. Besides, I doubt we can mess up the seats in your vehicle any worse," Kevin joked.

"Hey, now. Don't knock the machine that jump-started your heap," Brian growled.

Standing up from the steps, Kevin said, "You got a point there. I hope it just needs a battery." Turning to the door, he said, "I'll grab my wallet, and we'll jet."

"Here, take this," said Brian just before sucking down the rest of the can of beer, belching loudly and then handing the empty can to Kevin. "Grab my jacket while you're in there. It's getting chilly out here."

"That's how it's going to be?" Kevin chuffed.

"Home sweet home, brother. Now get moving—I'm getting hungry."

Kevin disappeared through the front door, and Brian slowly stood and stretched. He yawned and walked around the outside of the house to the driveway. The two brothers converged again at the tired-looking red Jeep Cherokee hitched to a box trailer. After Brian started the engine, Kevin stood in line with the rearview mirror and guided Brian while he made repeated back and forth maneuvers to turn the trailer around. When the Cherokee was finally pointed up the hill, Kevin climbed in the passenger side door and Brian drove the vehicle up the lane. Approaching the maintenance buildings, Mr. Warren appeared in a doorway and waved them down. The Cherokee braked to a stop and Brian rolled down the window.

"Hey, you must be Brian. I'm Earl Warren," he said, leaning on the window frame and shaking Brian's hand.

"Sure am," Brian replied. "Good to meet you, sir."

"Nice to meet you, too. I'm glad I caught you boys. I got a phone message for you Kevin. They must have just missed you at the farmhouse. Say, you don't have a cell phone?" Mr. Warren asked.

"Nah," Kevin said. I'm putting that off as long as I can."

Handing a folded sheet of paper to Brian, who handed it off to Kevin, Mr. Warren waved and said, "Can't blame you there. See you around," and walked back to the open door of the maintenance office.

Kevin unfolded the paper and examined the message. "Can you hit the dome light, Brian? It's too dark to read." Brian rotated a switch on the dashboard and the dim overhead light blinked on. Kevin held the slip up to the light and said, "Looks like we need to make a stop first. Work related."

"Crap," Brian responded. "Where to?"

"North Philly. Saint Malachy Rectory—1429 North Eleventh Street."

"Urgent?"

"No," Kevin replied. "Just a ghost sighting."

"You think this is going to take long? Because I'm really getting hungry."

"No idea. I haven't done this since turning pro."

"Then we'll get something for the ride," Brian said. "Nothing worse than showing up to the incident on an empty stomach."

"You would know. I'll defer to your judgment."

"Overbrook Pizza is just down on 63rd. We can get steaks to go," Brian declared.

Kevin said, "You're a better man than me if you can eat a steak while driving."

"Not how it works, boy-o. Since it's your call-out, you can drive while I eat."

14

Tuesday, October 9

8:05 p.m.

THE CHEROKEE AND attached trailer rolled to a stop on North Eleventh Street in front of St. Malachy parish. Cars were parked bumper to bumper, and the wide sidewalk and front steps of the North Philadelphia church were bathed in the pale, yellow glow of streetlights. The building's exterior was red brick, with arches over three sets of scarlet double doors. Above the level of the streetlights and web of utility wires, the bell tower blended into the darkness of the night sky.

Glancing up, Brian commented from the passenger seat, "Looks like the place."

Kevin nodded while moving the shift lever to park. "Tell you what, I'll jump out here and you pull this thing into that parking lot next door," Kevin suggested. Without reply, Brian exited the vehicle and walked around to the driver's side. Kevin crossed to the sidewalk and followed a path down the left side of the building marked with a sign that said *Rectory*.

At the end of the dimly lit path, Kevin climbed two steps and paused before the rectory door. He reached for the doorbell button, but before he touched it, a soft hissing sound drew his attention to the left. Startled, he froze in place at the sight of a dark figure approaching from a deep shadow. The hiss gave way to a gentle female voice. "We can't disturb Father."

Kevin exhaled and whispered, "Geez, you scared me!" Looking around, Kevin pointed back to the way he came. "How about coming over to the parking lot? Can we talk there?" He then retraced his steps back to the front of the church. The dark figure, once moving, took on the shape of a woman wearing a shawl. Turning right at the end of the sidewalk, Kevin made straight for the Cherokee and trailer, with the woman trailing behind in silence.

At the vehicle, Kevin gestured to the rear door. "Would it be all right if we talk in the car? We'll attract less attention that way." Shaking her head, she hesitated a few steps short.

"It's going to be okay. We're here to help," Kevin reassured, while opening the rear door and gesturing toward the back seat. The woman ducked her head, looking inside before climbing in.

Sliding into the front passenger seat, Kevin said, "You really gave me a start."

"I'm sorry about that," the woman replied in a meek voice.

"That's a good way to get hurt if somebody reacts abruptly," Kevin continued as he settled himself. Taking a deep breath and letting it out slowly, he looked to the back seat and explained. "Let's try this again. I'm here about some kind of strange sighting. Was it you that called for help?" The woman nodded then dropped her gaze to her lap.

"I asked Father Santos what I should do, and he said he'd find some answers." She then added, "He must have found you?"

"I guess so," Kevin agreed. After a quick glance at Brian, he asked, "Let's start with the basics. What's your name?"

"Michele Fields. I'm the rectory housekeeper."

"Good. That's a start. I'm Kevin and this is Brian."

Brian looked up at her reflection in the rearview mirror and said, "Nice to meet you."

Kevin continued. "We're going to try to help you get to the bottom of your situation. Is it okay if we ask you some personal questions?"

Raising her head and pulling back her shawl, the woman's large eyes reflected the glow of the illuminated dashboard. "Um, honestly, you two aren't really what I was expecting."

Brian looked down at his shirt and then pulled the collar up toward his nose. Making a sniffing sound, he said, "We're sorry about the body odor and all. Kevin and I were moving furniture and stuff." Looking at Kevin, he added, "Should probably have more professional attire. Maybe like the Ghostbusters, eh? Or were you expecting something like the Spanish Inquisition?"

"Come on, Brian, this is serious," Kevin groaned.

"Lighten up a little," Brian mocked.

Michele's emotionless face cracked a slight smile. "That's a funny joke, because nobody expects the Spanish Inquisition. Right? Like the old Monty Python movie. I just thought there would be something more formal."

"Okay, okay," Kevin exhaled and rolled his eyes. "Look, I'm the guy they hired to fix . . . things, and we just came from moving into a new place," Kevin asserted. Staring at his brother, Kevin said, "Let's see if we can zero in on the problem. All right?" Kevin looked back at Michele.

The woman nodded and looked back down at her hands while asking, "So, are you an exorcist or something?"

"No, no, nothing like that." Kevin said.

Then Brian chimed in. "If he's anything, he's more like"—he grinned while stretching out the last word—"an ex-or-cis-tant."

Looking at his brother, Kevin said, "Come on. Knock it off with the bad jokes."

"All right, all right," Brian relented, shrugging his shoulders.

"I suppose you been saving that for just this occasion, haven't you," Kevin said to Brian.

"Nah. Just came to me. You know I can't stand to see a lady all sad and everything," Brian replied. Then turning to face the back seat, he said, "You'll be all right, Michele."

Michele's eyes widened at the mention of her name, and she smiled at Brian.

Kevin said, "Okay. How about we hear Michele's story. Would that be all right?"

Brian nodded and Michele shifted in the seat. After a long moment, she sighed and said in a choked-up voice, "My mother—her name was Marcie—was killed in a really bad hit-and-run three weeks ago. The police are still looking for the driver." After a long pause, she continued. "We had a funeral mass here at St. Malachy, then she was buried at the New Cathedral Cemetery." Pausing again, Michele covered her face and began a quiet sob. Through the soft sobbing she said, "I was there for all of it. I saw her casket, in the ground, before it was covered and buried. My mother's body is in there."

Brian reached back with his right hand and touched her shoulder saying, "It's okay."

After waiting for the sobs to subside, Kevin then asked, "I take it that's not the end."

Michele looked directly at Kevin with wide eyes and nodded.

"You've seen her since the burial. Where, when?"

"She was . . . she was walking down the street, a few blocks from here. Three days ago. Then yesterday I saw her again near the supermarket. I knew it couldn't be her, but it was uncanny."

"Do you have a photo of her?" Kevin asked.

"No, I'm sorry. I should have brought one," Michele answered.

"Did she have any distinguishing features? You know, something that made your mother easy to recognize?" Kevin suggested.

"Mom had an underbite." Michele then thrust her jaw forward in demonstration. "Like that, you know? Her jaw was very distinctive."

"Did she ever get any kind of surgery for it, that you know of?" Brian asked.

"No. I don't think so, why?" Michele replied.

"Things change, you know? Tell me about her face or hair," Kevin suggested.

"Mom was pretty. She had the classic cheekbones like a supermodel, and her hair was blond when she was young, but went snowy white in her fifties."

"And the person you saw yesterday?" Kevin prompted.

"Well, I'm not sure, but I didn't really see any hair. Maybe she was bald? I couldn't see very well because she had a coat with a hood."

"Was there anything about the shape of her face that looked unusual?" Kevin continued.

"Maybe. She might have been a little puffy, you know?" Michele answered and then asked, "Was I seeing a ghost? Is she haunting me?" After a deep breath in and out, she said, "I loved my mom, but we didn't always get along too good."

"I don't think you saw a ghost," Kevin explained, "and it wasn't your mother either."

"But who was it? She really looked like Mom," Michele croaked.

"It's hard to describe, but basically, there's this thing that happens right after some folks die," Kevin explained. "It's this transformational process, and if this certain animal comes in contact with the corpse, it can assume the form of the dead person."

Her jaw quivered at the description, and she buried her face in her hands again. "Father said he wouldn't trust the explanation. I'm not sure what to think," Michele declared.

Kevin continued. "Look, it will be all right. I . . . we," Kevin gestured to Brian, "know what it is and how to make it go away. We just gotta catch it, that's all."

In a soft voice, Brian asked, "Have there been any stray cats around here?"

Michele answered, "I don't know. I never noticed. Mom and I are both allergic to cats, so we never went looking for them."

Kevin explained, "That's fine. But to solve this problem, the first thing you need to do is start paying attention to the cats."

"You're serious about this? Cats?"

"Yes," Kevin said.

"What am I looking for? I don't really know anything about cats."

"The cat we're looking for will be inclined to hang out with folks who are old, infirm, or vulnerable. Sometimes they befriend street people. Do you know what I mean?" Kevin asked.

Michele nodded and said, "Can I ask around about the cats? I know a lot of people in the parish. Maybe somebody has seen a strange cat."

"That would be great," Kevin agreed. "If I can suggest, however, you probably don't want to try to explain the connection between the cat and your mother." Looking at Brian, Kevin softened his voice, "If nobody's seen a suspicious animal, we'll have to search for it, and that takes a lot of time. I don't think it will be long before it goes again."

Brian nodded understanding before turning to Michele. "The cat we're looking for doesn't want to eat anything. Most people will notice the unusual behavior if they try to feed it."

Kevin then instructed, "If you see or hear about a cat that doesn't belong, or see the person that looks like your mother, don't touch them. Get a good look if you can, but don't get too close. Then give me a call."

"What happens if you touch them?" Michele asked.

"The cat will scratch for sure. And the wound will bleed like crazy," Brian described. "And the one that looks like your mom? Well, touching it can damage your skin."

"Okay," Michele agreed in a soft voice.

Kevin handed Michele a card with just a phone number on it. "Here is how you can contact me. There's a machine, so if you don't get me, just leave your name and a number. Don't leave any other details. I'll know what it's about, then I'll call you back. Okay?"

Michele nodded again.

"Good. Look, we're going to resolve this. The person you saw isn't your mother, and she's not haunting you, but it is something we need to take care of."

"Is there anything else I should do?" she asked.

"Just call. We'll be around, but we like to work in the background, so kinda pretend we're not here. See? So, go home and know it'll be fine."

Michele nodded again. Reaching forward she briefly touched Brian's shoulder and sniffed, wanly smiling before saying, "Thank you for trying to cheer me up."

"Good night," Brian whispered as she exited the vehicle and walked off into the darkness.

When Michele was out of sight, Kevin looked at Brian and hissed, "What the hell's got into you! You shouldn't be flirting with a lady right after her mother dies and she's seeing ghosts and needing help."

Brian started the Cherokee and dropped the transmission into gear. "I wasn't flirting with her. I was just trying to lighten the mood. She's clearly in a bad place and needs a little levity in her life."

"I'm not sure I can bring you to these meetings if you're going to act like that. This is serious business."

Brian grinned. "I know it, and I know this is your livelihood and these people need help, but you gotta take yourself a little less serious."

"What do you mean?" Kevin asked.

"If you act all scared and freaked out, they're going to reciprocate. You don't want that."

Kevin was quiet for a minute as Brian drove the vehicle back onto Eleventh Street and accelerated away from St. Malachy. "Okay.

You may have a point there. My actions and reactions will set the tone for the folks I'm working with. They won't believe I've got it under control unless I act like it's under control."

"Exactly," Brian agreed. After a pair of left turns, Brian continued driving south. At a stoplight, he looked over at Kevin and asked, "I noticed you didn't give a lot of details about what the cat does or the end results for the victims."

"Yeah," Kevin acknowledged. Looking out the window, Kevin remained silent until the vehicle moved again. "I figured I should offer the least explanation that was satisfactory for Michele." Looking over at his brother, Kevin said, "I mean, what do we really know about this thing? Until we get to the origin of it, if we can get that far, we'll never really know what it does or why."

"It looks like a cat. It can look like the last person it sucked the soul from, it doesn't like liquids, and we don't know why," Brian summarized.

"See what I mean? That doesn't really satisfy the 'what happened to my mom' question."

"I think you're right. The less she knows, the better. For now, anyway," Brian agreed.

"No matter what, we're short on time. That thing is already stalking its next victim, and it will probably transition before we find it. Then we'll be screwed because we won't know what we're looking for next."

15

Thursday, October 11

8:14 p.m.

BRIAN WALKED INTO the farmhouse and found Kevin asleep on a brown leather couch in the living room. A small, black flashlight and a book were lying on the floor next to him. The old picture tube television on the opposite side of the room displayed images of three awkward men and an attractive blond woman sitting in a small apartment.

Entering the room, Brian asked, "Rerun or new episode?"

"Huh?" Kevin responded in a startled flinch.

"On TV, the show," Brian explained. "Never mind. How long have you been napping?"

"What time is it?" Kevin asked.

"Quarter after eight. You got somewhere to be?"

"Yeah. I'm going back over to the North Philly area. Wanna go?" Kevin asked.

"Not really." Brian then added, "I'm working tomorrow, so staying out late isn't on my list."

"Too bad."

"Why? What's up?" Brian asked.

"Nothing," Kevin said. "It's just that hunting for an unknown cat in an unfamiliar neighborhood by myself kind of sucks."

"I imagine so. Did you try Mark? It's been a few days since he's been around," Brian suggested.

Kevin answered, "Out of town."

"How about Johnston?" Brian offered.

Kevin replied, "Down the shore, visiting her mom."

Brian shrugged his shoulders and said, "Then it looks like you're on your own tonight."

"I guess so."

Brian asked, "Did you learn anything this morning?"

"I spent most of the time getting oriented to the surroundings," Kevin replied. "Didn't see a single cat or any potential victims."

"I wonder if this is how it usually goes?" Brian inquired. "The last cat might have been just dumb luck, because it seemed like you were stumbling across it all the time."

Kevin offered, "I hope not. I didn't even see any street people on this trip, which I thought was kind of odd. But then, it was raining shortly before I got there."

"Speaking of getting there," Brian said, "Are we still having the housewarming shindig this Saturday? You haven't mentioned it since the first day we moved in, and time's getting short."

"Yeah. I told Uncle Matt, Johnston, and Mom about it, so I guess we're having a get-together," Kevin agreed. "I should probably tell Mark too."

"Okay. You planning to cook? If you don't want to, I can get Skinny to cater," Brian said.

"What?" Kevin asked.

"It's a new thing he's doing. He bought this smoker-on-wheels business, and he's looking for gigs."

"Right. How much is this going to cost?" Kevin asked. "I mean, I'd be happy to let him do it, but it's not like I've got extra cash burning a hole in my pocket."

"I don't know, but it can't be too much. I'll find out tomorrow," Brian said. "How many folks you think?"

"Me and you"—Kevin paused and looked up at the ceiling while counting on his fingers—"Six? You think we should ask Mr. Warren?"

"Don't know about that. Let me work on Skinny before you go inviting more people."

"Good idea," Kevin agreed as he rolled his legs off the couch and sat upright. Reaching to the floor, he picked up the book and said, "I guess I ought to get going."

"Those cats aren't going to find themselves," Brian agreed as he switched on the overhead light fixture. "What's with the book and that fancy flashlight?" Brian asked while reading the book cover. "Cat behavior? That's probably a good idea."

"It seemed like it when I got it, but I'm not sure any of it applies, since this thing doesn't eat or poop like a regular cat."

"You got a point there, boyo, and that thing?"

Pointing it toward the ceiling, Kevin clicked on the flashlight momentarily. Blinding white light flashed through the room. "Eight-hundred-lumen tactical flashlight."

"Gotcha. You could get a suntan with that," Brian said as he blinked and dropped onto the far end of the sofa.

"Hoping it helps me see the people with eye-shine," Kevin replied.

"Ah, since only the cat victims should reflect back?"

"That's the idea," Kevin agreed.

After running his hands over the leather, Brian added, "You know this couch is way better than the one we left in the apartment."

"Yes, it is. In fact, I'll bet you're still on it when I get back tonight," Kevin said.

Brian smiled back and said, "Maybe."

16

Thursday, October 11

9:49 p.m.

KEVIN BROUGHT THE white Jeep to a stop at the intersection of North Broad and Jefferson Streets. He surveyed the surroundings while waiting for the traffic light to change. The streets were wet from an earlier rain shower, and the lights of the passing cars reflected in the lingering puddles. Pedestrians moved in ones and twos along the sidewalk, and several people were gathered near the bus stops on the east and west side of the street.

When the light turned green, Kevin eased out the clutch and feathered the gas pedal. He matched the slow creep of the cars ahead until he reached a shopping center on the east side of the street. He maneuvered into a space in the center of the parking lot then shut off the engine.

Kevin sat in the vehicle for what seemed an eternity, watching through the open driver's window. Six of the seven stores were closed for the night or vacant, but at the supermarket to his left, occasional pedestrians walked in or out. When the dashboard clock read 10:45, Kevin closed the window, grabbed his dark gray jacket, and exited the vehicle. Walking to the northeast corner of the parking lot, he ducked into the shadows along the east side of the supermarket. He continued toward the rear of the store, where a few empty cardboard boxes and food containers were scattered along the pavement. The unseasonably warm temperature accentuated the smells issuing from the bank of trash receptacles behind the building.

Penetrating farther into the shadows, Kevin slipped a hand into his jacket and withdrew the new flashlight from a pocket. Holding it in his left fist, near his ear, he clicked the thumb button on the tail of the light. The beam slashed into the black recesses and reflected off beady rodent eyes that quickly scattered from the light. Kevin clicked off the light again and continued to search the back of the supermarket.

Beyond the corner, the glow of yellow security lights revealed loading docks and the trash collection containers, but there was no sign of human or animal activity. Kevin walked slowly, directing the beam of his light into the dark recesses. Still finding nothing of interest, he continued around the building until he was standing under a floodlight at the opposite end of the store from where he started.

Looking south, Broad Street stretched out to the skyline of Center City. To the north, a movie theater's colorful marquee stood in contrast to the white exterior lights of the Temple University buildings. A steady stream of cars passed his location, but the number of pedestrians had dropped off since his arrival. Scratching his head, he mumbled to himself, "Come on cat, show yourself."

Kevin remained stationary for some time. He leaned against the wall of the supermarket, scrutinizing the faces of the few people walking by. Except for two men dressed in dark hooded sweatshirts and lingering in the shadows on the opposite side of the street, the passing pedestrians appeared normal and moved with purpose.

After a long period of time where nobody passed Kevin's location, he checked his watch and began walking south. Moving at a casual pace, Kevin glanced in the windows of the shops and occasionally illuminated dark recesses with his light. At the end of the block, he scanned the cross street and then continued south. Surrounded by a chest-high metal fence, the Mount Olive Temple church building occupied the north end of the next block. Beyond it, a grove of trees with benches and picnic tables bordered an athletic field. Turning left into the grove of trees, Kevin sent the beam of his flashlight into the darkness, revealing nothing unusual. "I'll give it another fifteen minutes," he said to himself as he took a seat on a bench.

Sitting in the darkness, Kevin watched his surroundings. He looked to his left and right, then behind himself. Nothing moved except a group of people walking north on the far side of Broad Street. When they disappeared behind the corner of the church, Kevin stood up and walked east. Reaching a large building on the far side, he turned north toward the shopping center. At the top of the block, Kevin alerted to a police cruiser parked nearby. Backlit by the streetlights, the silhouette of two officers were visible in the darkened car. The front windows were down, and the muffled voice of the radio dispatcher could be heard above the low hum of the city.

As Kevin approached the car, a voice from inside addressed him, "Sir, would you mind coming over here? Where are you headed?"

Kevin gave a short cough and hesitated for an instant before saying, "I'm, ah, looking for cats."

The near officer glanced at the other before returning his gaze to Kevin and saying, "What's your name, and are you looking for a particular cat, or just your general garden variety of stray?"

"It's Kevin Maloney, and feral cats mostly. And strays too," Kevin replied. "Anything that poses a public health hazard, or you know, threatens the natural eco-diversity of the urban landscape.

It's a kind of side thing I do. Catch and sterilize them. You know, population control."

The officer grinned and then said, "Did you hear that Smitty? That's a new one."

"I'm not causing any problems, am I?" Kevin asked.

"Naw, Kevin. It's just that I wouldn't recommend wandering about this late at night by yourself. We don't want to see you get hurt or worse. See?"

Kevin nodded saying, "I agree, officers, but the cats, well, they kind of like doing their thing in the dark, so you know, that's when it's easiest to find them. I usually bring some help, so I appreciate you looking out for me, and if I'm straying toward trouble, or you see a cat that's not exactly tame, well, just let me know."

The officer said, "Okay, cat hunter. We'll do that, but for now, you might want to head home for the night."

Kevin gave a brief smile and called out as the cruiser slowly motored off into the night. "Thanks, officers!"

When the car disappeared around the corner, Kevin crossed the street back into the parking lot where he'd started. Approaching the white Wrangler, he fished in his pocket for the ignition key with his right hand, just as a dark-hooded figure appeared in front of him. Kevin paused and said, "Yo," just as a piece of two-by-four landed a blow across his upper shoulders from behind, forcing him to his knees. An involuntary groan escaped his throat as Kevin's hands shot up to shield the back of his head and dropped the key ring on the pavement in front of him.

"Stay down!" a voice spat from the assailant behind him. The figure in front snatched the key ring from the ground just as another blow from behind landed on Kevin's raised arm and glanced off his head. A bright red splotch appeared at the base of his skull, and he collapsed to the pavement.

The two-by-four clattered to the ground as the two assailants opened the doors and climbed into the Jeep. The red brake lights came on and the ignition chime began echoing across the parking lot. A voice issued from inside, "You see that Busta? I don't drive stick!" The hooded figures immediately exited the Jeep, leaving the door ajar and the key in the ignition. One of the assailants returned to Kevin, where he was lying on the pavement clutching his head. "This is for driving a stick!" he shouted while delivering a hard kick to Kevin's gut, then sprinted into the darkness. Kevin contracted into a fetal position on the ground, groaning and gasping in blinding pain.

17

Friday, October 12

12:06 a.m.

SILHOUETTED BY THE yellow glare of floodlights, a small cat silently trotted across the deserted supermarket parking lot. It slipped underneath the lone white vehicle and crouched near the left rear wheel. Ignoring the lights and chimes emanating from inside the Jeep, it watched the wounded human lying motionless on the pavement nearby. The tail flicked twice before the feline crept across to the curled-up shape. Its nose pitched up and down, sniffing the body. Then it turned its attention to the head and licked at the blood smears near an oozing wound. After several laps of the tongue, the human form moved, slow rolling from its side to its back. The cat leapt away, retreating toward the vehicle, where it sat down.

Kevin groaned and continued the roll onto his other side. He cradled the back of his head and slowly pushed himself to a seated position with his uninjured arm. Patting his neck and head, then looking himself over, the glow of the floodlights revealing blood on his hands and arms. "Son of a bitch," he spat. Looking toward the Jeep, he startled at the sight of a cat staring back at him. It was mostly black, with a white face and mittens.

"You wonder if it's my time, don't you?" he growled at the cat. "Screw that. You're not getting me that easy." Collecting his legs and feet under himself, Kevin slowly stood up and staggered to the Jeep. He mumbled to the cat, "I guess this wasn't a complete waste; now I know what you look like." Looking back, directly into Kevin's eyes, the cat meowed and then disappeared under the Jeep. Emerging on the other side, it scampered into a dark corner of the parking lot.

Kevin slumped against the rear fender, breathing deep, slow breaths. His right hand probed the back of his neck, head, then his left wrist. "Not dead yet, you stupid cat."

Rocking forward, Kevin steadied himself against the spare tire mounted to the tailgate. Working around to the left side of the vehicle, he shuffled forward. The door was open. A chiming still came from the interior, and the dash lights glowed dimly. Kevin muttered to himself, "Crap," as he dropped into the seat. Using his right hand, he guided his legs into the vehicle, then closed the door.

Depressing the brake and clutch pedals, Kevin jammed the key forward to the start position, but nothing happened. He recycled the key to the off position and all the lights and sounds ceased. Rotating the key forward once more to the start position yielded the same silence, with all the engine warning lights dimming to black. Turning the key off again, Kevin dropped his forehead onto the steering wheel. He let out a long groan of exasperation and pounded his right fist on the dashboard. Coming upright, he looked around and asked, "Come on. The battery is brand new! What the hell is wrong? Why tonight?"

He climbed out of the Jeep, shut the doors, and began slowly walking across the parking lot toward the supermarket. Inside, visible through the front window, there was an employee leaning against the customer service counter. Kevin staggered in the door with his right hand pushing ahead of him, leaving blood smears on the glass. Once inside, he said, "Can you help me?"

The tall young man turned to look at Kevin. He was dressed in a black shirt and baggy trousers. His name tag read *Seven*, and he said, "Yo, are you okay? You got blood all over your face and jacket!"

Kevin responded, "I've been worse. Can I use your phone? My car won't start."

"Forget the car. Really, you look like a horror show."

"I think they cut my scalp in the back. It's not as bad as it looks. Just bleeds a lot."

"Did somebody jump you?"

"Yeah. Two guys in black hoodies. Tried to steal my Jeep," Kevin panted. Then with a slight grin, he added, "Took off when they couldn't get it started."

"Aw man. Should we call the cops?" Seven asked in an excited voice. "We've had a few incidents around here recently."

"Can I get something to hold on this cut and then can you point me to the phone?" Kevin asked.

"Sure," he said and led Kevin to the customer service counter. Seven retrieved a roll of paper towels from under the counter and began tearing off towels. After packing a wad into his left hand, Kevin pressed them against the back of his still-oozing head.

The young man pointed to the end of the counter and said, "The phone is right there. Can I get you some ice or something?"

"Nah," Kevin said and picked up the handset. He entered a number from memory. A voice squeaked from the speaker and Kevin responded.

"Yeah, I'm okay. Look, I'm in the Fresh Grocer at Broad and Oxford. I'm stuck here because the Jeep's battery is dead. I'll tell you about the rest later."

Kevin listened longer and then completed the call saying, "Yes.

I'll see if I can get someone here to help me, if not, I'll call you back." Replacing the handset, he turned to the young man. "I don't suppose you could give my car a jump?"

"They don't let us do that, you know, for safety reasons. I can call a tow truck for you."

"Huh," Kevin paused. Then, looking at the employee's name tag, he asked, "Is your name really Seven?"

"Nickname," he replied.

"How'd you come by that?" Kevin asked.

"I have six older brothers and sisters."

"Of course. I'm the youngest. So, about that jump? I have jumper cables. It won't take but a second," Kevin prodded.

"I'm sorry, sir. I can't. But if it helps, the tow guy doesn't charge. The store pays him in groceries."

"That's a great arrangement." After a pause, Kevin said, "Okay, I guess you'd better call the tow truck."

"It's no problem; he's just a mile away," Seven smiled.

"Thanks, Seven. You're a big help."

18

Friday, October 12

10:56 a.m.

KEVIN PAUSED AT the top of the staircase outside his bedroom door. A bundle of clothes was tucked under one arm, and a blood-stained towel hung over his opposite shoulder. Sniffing at the air, he said, "Why do I smell smoke?" Then, with a firm grasp on the handrail, he descended the stairs, his bare feet thumping one at a time on the wooden treads. At the bottom, he glanced around the living room and then turned into the bathroom, closing the door behind him.

Just as the sound of water flowing in the shower began, the kitchen door opened and a large man with a long blond ponytail stepped into the house. He wore half-laced boots, work-worn tan cargo shorts, and a black *The Who- Quadrophenia* concert T-shirt that strained to contain his belly. He laid a faded and stained barn coat over the back of a kitchen chair, then crossed into the living room. He flopped onto the couch and quickly faded into a rhythmic snore.

Soon after the sound of flowing water ceased, Kevin emerged from the bathroom freshly dressed and shaved. He paused at the foot of the stairs and observed, "Something's on fire." Then looking right, he saw the scruffy man sound asleep on the couch. Sniffing the air again, Kevin approached the stranger on the couch and whispered, "Maybe it's you. And who the hell are you, anyway?" The sleeping man didn't respond but only continued to breathe loudly.

Crossing to the kitchen, Kevin looked out the window. A rust-eaten, flat-black Ford Econoline van and an equally large barbecue smoker occupied the driveway. There was a pile of split firewood in the grass, and a steady column of white smoke issued from the chimney of the smoker. Painted on the side of the van in red, white, and blue letters over a Texas state flag were the words *Uncle Jimmie's Bigger, Better Bones.*

"That explains the smoke," Kevin grumbled as he turned to the refrigerator.

After retrieving a jug of milk, he collected a box of Frosted Flakes cereal, a spoon, and bowl, then assembled his breakfast. Just as he took the first bite, the figure on the couch yawned and rolled over, squeaking the leather upholstery as he moved. Taking another bite, Kevin turned to watch. The man rolled off the couch and stood upright. Stretching and yawning some more, he shuffled through the kitchen and out the door without looking at Kevin or saying a word. At the pile of wood, he collected an armload and fed it into a hatch beneath the chimney. Moving to the side of the smoker, he adjusted a damper and looked at a thermometer. Rubbing his eyes and stretching again, he climbed up the steps and entered the kitchen. Upon seeing Kevin, he mumbled, "Hey, who are you?"

Rocking back in his seat, Kevin replied, "I was wondering the same thing. My name's Kevin Maloney. I live here."

"Oh yeah, okay." Standing up straighter and extending a hand, he said, "I'm Jimmie. Brian said I should make myself at home."

Kevin shook hands and said, "Jimmie, huh?"

"The one and only. Pitmaster for Uncle Jimmie's Bigger, Better Bones, LLC."

"Pitmaster. That's a good title." Pointing to a chair, Kevin said, "You work for Skinny then?"

Dropping onto the chair, Jimmie nodded. "Yeah, I sold him the business last month. Now he finds gigs and manages the taxes and stuff, and I just do the cooking."

"What made you sell the business?"

"I wasn't so good at keeping out of trouble with the city and the IRS, so Skinny formed a new company and hired me and leased my equipment."

"An LLC, eh?"

"Yeah, I'm not sure what that is, really, but Skinny says it's a good thing."

"Gotcha. So how does all this work? The smoker and stuff. Did Brian make all the arrangements?"

"All taken care of," Jimmie said as he reorganized his ponytail and secured it with a rubber band.

"That's good. I guess." Kevin said as he scooped up more cereal. Before filling his mouth, he asked, "What's on the menu?"

"Pork ribs and brisket slow-smoked on my old gal Deirdre out there. Two kinds of beans. Corn muffins and some banana cream pie with vanilla wafer crust."

Kevin nodded while he crunched his cereal, and after swallowing said, "That sounds good."

"Oh it's good," Jimmie smiled. "For sure it's good."

"Did Brian happen to mention how many folks you're feeding?" Kevin asked.

"Yeah, it's small, just forty or so servings."

"Forty? I don't think I know forty people."

"Some of the firehouse bubbas are coming. They eat a lot, so I think it'll be somewhere around thirty real people."

"Well, that's better."

"Any chance I could get a bowl of cereal? That's kinda making me hungry," Jimmie asked.

"Help yourself. It's Brian's box, so it'll be fine." Looking and pointing over his shoulder, Kevin said, "Grab a bowl and spoon."

Jimmie went to the indicated cabinet and then returned to the table. He filled the bowl with cereal, splashed it with milk, and took a bite. Talking through a full mouth, Jimmie said, "I can't remember the last time I had a bowl of cereal."

"Yeah, me too," Kevin replied. Then he asked, "So you'll just crash on the couch until you've got all the meat smoked?"

"It's a long process. I gotta burn down the coals and get the smoker all set, then I gotta maintain it pretty regular all night. It usually takes a couple cases of beer."

"That's one way to measure time," Kevin remarked. "You'll be here tomorrow night too?"

"Yep. Two meats, two sides, dessert, setup, entertainment, cleanup. It's all included with the package."

"Okay. Well, I'll just stay out of your way then," Kevin said. Then, looking at Jimmie as he took another bite, he asked, "How much does this setup cost?"

Crunching loudly, Jimmie said, "You'll have to ask Skinny. I'm sure he and Brian have got some kind of deal."

Rolling his eyes, Kevin said, "I'm sure they do." Scooping the last bite of cereal in the bowl into his mouth, he sat back in the chair and crunched quietly and looked Jimmie over. After swallowing, he resumed the conversation. "What's the entertainment? You said that was included."

"Yeah, that's my favorite part," Jimmie bobbed his head.

"Can I ask what it is?"

Jimmie grinned and said, "Some music and storytelling."

"I suppose you're the performer?' Kevin asked.

"You'll like it." Jimmie reassured him as the wall telephone behind him began ringing with a dissonant electronic tone.

Pushing up from the chair, Kevin smirked and said, "It'll be great. Excuse me while I take this call."

"Yeah, no problem," Jimmie said as he took his unfinished bowl of cereal and retreated to the leather couch.

Kevin walked around the table and laid his right hand on the phone, not picking it up from the cradle until Jimmie was out of the room. Holding the handset to his ear, he said in a flat tone, "Hello."

Listening for a minute, Kevin stretched the cord as he walked toward the exterior door. "Okay. Hang on a second," he said as he lowered the handset and covered the mouthpiece. Craning his neck to look back at Jimmie seated on the couch, Kevin saw him continuing to eat. Turning back to the door, Kevin opened it and stretched the cord farther until he could sit on the top step. Mumbling to himself, Kevin said, "I guess that explains the long cord."

Returning the handset to his ear, he resumed, "Michele? You still there? Good. Okay. Look, don't worry about finding stray cats. I've identified the culprit. I'm hoping to get this wrapped up soon, so you won't have to worry any more. Okay?" Listening again, Kevin bobbed his head twice, then promptly stopped and clutched the back of his scalp with his free hand. Mumbling again, he said, "Ow, that hurts." Then listening and responding to the voice on the phone, he said, "Yes, I'm okay. Just took a spill last night. And yeah, my brother's fine. Sorry, he's not available. He's working." Looking at his free hand after touching the back of his head, Kevin rubbed the fresh blood between his fingers until it became sticky and stained the skin. In a soft voice he said, "You have my word, it won't be long before there's no more sightings. Okay? Good. We'll be in touch."

19

Friday, October 12

11:49 a.m.

KEVIN WALKED FROM the farmhouse toward the maintenance buildings situated on the northwest edge of the St. Charles seminary property. A warm southwest wind gusted at his back and irregular layers of gray clouds scudded across the sky. Out to his right, Mr. Warren sat behind the wheel of the red Toro lawn mower, buzzing in a circle around a tree. Completing the circuit, he straightened out on a path toward the open pavement next to a white corrugated metal equipment shed. Kevin watched as Mr. Warren brought the mower to a stop and set the parking brake. Then, with the whirring of a hydraulic pump, the batwing cutting decks folded up against the side of the machine. When the engine fell silent, Mr. Warren stepped down from the driver's seat and said, "Hey, Maloney. You look like you're moving a little slow. Everything okay down the hill?"

"Rough night," Kevin replied, "and to top it off, my vehicle is dead, again."

"Sorry to hear it. What can I do to help?"

"Can you recommend a mechanic and maybe loan me some wheels?"

Mr. Warren grinned and pointed toward the door on the side of the shed. "I'm just pausing for lunch break. Why don't you come in and we'll see about getting you fixed up."

Kevin said, "Thanks," and followed Mr. Warren into the maintenance office.

Mr. Warren opened the door into a space that functioned as a break room. The air was heavy with a complex scent of fuel and oil mixed with dirt, grass, and sweat. On the left side, a row of lockers filled the wall. On the right, a kitchen-like counter and sink butted up to an avocado-green refrigerator. A rough wooden picnic table took up the center of the bare concrete floor. On the far wall, a steel door with a small window opened into a garage bay. A second door, just beyond the refrigerator, opened into an office.

Approaching the refrigerator, Mr. Warren asked, "Want a Coke or something?"

Kevin shook his head. "No thanks."

Pointing to the office, Mr. Warren said, "Grab a seat," while he retrieved a crinkled paper bag from the refrigerator. Kevin stepped into the windowless office and sat on a chair positioned in the corner of the room. The space was lit by a frosted glass globe light fixture in the center of the ceiling. The silhouettes of dead insects were visible in the bottom of the globe. A noticeable amount of dust layered the seldom touched items. A moment later, Mr. Warren stepped around the desk and dropped heavily into the worn vinyl desk chair. He set the paper bag on the desk and asked, "A pickup truck work for you?"

"Yeah, anything."

"It's a bit rough. Regular cab, four-by-four Chevy work truck, with a vinyl bench seat and an AM radio that doesn't work. We mostly use it for plowing snow and other nasty jobs."

"Sounds great," Kevin said.

"I've also got the black Chevy Malibu," Mr. Warren explained. "It's my loaner for the seminarians. You can take it, if you'd rather have a car."

"No, no. The truck will do. Rough is better."

"Good. That solves that problem, at least until garbage day or the snow flies. Now. Have you met any of the other guys?" Mr. Warren asked.

"Naw. Not yet, but I probably should."

"Tell you what. Let's go look at that truck, and by the time we get back in here, they'll be rolling in for lunch." Mr. Warren heaved himself up from the chair and led Kevin back into the outer room. Turning right, they passed through the door to the garage bay. Crossing the empty bay, they exited the building at the other side. Parked next to the wall was a white Chevrolet 2500 pickup truck. Hand-high gray letters on the side of the bed read *4x4*. Pockmarks of rust showed above the wheel wells. Under the front bumper and extending in front of the grill was the attachment frame and hoist for a snowplow. Auxiliary headlights were perched at hood level on the ends of antenna-like steel posts. The slight scent of garbage swirled in the turbulent air around the truck.

"It's unlocked. The keys are in the door pocket," Mr. Warren said. "Why don't you bring it around to the front of the shop, and I'll see you back inside."

Kevin nodded and climbed into the cab while Mr. Warren disappeared the way they'd come. Kevin reached down to the left door pocket and found a ring with two keys and a yellow plastic tag labeled *Bill Marine Ford, Wilmington, Ohio*. First, he tried the oval shaped key in the ignition, but it didn't fit. Trying the square key, it slid home easily. Kevin muttered, "A long way from Ohio," and started the engine.

Kevin lowered the windows and adjusted the outside mirrors.

A low rumble, with a side note of rhythmic ticking, echoed off the wall of the garage and filled the interior. Kevin twisted the interior mirror and then turned on the radio. Loud static issued from the speaker. Kevin switched the radio off again and dropped the column mounted shift lever into reverse. Immediately, a piercing beeping sound added to the rumble and tick. "That's annoying as hell," Kevin mumbled as he eased the truck backward from its parking place. Shifting into drive, the beeping ceased, and he wrestled the wheel around to the left and idled forward to the office door. He set the parking brake, shifted to park, then left the truck idling as he returned to the interior of the building.

Mr. Warren stood at the head of the picnic table and four men of various ages and builds sat evenly spaced on the benches. Seeing Kevin enter the door, he said, "That going to work for you?" Kevin nodded as Mr. Warren continued. "Fellows, this here's Kevin. He's been assigned to us for supervisory and payroll purposes, but he'll mostly be working off campus. He's the guy living down in the old farmhouse."

Kevin smiled and added, "With my brother Brian, in case you see him around."

Mr. Warren gestured to the gray-haired man seated at his left. "Kevin, this is John the Baptist. He's my assistant supervisor." Pointing to the skinny teenager with a peach fuzz beard, he said, "That's Fast Eddie. After you, he's our newest guy." Switching to the similarly shaped middle-aged men on the right side, he said, "And these two characters are the brothers Mike and Matt."

"Good to meet you." Kevin stepped forward and shook hands with each of the men.

Fast Eddie looked Kevin over and said, "You been in a fight or something, mister man? You got some dried blood in your hair and some big-ass bruising on your neck. I grew up in the hood, so I seen some fights go down."

"Had a mishap last night," Kevin shrugged, wincing a little as he did so.

Mr. Warren continued. "Now, if I'm not around and you need something, John will fix you up. He's been here nearly as long as me. If you need to know how to use a piece of equipment or find a good steak, the brothers can help you out. And Eddie here, he just came to us from the vo-tech school. He doesn't know much of anything about anything, especially interpersonal relationships and tact, but, on account of the fact that he's a savant when it comes to fixing engines and equipment, he'll be down to look at your Jeep after lunch."

"That's great, Mr. Warren. I can't thank you enough." Looking at Eddie, Kevin added, "I'll leave the key on the visor for you."

Eddie grinned and said, "Sure thing."

Mr. Warren chimed in, "Like I said. You're one of us now, and we stick together. Besides, I'm going to get you on a mower next spring, and that'll be thanks enough."

"Hey, since I'm here," Kevin said. "We're having a housewarming and bon voyage party for Father O'Conner tomorrow. I'm sure you noticed the smoker. Anyway, there will be plenty of food and beverages if you fellows want to stop by." Kevin paused for a moment, then added, "Maybe after four."

The men all looked at each other and mumbled and murmured. "Sure, yeah, okay..."

"Great," Kevin exclaimed. "Look, I left the truck running, and I gotta get going, so see you around. Maybe tomorrow."

20

Friday, October 12

12:40 p.m.

KEVIN ROLLED THE truck to a stop in front of the farmhouse, blocking the end of the driveway. The parking area was full. The Jeep was boxed in by the house, Uncle Jimmie's van on one side, and Brian's red Cherokee on the other. Turning off the engine, he tucked the key into the door pocket and exited the vehicle. Walking around to the kitchen door, Kevin was overcome by plumes of wood smoke from Jimmie's equipment. He immediately broke into a fit of loud sneezes. Ducking into the house as he covered another sneeze, he was greeted by Brian and Jimmie sitting at the kitchen table.

Brian turned and grinned at his brother. "Gesundheit!"

"Thanks," Kevin replied.

"Hey. Have you met Jimmie?" Brian asked.

"Yeah, we met earlier." Kevin half grinned, and Jimmie waved in reply. Kevin asked Brian, "How was your shift?"

"Same as it ever was. Sorry I didn't get a chance to fill you in on the party plan. Jimmie here said you might have been a little surprised to see him and all his gear."

"Yeah, but compared to my night, it wasn't a big deal."

"What happened?" Brian asked.

"I met a couple of locals and their pet two-by-four. Then the Jeep wouldn't start."

"How bad did they rough you up?"

Pointing over his shoulder with his right hand, Kevin said, "Got me good across the shoulders and then it cut the scalp at the base of my noggin."

"Sore?"

Kevin shrugged, "Yeah. Black and blue too. I bled all over from the cut. Looked worse than it was."

Brian then offered, "How about you let me look at the cut. Don't want it getting infected."

"Sure," Kevin replied and turned his back to Brian. Brian stood up from the table, grasped his brother by the shoulders, and placed him under the kitchen's flower-decorated ceiling light fixture.

Running his fingers along the back of Kevin's head, Brian spread apart the short cropped red hair. "Yep. About an inch long and pretty deep. Probably should have got a stitch or two in there."

"It isn't still bleeding, is it?" Kevin asked.

"Nah. But I don't recommend moving your head around too much. Where were you?"

Kevin hesitated a moment and answered, "I was working the job for Michele."

"Right," Brian replied, his head tilting slightly toward Jimmie. "How's that going?"

"I think I know what it looks like. The cat I mean."

"That's good, right?" Brian encouraged as he resumed his seat.

"Yeah, it is. It'll go faster that way."

"How'd you figure that out?"

"When I got the beat down, it came over to check me out," Kevin declared.

"Ugh. It thought you were—"

"Yeah."

Jimmie, observing the exchange, said, "Sorry man, I didn't realize you were busted up."

"Don't worry about it." Kevin waved off the apology just as the wall-mounted phone began ringing. Stepping over to it, Kevin picked up the handset and placed the speaker to his ear. "Hello." After a moment he continued. "Great. Perfect timing. Thanks, and I'll be up to get it in a little while."

As Kevin hung up the handset, Brian asked, "What's that about?"

"That was Mr. Warren. Some stuff I ordered for the job just came in."

"What did you get?"

"A catch-all pole and a carrier. Pretty much the armor plate version of the stuff we used down at Penn's Landing."

"That's a good idea," Brian complimented.

"Just trying to build a playbook and collect the tools of the trade."

"Well, I suggest you avoid interacting with the local lumber distributors next time. Which reminds me, you are going to be here for the party tomorrow, right?"

"I'm going back down again this evening, but I plan to come home around midnight," Kevin said. "Unless I get a hot tip."

"You got help tonight?" Brian asked. "Like, maybe somebody to watch your back?"

Kevin shrugged, "I was planning to go solo, but I was thinking I'd stay in the vehicle as much as possible. Maybe avoid getting the treatment again."

"Any idea what made you stand out as a target?"

"I've been thinking about that." Kevin paused and then said, "I'll bet some local network doesn't like me working in their territory. Or they think I'm a snitch."

Jimmie chimed in from across the table. "You know the gang saying, 'Snitches get stitches.'"

"I'll just have to be more careful," Kevin concluded.

21

Friday, October 12

9:01 p.m.

KEVIN WAITED AT a traffic light on east-bound Fairmont Avenue. His right hand lightly gripped the bottom of the steering wheel. Hanging out the truck's open window, his left hand rested on the exterior mirror. The sound of the tailpipe rattling against some part of the vehicle's frame echoed off the walls of the surrounding buildings. "Not real stealthy, Kev," he mumbled to himself. "Maybe I should've gone with the Malibu." Glancing up at the rearview mirror, the dark boxy shape of the heavy-duty animal isolation cage was showing above the tailgate. "But on the bright side, there is plenty of room for gear."

When the light changed to green, Kevin let the truck ease forward a few feet before giving it a little gas. "Good, it can do something a little less noisy," he observed as the tailpipe rattle abated. Making his way through easy evening traffic, Kevin looked for cat-like eye-shine from the faces of the pedestrians illuminated by the headlights.

Crossing over North Broadway on West Girard Avenue, the four-lane road widened to make way for trolley tracks embedded in the pavement. On the right, older buildings contained shops and storefronts. Across the street, Temple University facilities gave way to apartment buildings. Ahead, clouds reflecting the city lights silhouetted the bell tower of an old church.

The roadway dipped slightly at North Ninth Street to pass under the four-track railroad viaduct that extended out from the city center. Kevin slowed the truck in the deep darkness of the underpass and signaled a right turn at the next intersection.

Turning on Eighth street, the pavement was lined with medium-sized trees. A fenced athletic field and old brick apartment buildings occupied the street. A block ahead and to the left, the illuminated gold dome of the now-familiar Ukrainian Catholic Cathedral rose above the treetops. To the right, scrub and wild undergrowth lined the railroad viaduct. Kevin searched the street as he rolled along in a slow search. "Good hiding in there," he said as he scanned the brush.

Continuing south, he passed the west face of the cathedral and its associated buildings. In another block he turned right on Fairmont Avenue to pass under the viaduct superstructure merging with North Ninth Street. Steel commercial buildings with faded and peeling paint took the place of brick apartments. An electric power substation occupied the corner next to the elevated tracks. Kevin circled north under the railroad superstructure. For seven blocks, he examined the open grid of steel girders supporting the railway like a bridge. The square uprights were anchored to concrete pillars extending waist high above the pavement. Reflectors and yellow paint on the concrete were topped with graffiti slogans and tags.

With the wheels of the truck barely rolling forward, and the exhaust pipe rattling in time with the engine, Kevin craned his neck out the left window of the cab, searching the backlit recesses between girders. "Man, oh man. This is a good place for a cat that doesn't want to be found."

Kevin followed the superstructure north. After crossing Master Street, the railway deviated slightly west and by Jefferson Street it descended to ground level. No longer aligned with the north-south streets, the rails carved through city blocks, leaving small polygons of land that were too small to develop and were mostly left overgrown.

At Oxford Street, Kevin turned left, crossed under the railway, and slowly motored west toward Broadway. Stopping at the next intersection for a stationary car with its left taillight blinking, he scanned the surroundings in more detail. A grin erupted on his face. Slapping the empty bench seat next to him, Kevin said, "A source of water. That could be good to have nearby when it's time to corner them. I wish I'd thought of that sooner."

Once Oxford Street was clear of traffic, Kevin hastily followed the car ahead of him as it turned left onto Tenth Street. He pulled the truck into the first open parking space on the block and shut off the motor and lights. He sat still in the cab of the truck, watching the surroundings. The street was free of traffic, except for the southbound car motoring into the darkness. The west side of the block was filled with brick two-story apartment buildings. Each of the individual units had a small front lawn, surrounded by a chest-high chain-link fence that enclosed flower beds and trimmed shrubbery. Window shades glowed from interior lighting, and the occasional propped-open front door revealed scenes of domesticity inside.

On the east side of the roadway, illuminated by streetlights, was a city recreation center. The sizable lot was separated from the rest of the block by the railway. A baseball diamond and athletic field filled half the space, and a playground, basketball courts, and a half-filled swimming pool occupied the remaining area.

Seated on a deeply shadowed bench on the far side of the basketball courts, several human figures were barely discernible in the darkness. Only the occasional bounce of a basketball and outburst of muted laughter drew Kevin's attention to them. Kevin watched for a dozen minutes, staying perfectly still in the cab of the truck. Above the park bench, the red glow of a cigarette danced in the dark, occasionally glowing brighter before being passed to another of the dark figures. Kevin continued to monitor the block until the red point of light disappeared and the cluster of dark human shapes broke up. "Probably not a good night for making new friends," he said to himself. Glancing down, he reached for the ignition key. Cranking the engine to life, and flipping on the lights, he looked up again to see several figures blocking his way forward.

"Hey Johnny! I think this is the same guy we schooled last night," the closest voice called out.

"Yeah, it sure is," replied a second from outside the light cast by the truck's headlamps.

Addressing Kevin directly, the first speaker said, "You don't learn too fast, huh, Ginger?"

"I think he needs another lesson in minding his own business." Another voice laughed from behind the truck.

"Hey fellas, I'm just looking for feral cats. That's all," Kevin declared.

"Sure, you are. Feral cats. Right. Who's running with them? I never heard of that crew. This is Johnny Square's hood. Nobody comes in this territory without his okay, right Johnny?"

"You don't understand, it's not people, it's the animals—" Kevin replied as the sound of plastic and glass cracking and crushing interrupted him, "What are you doing!"

The voice at the back of the truck yelled, "Be glad we aren't busting out your face!" followed by the sound of more plastic and glass breaking.

"What the hell?" Kevin cursed as he dropped the truck into gear and tried to inch forward. Three men were now close enough to start pounding on the hood of the truck and obstruct the way forward. Kevin stopped and jammed the shift lever into reverse. The truck jerked back until the right rear tire snubbed against the curb.

A fourth man climbed up into the bed of the truck from behind. He began banging on the top of the cab and yelled, "Come on, Ginger!" Just then another vehicle turned south onto Tenth Street at the intersection; its headlights flicked to high beams and flooded the confrontation in light. The men at the front of the truck raised hands to shield their eyes from the glare. A spotless black Lincoln sedan rolled to a stop next to the truck. "Come on, Ginger!" the man in the bed yelled again, continuing to bang on the roof of the cab, not noticing the car.

The dark-tinted right front window silently lowered halfway to reveal Borys, the driver for the Ukrainian archbishop. A dark, dangerous shaped object was resting in his lap. Borys said abruptly in his thick accent. "Stop what you are doing."

The man in the bed of the truck looked over at the open window. He declared, "Ain't this some kind of bullshit!" and immediately dismounted the bed of the truck. He motioned to the others saying, "It's that Russian bodyguard and he's got some big-ass gat in there."

The three others cleared out from in front of the truck, the tallest of them saying to Borys, "He's been snooping around two nights in a row. He's a cop—or he's working for the cops."

"His business is more important than that," Borys said in a forceful tone. "Clear?"

Silently, the four men quietly shuffled off the street and dissolved into the darkness.

Borys looked at Kevin. "Sorry about the damage to the truck. They will not bother you anymore."

"I can't thank you enough. You got here just in time. How did you know I was here?"

"Let's call it guardian angel," Borys said, interrupting Kevin.

"Some of God's children," he waved his hand in the direction of the retreating figures, "only respect force. Good night." Then the window slid closed, and the car pulled away with only the sound of crunching pebbles under the tires.

22

Saturday, October 13

10:16 a.m.

THE KITCHEN PHONE was on the fourth ring when Jimmie picked up the handset. He said, "Hello, Jimmie speaking." Listening for a moment, he then replied, "Who am I? I'm the pit master for the barbecue happening later today." Following a pause, he said, "Yeah. The party is still on." Then after another pause, he responded, "Huh. He came home about midnight, but I think he might be in rough shape, you know, like he got into it with somebody again." Then Jimmie listened again before saying, "Because both headlights and a taillight are busted out on that truck he borrowed, but yeah, I'll tell him. I'll go get him right now. See you in a few minutes."

Jimmie placed the handset in the cradle then made his way across the living room to the bottom of the stairs. Looking up into the dark recesses of the upper floor, he called out, "Yo! Kevin.

Detective Johnston is going to be here in about ten minutes. You got a call out!"

Jimmie reversed course back to the kitchen and retrieved a can of beer from the refrigerator. He popped the top and took a swallow, then stood perfectly still, listening for a long moment. Unsatisfied, he grunted and returned to the bottom of the stairs.

"Kevin! Did you hear me? You got a call out!" Jimmie called again. A clunk originating somewhere above Jimmie's head caused him to direct his attention to the ceiling. "Must be awake now." Jimmie took another swig and called out again. "The police are going to be here in about eight minutes!"

On the upper floor, a door opened, filling the stairway with light. A voice called out, "I heard you. I'll be down in a sec. Did you say Johnston was on her way?"

"Yup. Johnson, or Jasmine. Something like that," Jimmie huffed. The door at the top of the stairs closed again and Jimmie headed back to the kitchen mumbling, "What am I? A den mother?"

Jimmie continued through the kitchen and stepped out the exterior door. He crossed over to the smoker and began feeding wood into the bottom of the offset firebox. "Good, good," he mumbled to himself as he clanged the door shut. He checked the temperature gauge on the main hatch and then looked at the puffs of smoke lifting away from the chimney. "Huh," he grumbled and returned to the damper at the side of the firebox. After making a slight adjustment, he stood up and watched the smoke again until an approaching car interrupted him. Finishing the beer, he tossed the empty can into a box of firewood.

The silver sedan came to a stop at the end of the crowded driveway. Detective Johnston stepped out of the car and walked up the pavement. She glanced at the white pickup with three broken lights, the white Jeep with its propped-up hood, and the rust-eaten black van. "This place is really starting to look like a junkyard," she observed out loud. Arriving at the trailer-mounted barbecue pit, she greeted Jimmie. "Uncle Jimmie! I didn't make the connection. We've met before."

"I believe we have, but this time I'm all legitimate. Just an employee."

"Good to hear." Gesturing toward the kitchen door, she asked, "Kevin up and moving?"

"I think so. Come on in. Want a beer?" Jimmie asked.

"Thanks for the offer, but it's only ten o'clock. Maybe later," Johnston replied.

"Yes, ma'am. I'll check back with you in a couple hours."

23

Saturday, October 13

10:31 a.m.

KEVIN PAUSED IN the living room doorway, freshly showered, dressed, and carrying a pair of shoes and socks. Seeing Jimmie and Detective Johnston sitting at the kitchen table, he said, "I see you two have already met."

"Old acquaintances," Johnston replied to Kevin while Jimmie said nothing. Turning back to Jimmie, Johnston asked, "How long since I arrested you the first time? Maybe three or four years?"

"Uh, something like that," Jimmie shrugged.

"Back in my uniform days." Johnston smiled at Jimmie and then turned her full attention to Kevin. "So, you've been busy?"

"I guess you could call it that," Kevin replied as he pulled a chair out from the table and sat down. Bending over, he inserted his feet into his shoes and began tying them. With his head down, the bruising up the back of Kevin's head was visible to Johnston and

Jimmie. Johnston's eyes widened and she leaned closer to Kevin.

"That's from the other night," Jimmie commented. "He has a good size cut too."

"I see it," Johnston replied as she reached over and touched the back of Kevin's head.

"What are you doing?" Kevin flinched as he finished tying his shoe. "It just looks bad, okay?"

"Who gave you that?" Johnston asked.

"A couple of punks who run with some small-timer named Johnny Squares. It's nothing. They're taken care of."

"Are they the same ones who did the work on the truck?" Johnston asked.

"Yeah, but like I said. I don't have to worry. They've been called off."

"I'd like to hear that story," Jimmie interrupted. "Those guys hold grudges."

"I agree," said Johnston.

"Maybe, but I got a job to do."

"Yes, you do, which is why I'm here," Johnston exhaled. "Grab a jacket. The boss wants your opinion."

"Okay. I figured. You driving?" Kevin asked.

Johnston said, "Yes. You ready?"

Retrieving a can of Coke from the refrigerator and a light jacket from a hook next to the door, Kevin said, "Let me get something to eat for the ride." Then he asked, "Are we going to be done in time for the party?"

"Should be, and there's some breakfast in the car for you," Johnston offered as she stood up. "Nice to see you again, Jimmie. I'm looking forward to some of your ribs."

Jimmie waved in response and watched Kevin and Johnston step out the door. After the screen door slammed shut, he said, "Now that the house will be quiet, maybe I can get a nap."

Walking down the driveway, Johnston said, "Is he sleeping here?"

"Just for the duration of the party," Kevin replied as he stopped and turned to Johnston. Johnston paused and faced Kevin, who reached out and pulled her into a kiss. Then he quietly said into her ear, "It's been a long week, and I've missed you."

"I've missed you too. A week of my mom is almost more than I can take."

Kevin chuckled and she kissed him on the cheek. "All right sailor, you need to let go. We're on the clock, so no public displays of affection." Continuing toward the unmarked police car, Johnston commented, "You've clearly been busy wrecking stuff. Have you learned anything?"

"Yeah. A few things, like to learn more about a neighborhood before you go wandering around in the dark by yourself."

"I was really asking about the cat creature you get paid to exterminate, but yes, that is a valuable lesson," Johnston said.

"Sure, well, I know what the cat looks like."

"That's a good start. How did you figure that out?" she asked.

"When I got the beatdown," Kevin said as he touched the back of his head, "this cute little cat appeared out of nowhere to check me out." After wincing as he touched the wound, he said, "If I'd been on my game, I'd have snatched it right there and been done with it."

Arriving at the car, Johnston said, "That's too bad. You can tell me about the rest on the way. Come on, the boss is waiting."

24

Saturday, October 13

10:58 a.m.

DETECTIVE JOHNSTON GUIDED the unmarked police cruiser east on Diamond Street through old neighborhoods of three-story row houses. An endless line of parked cars filled the curb space on both sides of the street. Approaching the Temple University campus, the walls of red brick gave way to steel and glass apartment and commercial buildings, mixed with multistory academic facilities. The mature trees lining the sidewalks were showing patches of fall colors in contrast to the featureless gray sky reflected in the glass facades of the buildings.

Kevin looked across at Johnston from the passenger seat and said, "You know there's a public swimming pool a dozen blocks south of here. I stopped for a look last night. That's where I met my friends."

"Are you referring to the Dendy Rec Center?" Johnston asked.

"Yeah, that's the place. It occurred to me that not every place has a handy river for dissolving these cats, and a pool could do the job."

"I guess that might work," Johnston agreed.

"And pools are usually below ground. If I can get the cat in there, even if there's no water, it should go limp, which would mean a lot less chance of me getting injured."

"I think I've underestimated your commitment to the task."

Kevin shrugged, then said, "It's what they're paying me for, isn't it?"

Johnston chuckled as she brought the car to a stop for the traffic light at Eleventh Street. She looked over at Kevin and smiled. "You are something else, sailor."

Kevin shrugged in reply.

Johnston eased the car forward when the light turned green. On the far side of the intersection, Diamond Street became one way and then narrowed for a railway underpass. On the east side of the railway viaduct, the architecture abruptly transitioned from clean and modern multiuse buildings back to century-old red brick. Grass sprouted from the cracks in the pavement. Graffiti, rust streaks, and climbing vines dominated the neighborhood scenery.

Johnston slowed the car, looking up at the street signs. The blocks were long and narrow, with the main axis running north and south. Cars in various conditions were parked on both sides of the street, many halfway up onto the deteriorating sidewalk. She called out the names as they passed. "Delhi, Percy, and there it is, Ninth Street." She stopped the car in front of an old brick building labeled *The Diamond Deli*. A large faded yellow sign advertised BEER TO GO.

Johnston asked, "Does that say twenty-one hundred block to the left?"

"Yep," Kevin confirmed, and she turned the car north.

"Twenty-one twenty-eight, and there's the other city vehicles. This must be the place." Johnston stopped the car in the middle of the street behind the medical examiner van and turned off the ignition. "I guess you're up. Time to see what they've found. Hopefully, it's something more identifiable than the pile of ash back at Eastern State."

Exiting the car, Kevin slipped on his jacket and crossed the street to the edge of an empty lot where two row houses had once stood. He looked up and down the street, and Johnston stopped behind him. She said, "Nothing but old row houses as far as the eye can see."

Ahead of them in the grass, a small crowd of people were huddled at the base of a tree on the far end of the lot. A woman in the group let out occasional and irregular wails of grief. Not far away, there were several police officers and technicians inside a cordon of yellow plastic police tape. They were looking at an unidentifiable form on the ground. "I didn't know how lucky I was until I started coming to places like this," Kevin said.

"It can kinda get to you," Johnston confirmed. "But you know, you're doing your part to make it better."

"I guess you're right. Okay, let's go." Kevin led the way toward the clump of police. Calling out as he walked through the ankle-high grass, "Hey, I'm Kevin Maloney, your special consultant. What have you got?"

The nearest officer, standing with his back to them, turned to look at Kevin and Johnston and grinned. "You're back for more, eh?"

Kevin said, "Yeah. Nice to see you again, Officer Hertz."

Hertz waved at Johnston and said in a too-friendly voice, "My favorite detective." Without missing a beat, he said, "The body was found this morning by a local resident when he came to mow the lot. Mr. Thomas Reed was able to identify the deceased as Ike Mason. Around twenty years old. He described him as a good kid. Seems that the deceased had trouble with diabetes ever since he was a child. Lived in the house right there with his mother. That's her over there along with several other family members and neighbors.

Mr. Reed said the deceased often cut across this lot when he was walking to and from work."

"Any idea how long Ike's been here?" Johnston asked.

"Reed said the lot was empty last night. He checked just before dark, yesterday, to see if the grass needed mowing," Hertz replied, looking Johnston up and down with a grin. Then he said, "I like mowing the grass. How about you, Detective?"

Johnston rolled her eyes and lightly pushed Kevin forward saying, "Get it over with so we can get out of here."

Without a word, Kevin stepped forward and crouched down to look at the body lying in a heap on the grass. The skin was shriveled tight across the bones of the visible arm and hand. The head was face down in the grass, and the uncovered ear was shrunken like a prune. The torso was twisted so that the chest was facing Kevin. A plastic name tag poked out from under the shirt.

In a soft voice, Kevin said, "The cat was following you, wasn't it? I'm so sorry, Seven. I am so sorry. You don't deserve this." Kevin quickly stood upright, looked up into the dreary overcast sky while running a hand over his red hair, and muttered, "Damn it all to hell." Looking down again at the body for a long moment, with tears welling up in the corners of his eyes, Kevin said to Hertz in a sinking voice, "Yeah. He's one of mine," and then turned back toward the silver sedan.

"I'll finish up here and join you in a few minutes," Johnston said to Kevin as he walked away.

Hertz looked to Johnston and said, "Is he okay? He needs to toughen up if he's staying in this line of work."

Johnston replied in a curt tone, "He's fine." Then she added, "Kevin must have recognized him."

Back in the isolation of the sedan, Kevin sat in silence, fidgeting with the zipper of his jacket. When Johnston finished her work on the scene, she returned to the car, dropped into the seat, and said, "Damn that Hertz!" Looking across at Kevin, she said in a quiet but firm voice, "Buckle up."

Kevin complied without a word while she started the engine and shifted the car into reverse.

Looking over her right shoulder, she backed down the block the opposite direction from their arrival. She slowed at the intersection and turned the car to resume following the eastbound flow of traffic. Dropping the car into drive, she drove a couple blocks and pulled into an empty parking space. Shifting back into park, Johnston shut off the engine and reached over to caress Kevin's shoulder. "Are you all right?" she asked in a voice softer than usual.

Looking down at his hands in his lap, Kevin replied, "That kid. His nickname is Seven. I met him the other night. He helped me when my Jeep wouldn't start."

"Ugh. That sucks. I'm sorry," Johnston replied. "The job is hard enough when they're strangers, but it's much worse when you know 'em."

"I can't say I knew him. We only talked long enough to get a jump start from his uncle." Pausing to look up at Johnston, Kevin continued. "Really, the only thing I knew about him was his nickname. He was Seven because he was the youngest of seven kids."

"But he was somebody," Johnston offered, "and he had a name. A name you knew."

"I guess I did. And now I've got to find and destroy the last image of him."

Johnston dropped her hand from his shoulder and returned it to the key in the ignition. "Come on. Let's go get a cup of coffee. It'll make you feel better."

"Sure, okay," Kevin agreed under his breath.

25

Saturday, October 13

1:41 p.m.

UNCLE JIMMIE STOOD at the end of the farmhouse driveway, watching the police sedan descend from the seminary's main road. He was dressed in black canvas sneakers, black jeans, and the outfit was topped with a black T-shirt. A tuxedo ruffle and bowtie were screen printed on the front. On the back was *Uncle Jimmie's Bigger Better Bones* with a phone number. The car stopped next to him, and the front window powered down. Johnston and Kevin looked out at Jimmie as he leaned against the window frame of the car and said, "Welcome to the party!"

"You do traffic control and parking too?" Kevin asked.

"Nothing but first class, my friend. First class!"

"The tux T-shirt is a really nice touch," Johnston added.

"Glad you like it," Jimmie grinned as he looked down at the black-and-white material stretching over his ample girth. "Custom graphics. As you know, advertising is a tax write-off." Jimmie pointed down the lane. "Would you mind starting a line facing back this way? Guests will be rolling in soon, and I want them to see where to park."

Johnston replied, "We can do that."

"Fantastic. I'll see you back at the pit." Jimmie smiled and walked back up the driveway.

Johnston coasted the sedan down to the end of the pavement and stopped at the unused gate along Lancaster Avenue. She executed a three-point turn at the end of the lane, then drove a short distance back toward the house. Stopping on the edge of the grass, she shut off the engine, and they exited the car.

Kevin met Johnston leaning against the front fender. She pointed up the driveway and said, "Is that your mom's car parked up there?"

"You ready to meet her?" Kevin asked.

"I'm sure she's as sweet as can be," Johnston said as she caught Kevin's hand and drew him closer. "She's your mother after all."

Leaning into an embrace, Kevin said, "Okay," and closed the distance, kissing Johnston.

Johnston pulled him closer and then eased him back after she ran out of breath. "That's enough sailor. You have a party to host."

"I suppose you're right."

"Time to switch gears," Johnston advised. "Put the morning behind you. Go hang out with your mom and really cool uncle. I promise the blues will fade away."

"I'm sure you're right. Let's go," Kevin relented and led the way toward the house, hand in hand with the detective.

Halfway to the kitchen door, Johnston said, "The weather guy on the radio said it might rain. It's kind of looking that way."

Kevin looked up from the driveway pavement and surveyed the sky for the first time since leaving the police cordon on Ninth Street. Dark patches of cloud had displaced the morning's uniform gray overcast. The previously still air had occasional gusts that rustled the distant, red-tinged leaves. "Huh. I missed that. He could be right."

They walked the remaining distance to the house in silence until they came across Jimmie standing next to the trailer-mounted smoker. A large white canopy on a metal frame covered two tables in the grass next to the house. An array of serving dishes and utensils held the table coverings in place against the puffs of wind. Under the tables, several open tubs were filled with cans of soft drinks and bottles of water. Next to the kitchen door, a beer keg stood in a trash can filled with ice.

"What's the plan if there's rain?" Kevin asked.

"As you can see, I got my canopy set up, so the serving line will be okay. If it gets too bad, I guess we'll move inside," Jimmie replied. "Plenty of room in the kitchen."

"Did we ever get a final estimate on people?" Kevin asked.

"Not really. I'm sure it will be fine," Jimmie replied. "We're getting close to the golden hour here, pretty much the most important thing in finishing a good barbecue, so I'm going to be pretty busy with this."

"Anything we can do?" Johnston asked.

"Skinny will be here shortly to help." He cocked his head toward the door and said, "You kids head inside and relax."

"Then we'll just stay out of your way," Kevin replied. Leading the way up the steps to the kitchen, he held the door open and then followed Johnston into the house.

They were immediately greeted by Brian, who was standing at the sink. "Hey, look who's finally here. Glad you could make it, Detective."

"Good to be here," Johnston smiled back. "It'll be nice to relax for a while."

Turning to the table, Brian gestured to the silver-haired woman seated there. "Mom, this is Kevin's lady friend. Johnston, this is our mom."

Mrs. Maloney rose from her seat and met Johnston with open

arms, embracing her in a warm hug. "It's nice to meet you! I've heard so many nice things, and a detective! That is very impressive."

"Aw thanks," Johnston replied, grinning at the brothers over their mother's shoulder.

"Now let me see my baby boy," Mrs. Maloney said while releasing Johnston. Johnston backed away a half step and let her pivot to Kevin. "Oh, it's so good to see you," Mrs. Maloney said as she embraced Kevin.

"You too, Mom."

"I know it's only been a couple weeks since you came by, but at my age, that can feel like forever," Mrs. Maloney declared.

"I'll try to get by more often, but you know this job here has me pretty busy," Kevin replied.

"Yes, yes. Your father always said that, but you're never too busy for your family. And that goes for you, too, Brian."

Unseen by Mrs. Maloney, but clearly visible to Kevin and Johnston, Brian rolled his eyes and said, "Yes, Ma. We'll both try to do better."

"Good boys. Now when is your Uncle Matthew coming down?"

"He should be here any moment," Brian replied, then asked, "Anybody want something to drink?"

Johnston shook her head and Kevin said, "I'm good." Turning back to his mom, Kevin asked, "Did Brian show you around the place?"

"He did. I never saw it, but I'm sure it's much better than the basement where you two were living before." Turning to Johnston, she asked, "Did you ever see that mole hole?"

"I did, and you're right. This is much better, but I haven't seen it since they got it fully furnished."

"I guess I should give you the ten-cent tour," Kevin offered, and Johnston nodded. "We'll be right back, Mom." Kevin and Johnston stepped through the doorway and disappeared into the living room.

After Johnston and Kevin had thumped up the stairs, Brian asked, "So, what do you think of her?"

"I'm sure she's a good catch," Mrs. Maloney replied with a slight shrug of her shoulders.

"You don't like Detective Johnston?" Brian responded in a surprised voice.

Mrs. Maloney explained, "It's just too early to tell. I was wrong before—about your marriage—so I'm going to play this one a little closer to the vest. You know what I mean?"

"I guess so. But Mom, from what I've seen so far, Della is the real deal. She doesn't put on airs or pretend to be something she's not. You know? She's practical. Hell, she could be just one of the guys. I think that's why she just goes by Johnston. Della sounds too girly." Then in a lower voice, Brian said, "Oh and don't say I told you her first name."

"Now you see there, that's a problem too." Mrs. Maloney continued. "A successful woman must blend in, and yet still stand a little apart. Especially in a male-dominated world like the police precinct or firehouse. That's why she goes by Detective Johnston, and not her given name. If she let the boys call her by something more familiar, she'd lose their respect."

"Yeah, maybe," Brian relented.

Mrs. Maloney continued. "I'll tell you though, the one I'm really worried about is Kevin. He doesn't look so good. I think he's feeling stressed. I don't think he's getting enough sleep, and did he get hurt?"

Brian looked at his mother and said, "How could you tell?"

"A mother knows these things," she said flatly.

"He had a run in with some thugs. He didn't get hurt bad. Just got scared, really, but you're right," Brian said before pausing. "He's so serious about resolving the problems of the dead that he's almost got no regard for the living."

Mrs. Maloney asked, "Is this going to be a regular part of this job?"

"I don't know, Ma."

"You've got to look out for your brother, Brian. I don't want anything bad happening to him. He's my baby, after all."

"Ma, he's a grown man. He's been to war. I think he can handle himself."

Mrs. Maloney looked Brian in the eye with a hard stare and raised her eyebrows until Brian said, "Yeah, I know. I'm trying."

"Thank you, dear," Mrs. Maloney responded. "That's all I can ask for."

26

Saturday, October 13

1:52 p.m.

DESCENDING THE STAIRS into the living room, Detective Johnston said, "Thanks for the tour. You boys have done a fair job of making this place habitable."

Kevin responded, "We're trying."

Johnston then pointed to an acoustic guitar case standing in the corner and said, "Who plays guitar? You didn't mention anything about musical skills. Is it Brian?"

"Um, neither of us." Kevin followed Johnston's gaze to the guitar case. "I'm going to guess that's Uncle Jimmie's. He said there would be entertainment."

"Well, this ought to be good," Johnston snickered as she led the way to the kitchen.

Standing at the door to the driveway, arms spread wide at the sight of Johnston and Kevin, Father Matthew said, "Here they are!"

"Hey! It's been a little while, hasn't it?" Johnston said as she approached him and allowed herself to be folded into a hug. "It's good to see you, and I'm a little jealous about the trip you're taking."

"The man of the hour! Uncle Matt, I'm so glad you could make it," Kevin chimed in.

Releasing his hold on Johnston, he stepped back, and said, "It isn't often an old priest like me gets a party in his honor."

"We're glad to do it," Brian said, then added, "We're going to have a great time. A big send off for your equally big trip to Rome."

Gesturing around the room, Matthew said, "This looks like a good start. Who else is coming?"

"Some of the crew from the firehouse and a few of the new friends we made over the summer," Brian grinned. "In fact, I think I hear somebody now." Standing up, Brian stepped to the door and said, "I'd better go attend to the parking."

Kevin followed Brian to the door, saying to the others, "You guys get comfy and catch up a little. I'll see how Jimmie is coming along."

"Let me know if you need help," Johnston called after Kevin and Brian as the door closed behind them. She then took a seat at the table, looked at Mrs. Maloney and Father Matthew, and started a conversation by asking, "When was the last time you two saw each other?"

* * *

Outside the back door of the house, Brian and Kevin watched a threesome of men dressed in shorts and casual shirts walking up the driveway. Kevin asked Brian, "Do I know these guys? I think I've seen them before, but I couldn't say when or where."

Brian replied, "You met them like six weeks back. The handsome guy is James Dunne. He was running the ambulance crew that pulled the guy out of the stairwell. The taller one is Tony Martini and the other is Glenn Carter. They're the guys that got all scratched up."

Kevin's eyes got big as he said, "Damn. That seems like a whole lifetime ago."

Brian spread his arms wide and called out to the approaching ambulance crew, "Hey fellas, glad you could make it! Come on up, come on up."

As the new arrivals reached the back of the house, Brian introduced Kevin and the crew to each other. He then pointed back toward the smoker while they all shook hands with Kevin. "We're going to have some of the best barbecue in town here in just a few minutes. In the meantime, there's coolers with beverages under the tent. Help yourselves."

James responded for the others with a big grin, "It was good of you to have us out."

Kevin added, "Yeah, I really appreciate you guys and what you did for us. I mean, you were right there with us." The three men nodded, and Kevin's eyes locked onto the red marks on Tony and Glenn's faces and hands. "Are the . . . are the wounds healing?"

Tony guffawed, "Yeah, yeah. Got us some extra paid days off. Just part of the job."

Glenn chuckled and followed Tony's casual response, "But I'll take a pass if you ask me to try cat-wrestling again." All five men responded with a laugh, and Tony and Glenn exchanged a fist-bump.

Brian then asked, gesturing toward the driveway, "Is Skinny down there?"

Tony responded, "Yeah. He's directing traffic."

"Okay, good. I'll go check on him. You guys talk amongst yourselves," Brian said as he stepped away from the group.

Glenn made his way to the keg and poured cups of beer. He handed them around, but Kevin waved off the drink. Then Glenn asked, "Have you figured out what that cat thing was? 'Cause I never saw something like that before." Pointing to the scar above Tony's right eye, he continued. "Tony's underselling it. That one there? It went to the bone and the docs tried everything to stop the bleeding. He was the freak show of the station house for weeks."

Tony looked away for a moment, then came eye to eye with Kevin and said, "It wasn't like that." After a swallow of beer, he continued. "No big deal. It was only a few times. Like when they'd make me squint or something. The scab would pull up and I'd be like, squirting blood from my eye for like five minutes. It's like any face or scalp wound. They just look like a lot of blood, but really, everybody would get a good laugh out of it. Eventually my granny heard about it. She's always got some home remedy, and she said to put a wet tea bag on it. So that's what I did, and it would stop the bleeding pretty quick."

James chimed in, "You wouldn't believe the ribbing he took until Glenn popped a scab, and he tried it. Seemed to work."

"That's one hell of a pro tip," Kevin replied. "Now I'll know what to do when I get scratched again."

James looked at Kevin with a more serious eye, "What do you mean 'again?' Are you saying there's more of those cats out there?"

Kevin looked down at the ground and then at the other half dozen people walking up the driveway before continuing. "Yeah. I'm trying to round one up right now. A little black-and-white furball in North Philly."

Glenn chimed in, "Glad it's not us. Our jobs are hard enough as it is. We don't need to be chasing wicked little beasties."

"Yeah, well, somebody's gotta do it. Might as well be me," Kevin shrugged. "So far, though, I haven't really had any problems with the cat. It's the folks in the neighborhood that have been giving me a hard time."

James nodded. "I hear you. A lot of runs require police escort. Amazing how ungrateful folks can be."

"Okay, enough work talk," Kevin said. He then pivoted toward the smoker and pointed, "My new roomie, Uncle Jimmie here, has some great-looking food, so help yourself. I'll catch up with you later."

The three nodded and Kevin broke free from the little group. He worked his way down the driveway greeting the other newcomers. At the lane descending from the main buildings, Kevin found Brian talking to a rotund older man sporting a gray walrus-style mustache and a bald head.

Brian turned to Kevin. "Hey, little brother, I want you to meet Skinny, and Skinny, this is my brother Kevin." The older man made a grand gesture of swinging his hand around to grip Kevin's in a prolonged handshake. A wide grin spread beneath the mustache.

"I'm so glad to meet you! Brian here has told me all about you and your adventures over in the Helmand Province and back here in the City of Brotherly Love."

Releasing the handshake, Kevin returned the smile and said, "I've heard a lot about you too. Apparently, you're well known throughout the civil servant community."

Skinny chuckled and said, "When you've been around as long as I have, people are bound to remember you—especially my enemies!" All three men laughed, and Skinny continued. "Is Jimmie working out? I got a lot tied up in this little sideshow, and he's got some personality. That boy is quite the talker, if you haven't discovered that."

Kevin chuffed before saying, "He's growing on me. If the food's as good as he claims, you'll be okay." Turning to Brian, Kevin pointed up the road at a half dozen cars coming toward the house and asked, "How many folks are we expecting? The last group coming through said they were pals of yours from the fire academy. You didn't invite all of them, did you?"

"Nah. It'll be thirty, or maybe a few more if folks bring their significant others."

Kevin held out a hand and pointed and counted on his fingers. "I've got seventeen already. You sure we've got enough stuff? And the weather's going to go bad soon. I'm not sure how many the house can hold if the rain comes down."

Brian shrugged off the statement. "You worry too much. It'll be just fine."

27

Saturday, October 13

5:09 p.m.

WIND GUSTS RIPPLED in waves across the wide lawn of the seminary, and scattered rain drops pelted against the dozens of cars parked around the farmhouse. The trees along the west fence line swayed in wide arcs, surrendering faded leaves to the building breeze. Uncle Jimmie, his ponytail breaking loose from the rubber band, rushed around the yard securing his equipment against the coming weather. When the last loose items were loaded in the back of the black van, he slammed the double doors and sprinted up the kitchen steps.

Finally, inside, with long blond hair plastered to his face by rain, Jimmie shuffled through the shoulder-to-shoulder crowd in the kitchen. There were empty plates and cups on the counters and table. The room was humid and warm from damp bodies and loud with voices trying to overcome the ambient sounds. He paused long enough to straighten out his ponytail and then began worming his way toward the living room. As he passed, he asked attendees, "Excuse me, did everybody get enough?"

At the doorway between the rooms, he called out in a raised voice, "If I can have your attention for a moment! Attention, please!" Someone in the living room made a loud whistle and the voices slowly abated. Jimmie looked around, bobbing his head saying, "Listen, this is a great party you've got going here. Thanks everybody for coming out. I mean, I lost count at fifty people. Wow! I'm sorry we couldn't stay outside, but, well, look, we're still going to have a great time, right? So about now, before you kids get too inebriated, Kevin probably has something to say, so I'm going to give him the floor, and when he's done speechifying, I'll be right over there for some acoustic entertainment. Right on?"

Kevin stood up from the kitchen table where he was sitting with his grade school pal Mark Francini and made his way to the center of the living room doorway. "Yeah, I guess I could say a few things here." Looking around, he locked eyes with his brother, then pointed at him. "First, I got to thank my big brother for his help and stuff. He put together this party on short notice and really brought out the crowd. Thanks for that."

Kevin continued. "Thanks, Jimmie and Skinny. You two put out a nice spread." Jimmie and Skinny both nodded, and several people called out, clapped, and whistled in acknowledgment. Kevin glanced at his mother and Uncle Matt. "Six months ago, when I separated from the Navy, I would never have guessed how many people in Philly would impact my life. I mean, I was part of the big Navy-Marine Corps team, and I thought that was never going to happen again. But look around this room. I moved back after being away for twelve years, and here you all are. Firefighters, EMTs, police. Nurse Nel, my former boss Daisy, from the *Moshulu*, Mark and Jessica, Mom, Detective Johnston. You guys are all great, and thanks for coming out. I mean it, thanks so much." After another round of brief applause and whistles, Kevin resumed, "Now, I've got to get to the heart of what this party is all about."

Pointing into the kitchen, Kevin called out Uncle Matt and Stepan. "Why don't you two come stand up so everybody can see you?" As the old priest and the towering deacon made their way toward the center of the crowd, Kevin resumed. "These two characters are going on a trip to Europe tomorrow afternoon. They're going to go see the queen of Denmark, the czar of Russia, and premier of Lesser Transylvania. And on the way back, they might squeeze in an audience with the pope. Now, I know Father O'Conner, otherwise known as Uncle Matt, hasn't been outside the seminary walls in something like a hundred years, so this is a big adventure for him. Protodeacon Stepan has agreed to show him the best holiday spots in all of Europe. They told me they'd be home in a month, but really, they're traveling for work, so you know, who can say when they'll get back. Right?" Chuckles spread around the room. "If you will join me, I want to hoist a glass for these two travelers." As arms and hands holding cups and bottles rose all around the room, Kevin looked the two men in the eyes. "May you have a safe journey, and wherever you go, may you enjoy God's protection!"

A chorus of "Hear, hear!" filled the house, followed by sporadic glasses and bottles clinking together around the rooms. Uncle Matt and Stepan were hugged, patted, and kissed endlessly as they made their way back into the kitchen.

Jimmie replaced Kevin in the center of the crowd and said, "That was great Kevin. Thanks for the inspiring words. Okay, if you want to take a minute to top off your glasses, we'll get together here in the living room and see who among you has a little rhythm!"

The crowd didn't move much, but several people began handing around cups of beer. Soon, Jimmie called out from the front corner of the living room, "Anybody else need a drink?" A voice replied from the vicinity of the stairs asking for a couple more, and soon a few more cups were passed from the kitchen toward the other side of the living room. Jimmie grinned as he lifted an acoustic guitar from the case propped in the corner. "You cats are a great crowd. We're going to have some real fun."

Jimmie set up a stool and microphone, then plugged a cable into the bottom of his guitar and adjusted a small amplifier next to the stool. With the instrument strapped in place over his girth, Jimmie began plucking at the strings. "Whoops, that's a bit out of tune," he said as he twisted keys on the head of the instrument. "That's better." Satisfied with the sound of a strum, he began playing a quiet intro and said, "Listen . . . here's how this works. I'm going to sing some songs that you might recognize. If you know how it goes, you sing along. Okay? Then, if you think of a song I should play, I got another mic up here for you . And don't worry about me knowing the tune. I know more than you, I promise. Everybody got it? All right, here we go . . . Since we're talking about taking a trip, this is a nice traveling tune by the Eagles you might recognize" Jimmie's strumming became more enthusiastic and he leaned into the microphone, "I've been running down the road, trying to loosen my load, I had seven women on my mind . . ." Within a minute, several of the younger firefighters and their dates were clapping and singing along with Jimmie.

* * *

With the rain ending around midnight, Kevin and Detective Johnston retreated to the steps outside the front door of the house. They watched the glow of the full moon illuminate the cumulus clouds from above. She clung to his arm and rested her head on his shoulder. Behind them, the door stood open, allowing the sounds of Uncle Jimmie and a few singers struggling through the verses of Don McClean's "American Pie" to escape into the night.

Johnston raised her head and looked at Kevin, saying, "This has been some kind of crazy-ass party."

Kevin huffed, "Yeah. One hell of a show." Looking back at Johnston, he leaned toward her and kissed the top of her head. "I'm a little bit thankful Mom and Uncle Matt called it quits shortly after Jimmie started playing. When he started handing out the tambourines and bongos, it kinda got out of control."

"But it was fun," Johnston chuckled.

"Yes," Kevin agreed, "crazy fun. That guy is something else. The wedding singer story and jokes were hilarious."

"A party for the ages," Johnston smiled and cocked an ear toward the door. No sounds were coming from the living room, and nobody appeared to be moving.

She said, "The music stopped."

"Don't you mean the music died?" Kevin quipped.

Johnston said, "Har, har," and released Kevin's arm as he pivoted toward the doorway. Kevin asked, "I wonder if Jimmie ran out of singers or songs?" Standing up, he leaned into the house and surveyed the wreckage of the living room. Jimmie was leaning on the frame of the kitchen doorway, tipping back a bottle of beer. Several people reclined on the couch, or next to the couch, mostly with eyes closed. Abandoned instruments were scattered around, and a man and pregnant woman were making out at the base of the stairway. Turning back to Johnston, Kevin observed, "Looks like he ran out of singers, except for Mark and Jessica over there, but they seem to have something more important going on." Johnston grinned at the remark and reached up to Kevin. He took her hand and helped her to a standing position. "Come on, let's see about sending the love birds home and cleaning up the carnage."

"Right behind you," Johnston said.

28

Wednesday, October 17

2:00 p.m.

KEVIN IDLED THE black Chevy Malibu to the apartment building located up the hill from the seminary's maintenance facilities. A scattering of orange and red leaves dotted the driveway. Blown down by the persistent west wind, the leaves contrasted with the gray overcast sky. Kevin stopped the car under the building's portico and popped the trunk lid.

Two unblemished royal blue roller suitcases stood on the front step. Exiting the car, Kevin set to work loading them into the trunk. When the second was secured, Father Matt emerged from the door wearing his usual blacks and collar. He was carrying a black jacket and a new carry-on bag that matched the suitcases.

Father Matt greeted Kevin as he approached the car. "Hello, Kevin!"

"Hey, there. You rested up from all the festivities?"

"That was some cook-out your brother put on. I must say I was darn tired by the time I made it back home, but it was worth it to meet the folks who've helped us out all summer. And your mother. We had such a nice visit."

"I think she really enjoyed it too," Kevin agreed. Father Matt handed the carry-on to Kevin, who placed it in the trunk and closed the lid. "That's some nice new luggage. Got it just for this trip?"

"Actually, it was a gift from your mother."

"Right on! Mom always knows exactly what people need. Speaking of which, is Stepan still meeting you at the airport?"

"I just spoke with him. He has a driver coming for him in a few minutes."

"Borys, I'm sure. That guy is everywhere," Kevin chuffed. "Okay, before you get in, do you have your flight information and passport?"

Father Matt patted his pocket. "Right here. American Airlines, 6:48 p.m. direct to Rome's FCO airport," Father Matt said as they walked to their respective doors and got into the car.

When the doors were shut, Father Matt continued from the passenger seat. "Thank you for driving me. It gives us a chance to talk for a few moments. This may be the last opportunity we have to discuss the cat and all it means in person. I suspect communications will become irregular once Stepan and I get to Italy."

"You know it isn't the Dark Ages over there," Kevin smiled. "Despite all the ancient Roman ruins and stuff, everybody has a cell phone that can make international calls."

"Yes, they do," Father Matt agreed. "And I don't care to share our business over the airwaves, even in friendly territory. No matter how routine all this may seem to you and me, it isn't part of the canon as most folks understand it." Looking right into Kevin's eyes, Matt said, "Your work has the potential to cause disruptions. You know what I mean?"

Kevin looked away from Father Matt and fidgeted with the key tag hanging from the ignition, "Stepan said something similar when we first discussed making this my full-time job. I will try to keep it in mind."

"Good," Father Matt declared in a relaxed but serious tone. "Now, let's go to the airport. I haven't been there in years. I suspect it has changed."

Kevin chuckled as he started the car and pulled around the parking lot and pointed the car toward the gate. "How long has it been since you flew on an airliner?"

Father Matt smiled and looked out the window. "Gosh, I don't know, sometime before you were born."

"I got to give you a heads-up about some things," Kevin said in a suddenly serious tone.

"What's that?" Father Matt inquired.

"You're going to get a security screening. They'll make you put your bag and shoes through an x-ray and make you go through a metal detector.

"Is that so?" Matt's eyebrows raised. "I suppose it's all related to the terrorists."

Kevin dipped his head once and added, "And just so you know, most of the airplanes don't have propellers anymore. So, when you can't see anything happening outside the window, it's okay."

With a deathly serious expression and gasp, Matt put a hand on Kevin's shoulder and said, "So, how do they fly?"

Kevin glanced over at his uncle and reacted to the expression on his face, "They have jet engines, now."

Father Matt turned away and began a deep belly laugh as Kevin brought the car to a stop at the gate. Kevin looked at his uncle and said, "You . . . really? That's how you're going to play this?" Father Matt continued to laugh as Kevin turned right out of the seminary and headed south on Wynnewood Road.

At the City Avenue traffic light, Kevin made a quick left followed by a right onto Sixty-third Street and motored south through the Overbrook neighborhood. Passing a stone church on the right,

Father Matt said, "That's Our Lady of Lourdes." His eyes continued to follow the scenery until the building was obscured behind a curve in the road. "I used to say Mass there, as a substitute. That church goes back to the 1890s."

Kevin glanced over at his uncle and said, "I've driven by it a few times, but never really paid attention. The parish seems to take care of it."

"They do. The building is English Gothic style intended to compliment the houses in the area. It is built of granite and trimmed in limestone and originally cost twenty-seven thousand dollars . . . but . . . anyway. You don't need to hear about that."

As Kevin continued south along the street, the stone houses on the east side gave way to some smaller brick structures. The west side was lined with large stone homes shaded by mature oaks and maples. Crossing Landsdowne Avenue, the large houses were replaced with the city's ubiquitous row houses. The farther south they traveled, the more the buildings appeared decayed. Approaching Market Street and the SEPTA elevated train line, the right side of the street was lined with the green space of Cobbs Creek Park. Coming to a stop at the Market Street intersection, Kevin looked across at his uncle and asked, "So what's your plan when you get there?"

Father Matt smiled back at Kevin. "Stepan has been busy planning everything. I understand somebody will meet us at the airport, and we'll be staying at a hotel near the Vatican."

"Not in the Vatican proper?" Kevin asked.

Father Matt said, "Stepan makes a very good point about keeping a low profile."

"Right on," Kevin agreed. "I'm sure they have factions, and the factions have watchers, just like anywhere else."

"He might be overly suspicious by nature, but since he's been in this line of work for a while, I'm going to follow his lead," Father Matt said.

Moving with the traffic again, the Malibu continued straight along the boundary of West Philadelphia until the street became the Cobbs Creek Parkway, following the stream for which it was named. After a left and right turn to cross Baltimore Avenue and a railway, the Parkway separated from the neighborhoods and dropped into the shallow creek valley and wound its way south with the watershed.

Father Matt continued the conversation. "Are you making headway with the next visitor?"

Kevin shrugged, "I guess so. I think I can identify the cat. I know the general area where it roams, and I'm certain I know its current human form, because I knew the victim."

"From the sound of your voice," Father Matt stated, "you're feeling some pressure to put this one behind you."

Kevin glanced at Father Matt and replied, "For a number of reasons, but mostly because I don't want to take another beatdown. If it weren't for Borys driving by last time, I might not be here right now."

"I'm sorry you found yourself in such a predicament."

"Yeah, me too," Kevin agreed, "but don't worry. I've got some new ideas for getting this thing resolved."

Father Matt patted Kevin's right shoulder and said, "Good. Keep trying new ideas, and remember, the sanctuary at the Ukrainian Cathedral is more than just a place of worship. You can count on them."

"I just hope it doesn't come to that," Kevin exhaled as he steered the car down the tree-lined road.

The Parkway followed the terrain until it eventually emerged onto the wide flood plain of the Delaware River and became Island Avenue. At Bartram Avenue, Kevin turned right and followed the traffic onto the ramps across Interstate 95 to Terminal A at the Philadelphia International Airport.

Slowing for the increasingly congested traffic, Kevin said, "I'm going to park in the garage and walk over with you, if that's all right.

I want to make sure you get checked in okay."

Father Matt said, "No need. Stepan said he'd meet me curbside at Departures."

"Oh, okay," Kevin blurted and quickly looked over his shoulder to find a space where he could move to the curb lane. Edging in between two slow-moving cars, he made his way to the right and brought the car to a stop where Borys, dressed in a black suit and matching black tie, was standing with a baggage cart. Kevin activated the remote trunk release and smirked. "I told you he was everywhere."

"So, it would seem," Father Matt agreed as his door was opened for him by the Ukrainian driver, who then disappeared behind the car and unloaded the suitcases. Father Matt turned to Kevin and extended a hand across the seat of the car. "Good hunting, and I hope to come back with some useful information to make your job easier."

Kevin gripped the hand and guided the old priest into an awkward embrace. He said, "Have fun and be careful over there. I can't wait to see what you find."

Father Matt exited the car just as Borys closed the trunk and rapped on it twice. Kevin waved at his smiling uncle as Borys came back to the open passenger door. Borys leaned in before closing the door and said, "Do not worry about your uncle. He is in God's hands."

29

Thursday, October 18

10:00 a.m.

THE KITCHEN PHONE began ringing just as Uncle Jimmie emerged from the bathroom. He turned to face the stairs and called out, "Brian! Kevin! Are you home? The phone's ringing. I'm sure it's for you!" On the third ring, and with no response from the upstairs bedrooms, Jimmie shuffled through the living room to the kitchen. Scooping the handset from its cradle, he held it up to his ear and said, "Hello, Kevin and Brian's phone. Uncle Jimmie speaking."

Jimmie leaned against the wall and replied after long intervals of listening, "Okay. That's great. Hey, listen, I'll pass that along. I'm glad you made it there in good shape. You take care. Okay. I'll write it down. No? Okay, I'll just tell them. See ya. Bye." Hanging up the phone, Jimmie crossed to the kitchen counter. He rummaged through the cabinets and refrigerator. Finding the box of Frosted Flakes, he shook the remaining cereal and crumbs into a bowl. The partial carton of milk wet the flakes, and he was happily eating breakfast when Kevin entered the kitchen.

"You're still here?"

Munching away, Jimmie hummed a reply through closed lips until the mouthful was swallowed. "Yeah. Still here." Bobbing his head up and down, he continued. "It was a big clean-up job, you know? But hey, I could be out of here later today. Right?"

Kevin squinted at Jimmie, "I kinda feel like we did most of the work yesterday while you were sleeping it off." Jimmie continued eating while Kevin circled around to the other side of the table. "What do you have left to do, and where did you sleep last night?" Kevin asked.

"I, uh, crashed out in the van. Now that it's mostly empty, I can get to my bed in there. You don't mind, do you? Anyway, I gotta finish the smoker," Jimmie offered, "and the outside area. It won't take too long."

Kevin scratched his chin and looked at Jimmie, "So, I'm going out for the afternoon. You'll be gone when I get back?"

"Yeah, I think so, probably."

Kevin pointed to the phone and said, "Did I hear the phone ring?"

"Hey, yeah, that was Father O'Conner, from Rome. He said to tell you they made it okay. The flight was good, and they are staying at the Hotel Della Conciliazione, on some street named Borgo Pio."

"That's good news," Kevin agreed.

Jimmie continued. "He said they'd get started tomorrow. I wasn't sure what that meant. Are they sightseeing or something?"

"No, but that's great. Will you leave a note for Brian?" Kevin asked.

"No," Jimmie blurted. "I mean. He said I wasn't to write anything down, I mean. I don't know why not."

Kevin interrupted Jimmie and said, "Actually, that's a good idea. I'll tell Brian, unless you see him first." Kevin pivoted back to the living room and disappeared into the bathroom, followed by the sound of water running in the shower.

Jimmie finished his bowl of cereal and took his used dishes to the sink, where he began washing the accumulated kitchen items stacked in the basin. When the bowls, plates, and utensils were rinsed, he arranged them on the drying rack and patted his hands dry with a dish towel. Reaching for the exterior door, he paused at the sound of the phone ringing again. "What am I, an answering service?"

Picking up the handset, he said, "Hello, Kevin and Brian's phone. Uncle Jimmie speaking." Jimmie remained silent for a long moment and then hung up the handset. He spun around and crossed the living room to the bathroom door and rapped loudly.

From inside the room, the sound of the shower stopped, and Kevin called, "What is it?"

Jimmie replied, "Another phone call for you."

"Who was it?"

Jimmie frowned as he said, "Didn't say."

Kevin made an audible groan and said, "Hold on."

Jimmie took a couple steps to the couch and dropped into the soft leather, closed his eyes, and leaned his head back. After some time, the bathroom door opened and Kevin emerged wearing only a pair of green USMC running shorts, with a towel over his shoulder. He asked, "What did they say?"

Jimmie's eyes popped open again. "Have you ever heard of an answering machine? I think you should look into it. Anyway, the mysterious caller, who wouldn't identify herself, said you're going to the Brandywine Airport today, and you need to pack an overnight bag."

Kevin looked Jimmie in the eye, "That's it? No other details?"

"Uh, oh yeah. She said Mr. Warren would pick you up at twelve. That's it. Then she hung up."

Kevin started up the stairs and then paused. "Okay. I guess I'm not going to North Philly today. Can you tell Brian about all this when you see him?"

Jimmie, closed his eyes and said, "Sure thing, boss," as Kevin bounded up the stairs.

30

Thursday, October 18

12:17 p.m.

THE BLACK CHEVY Malibu rolled to a stop in front of a two-level, red brick building. Built into the side of an embankment, the upper level was even with the paved apron of an aircraft parking area. From the passenger seat, Kevin read the sign under the edge of the roof, *Brandywine Airport*. Turning to Mr. Warren in the driver's seat, he added, "I guess we're in the right place."

Mr. Warren nodded and said, "Sister Elizabeth said I should wait for a few minutes to make sure you get hooked up with the right person. So, give me a wave when you're good to go."

"Good plan. Thanks for the ride," Kevin said, shaking hands with him before exiting the car. He retrieved his backpack from the rear seat and climbed the concrete stairway leading up the left side of the building. At the top, he pulled the door open and entered.

A tall man with salt and pepper hair and a handlebar moustache stood behind the service counter. He glanced at Kevin and held up a finger. "I'll be right with you." Picking up a walkie-talkie he spoke into the microphone and said, "Hey Stretch, when you are done with the Pennstar helicopter, take the avgas truck down to November-eight-niner-Mike-Juliet for a top-off."

While clipping the walkie-talkie to his belt, the man watched out the window as a white tanker truck with a Phillips 66 logo motor slowly up the taxiway. Then he smirked at the distinctly human, yet unintelligible sound emitting from the speaker of his radio. Turning back to Kevin the man asked, "You Mr. Maloney?"

"Yeah—Kevin. I guess I'm supposed to meet somebody here."

The man deadpanned when he said, "I'm Lou." Then he asked, "Any other bags?" Kevin shook his head as Lou continued. "The restrooms are around the corner. I suggest you take the opportunity now. Your ride will be ready shortly. Then I'll take you out to the ramp."

Kevin leaned his pack against the counter and stepped back to the door he'd just entered. Pushing it open, he leaned out and gave a thumbs-up to Mr. Warren. Then he followed the man's directions to the restroom.

Emerging from the restroom, Kevin saw Lou pulling up in front of the building in a white four-seat golf cart. Lou returned to the building and said, "Get your bag, I'm going to take you down now." Kevin complied without a word and followed Lou to the cart.

Driving down the aircraft taxiway to the west, Kevin held his pack on his lap and took in the surroundings. After passing a half dozen rows of prefabricated metal aircraft hangars, Lou steered the cart along a yellow line leading between two rows of T-hangars. At the end of the pavement, Kevin saw a man with a strange one-wheeled powered dolly pulling a sleek blue-and-white low-wing aircraft from an open hangar bay.

The smooth swooping shape of the fuselage was balanced on spindly landing gear with tires that seemed too small for the job.

A wide, gray metal propeller hung at the end of the pointed nose. On the left side of the cabin, a gull-wing door was propped open, revealing the large block lettering on the inside that spelled out *EXPERIMENTAL*. Lou said, "That's your ride. Lancair Four. Except for the jets, it's the fastest thing on the field."

Stopping the cart near the airplane, Lou waved at the man operating the dolly and trotted out to the aircraft with a pair of yellow wheel chocks. He crouched down from behind the wing and placed them under the now stationary left wheel. He then returned to the cart, where he instructed Kevin, "Follow me. Stay behind the wing. Don't want you meeting the prop."

Kevin nodded and followed the man across the pavement. Drawing up next to Lou as they walked, Kevin asked, "What does experimental mean?"

Lou grinned and said, "Amateur built, but don't worry about it," as they approached the left side of the aircraft between the wing and tail. The stocky pilot, dressed in khaki trousers and a sage-green military flight jacket, now stood on the ground at the back edge of the wing and opened a small baggage door. He pulled out a folding step stool, set it on the ground and held it in place with his foot. He said, "I'll take your bag. Use the stool and then step up to the wing. Keep your feet on the black painted walkway. Don't touch anything except the seat as you sit down. Then slide over to the right seat."

Kevin nodded, handed off his bag, then stepped where the pilot pointed. Reaching the open door, he carefully let himself down into the pilot's seat. Then he scooted over to the right seat, avoiding contact with anything but the tan upholstery.

Outside, the pilot climbed up onto the wing and turned around to watch Lou snatch the step stool and place it in the baggage compartment with Kevin's backpack. He then secured the hatch on the side of the aircraft. With a quick salute toward Lou, the pilot joined Kevin in the cabin and pulled down the gull-wing door. After engaging the door latches, he pointed to a pair of earphones and directed Kevin to put them on. The pilot donned a red baseball cap emblazoned with a stylized white P over his close-cropped hair and then added a pair of headphones. He buckled his seatbelt and then flipped some switches on the left side of the instrument panel. The pilot said into the boom microphone attached to his headphones, "Can you hear me?" Kevin nodded as the pilot gestured toward Kevin's seatbelt. "Put that on. Just in case we have a rough ride."

Lou stationed himself ahead of the left wingtip and watched the pilot. The pilot made a spinning gesture with his index finger that Lou mimicked with his own finger. The pilot then engaged the ignition key switch and the propeller swung to life with a couple of chuffs and then a low roar.

After moving more switches, consulting a laminated card, and touching several instruments, the pilot looked back to Lou and made a two-handed gesture with his thumbs pointing out. Lou duplicated the gesture and retrieved the wheel chocks from the left wheel before retreating to the golf cart. The pilot then reached over to Kevin's headphones and pulled the attached microphone into place in front of Kevin's lips. He then said into his own mic, "It's voice activated, just speak normally. So, how are you doing? It's been a few weeks since I came down to center-city with Mark, eh?"

Kevin replied, "Great . . . I guess. I'm a little confused. Have we met? And where are we going, if you don't mind me asking?"

The pilot chuckled and slapped his own thigh. "Hello, Maloney. You in there? It's me, Skip. Mark's brother-in-law. And we're going to Lunken Field in Cincinnati, Ohio."

Kevin stared at the pilot, squinting until his face slowly relaxed into a slight grin. "No kidding? Nobody told me anything. You're a pilot too? I thought you were just an Air Guard crew chief."

"I'm not one of those multi-million-dollar techno-babies the Air Force makes these days, but yeah, I got civilian pilot and mechanic certificates. Hell, my partner and I even built this airplane."

Stunned, Kevin said, "Okay. Well, let's get going then. I've got a case brewing here and I suspect I've got a cat to catch in Cincinnati too."

"Yes, you probably do." Skip's smiling face turned serious as he began manipulating the controls in the cockpit and the aircraft began rolling forward. Touching a button on top of the control stick, he spoke into his mic, "Brandywine traffic, Experimental One Mike Sierra taxiing from the T-hangars to Runway Two-Seven. Brandywine."

Back in the golf cart, and driving up to the brick building, Lou watched the aircraft near the end of the runway. After a brief stop, punctuated by intermittent accelerations of the engine, the plane taxied onto the runway, pointing west. On Lou's radio, the sound of Skip's voice crackled, "Brandywine traffic, Experimental One Mike Sierra departing Runway Two-Seven, westbound. Brandywine."

Lou picked up his radio and said, "Have a safe flight."

In reply, the radio made two clicks, then the throaty sound of the idling engine grew to a roar. Skip's aircraft accelerated down the runway, the pitch of the tumult rising with the increase in speed. Passing midfield, the wheels broke ground and the sleek aircraft nosed up toward the high overcast of cirrus clouds. A moment later, the landing gear folded back into the bottom of the fuselage, and the rapidly accelerating aircraft grew smaller, until it became a black dot that disappeared over the hills to the west.

31

Thursday, October 18

3:02 p.m.

A UNIFORMED LINEMAN LOUNGED behind the wheel of a small tanker truck parked on the transient ramp at Lunken Airport. He was engrossed in a paperback cowboy novel when the hand-held radio sitting on the seat beside him crackled with the voice of a woman calling, "Base to line, Four-one-one Mike Sierra five miles out and wants a top-off with avgas."

He picked up the radio and acknowledged the call. "Jay here. I'm in the avgas truck now." He turned his attention away from the paperback and looked out to the west. Thick cumulus clouds obscured the sky above eastern Cincinnati. The orange windsock next to the runway showed a gusty wind from the northeast. A handful of aircraft parked in front of the old 1920s art-deco terminal gently swayed in the breeze against their tie-down ropes.

Jay watched as Skip's airplane appeared as a sharp speck of

light over the Kentucky bank of the Ohio River, descending from the mottled gray clouds. Swinging around to the southwest to align with the runway, the speck became brighter, and soon the dark form of wings and a tail were visible behind the aircraft's landing light. Flaps extended from the wings, and the landing gear lowered out of the belly, reaching for the ground like the feet of a bird alighting on a rooftop. By the time the aircraft was crossing the flood control dike along the Ohio River, it was close enough to make out the blue-and-white paint scheme and see Skip and Kevin behind the cockpit windows.

Jay watched as the descent to earth was arrested just before the spindly landing gear touched the ground. For what seemed like a long-held breath, the aircraft floated just a hand's breadth above Runway 7 until it finally touched the pavement with a chirp of the tires. The aircraft coasted the length of the runway before the sound of the idling engine increased slightly, and the nose swung left onto the taxiway that brought the sleek machine back toward where Jay was walking across the parking ramp.

Turning off the taxiway, the aircraft slowed to a crawl. Jay directed it with arm signals to a halt in front of a modern glass-fronted building. The engine fell silent, and the propeller slowed to a stop. Jay met the plane and placed chocks under the nose tire. Then, looking at Skip, he swung his hands up over his head with thumbs pointed toward each other. When Skip repeated the gesture, Jay retreated to the fuel truck.

Skip opened the gull-wing door and slowly extracted himself from the left seat. Reaching his full height, he removed his red cap and tossed it back into the cockpit. He then gingerly stepped to the front edge of the wing and hopped down to the pavement. Kevin, unfolding his taller frame out of the cramped cockpit, followed Skip and stepped off the wing to stand next to him. The two men walked around the waist high wing and retrieved two bags and a backpack from the baggage compartment. They returned to the wingtip just as the fuel truck came to a stop in front of the aircraft.

Jay stepped down from the truck's cab and approached Skip, who replied without being asked, "Top it off, hundred low-lead. I don't know how long I'll be, could be a couple hours or overnight, so go ahead and park it wherever you need to."

"Okay. Brakes off?" Jay called back over the noise of the truck's idling engine.

"Affirmative," Skip answered while slipping a twenty-dollar bill into Jay's hand. Turning back to the airplane, Skip pulled down the gull-wing door and latched it closed. The two men then started across the windy ramp toward the glass building. "Come on, the coffee is begging to be set free," Skip said to Kevin.

Inside the building, a middle-aged woman wearing a blue blazer with a silver name tag that read *Marlene* stood behind the counter. She called out to the men in a friendly voice, "Good afternoon. Welcome to Signature Flight Support Cincinnati. How can we help you today?"

"Restroom?" Skip asked.

The woman replied, "Just ahead on the right."

He nodded and the two disappeared into the men's room. When they emerged, Skip approached the counter while Kevin hung back a step. "Good afternoon, Marlene. Four-one-one Mike Sierra, and it looks like I'll be here for the afternoon, but maybe longer." Reaching into his pocket, he extracted a wallet and retrieved a credit card. Handing it over to Marlene, she took the card and smiled. She examined both sides of the card and then handed back a sheet of paper and pen. "Would you mind filling out this form, please, Mr. Campbell."

"Yes ma'am," he replied and leaned into the counter, scrawling on the form with the pen.

While he was writing, Marlene asked, "Since you were not on my list of inbound flights, Mr. Campbell, would you like me to arrange ground transportation?"

Skip shook his head. When he was finished, he handed back the form and said, "Skip. Everybody calls me Skip. I think we're covered, but thank you anyway."

Marlene said, "Here's your AmEx. And here's my card if you need anything. We're here from five until midnight."

"Great." Skip pocketed the cards and then asked, "One more thing. If the weather turns bad, or you don't hear back from me by, say nine o'clock this evening, can you put my airplane in a hangar for the night? I'd really appreciate it."

"Not a problem," Marlene smiled again. "Enjoy your stay in the Queen City."

"We'll try!" Skip said with a jaunty salute toward Marlene. Turning to Kevin, he said, "All right, let's go see what this is all about."

32

Thursday, October 18

4:18 p.m.

A METALLIC TAN TOYOTA Camry idled several car lengths from the glass front doors of the Signature Flight Support building. When Skip and Kevin emerged from the doors, the car rolled forward and came to a stop opposite the building entrance. The front passenger window lowered and a white-haired man wearing a blue-and-white-striped railroad engineer cap and a black-and-orange Bengals football jacket leaned across the seat to address them. "You're the folks from Philadelphia?"

"We are," Skip nodded.

"Fine," the driver replied. "I'll pop the trunk."

A moment later, the trunk lid raised an inch with a click sound. Skip rounded the back of the car and lifted it open. They dropped their bags into the trunk and Skip slammed the lid shut, saying, "I love it when a plan comes together!"

Kevin dropped into the tan upholstery of the car's right front seat and shut the door behind him. Turning to the driver, he introduced himself, "Kevin."

The driver extended his right hand, "I'm Dave."

Kevin gripped Dave's hand and shook it while cocking his head toward the back seat. "That's Skip."

Skip reached between the seats and grasped Dave's hand. Shaking it firmly, Skip said, "Yo, Dave, thanks for the ride."

Dave looked from Kevin to Skip and replied, "My pleasure. From your comment, I gather you're an A-Team fan."

"Hannibal Smith is one of my personal heroes," Skip beamed.

"They haven't made a good action television show since," Dave chuckled. Returning his attention to driving, Dave shifted the car into drive and quietly eased away from the curb. At the parking lot exit, he turned left on Wilmer Avenue and then made a sharp right on Airport Road.

The Camry rolled through a commercial area bisected by a railroad crossing. After another block, Dave made a quick right and left onto Eastern Avenue and proceeded west.

"Did you have to come far to pick us up?" Kevin asked.

Dave smirked, "Farther than I want to walk, but no. We're almost there."

The car decelerated after passing three blocks of old two-story frame houses and brick school buildings. They turned right onto Donham Avenue and Dave idled the car forward, parking against the curb next to a Romanesque-style church built of tan bricks with a red tile roof. Dave said, "This is the place." Dave exited and walked around the front of the car. Kevin and Skip climbed out and met Dave on the sidewalk. Pointing to a rectory built in the same style as the church, Dave said, "Father Myers is the pastor of St. Stephen. He'll take it from here." While Kevin glanced at the buildings, Dave continued. "You'll want these," and handed Kevin the car keys. "If you need anything, I'm not far away. The last house up the hill. Follow the stairs to the top, I'm on the right."

Kevin nodded and said, "Thanks," as Dave turned and started

walking toward the end of the short street. Kevin looked at Skip and shrugged his shoulders. "I guess we'll go see the padre."

Kevin and Skip made their way up the walk to the front steps of the rectory. The building featured a tile roof and arched windows. The arched front door had a keystone accent, and nineteen detailed glass panes made up the window. At the top step, Kevin pressed the doorbell button set into the tan brick. After a brief wait, a middle-aged man with a handlebar mustache and dressed in a tracksuit appeared on the other side of the windowpanes.

Opening the door inward, the man said, "You must be my visitors from Philadelphia. Welcome. Come in, come in."

"I'm Kevin, and this is Skip," Kevin replied.

"I'm Father Myers, the pastor, but you can call me Karl." Leading the two men inside, Karl said, "I'm glad you're here. Follow me." The dimly lit central hallway had several doors leading off either side. Karl took the second door to the right and walked around a large desk and dropped into a high-backed desk chair. He gestured for Kevin and Skip to take seats in the two chairs opposite him.

Sitting down, Kevin said, "I don't have any background on the situation here, so maybe you can fill me in?"

"Yes, of course. I really appreciate you coming out so quickly," Karl agreed. "First, I want to get this thing out in the air. Make sure we're all on the same page?" Kevin and Skip glanced at each other, then Kevin nodded.

Karl said, "Um," followed by a long pause. "I, uh, am not sure exactly how to phrase this, but . . . I feel like I'm speaking it into existence."

The room went silent again until after Kevin leaned forward slightly and offered, "Let me see if I can help here. Our community spends a lot of time talking about love and serving God, but when it comes to identifying and confronting actual threats to our souls, well, we're uncomfortable with it." Kevin paused as Karl's eyes settled on his. "Why don't we try this? I'll describe a situation, and you tell me if it sounds familiar. Okay?"

"Sure. We can do it that way," Karl exhaled. Then he sat back in his chair, looking slightly less anxious.

Kevin interlaced his fingers in his lap and took a breath before beginning. "You, or somebody you know, has recently seen a person who looks similar, maybe very similar, to somebody you know to be dead and buried. Probably within the last several weeks. And now you think you've got a ghost or some other supernatural entity. You don't know what to do with it and you're worried nobody will believe you if you talk about it."

Karl looked at Kevin with wide eyes and folded his hands together, as if in prayer. "Yes. That's it." Karl perked up slightly, "How did you know?"

"Let me ask you some questions," Kevin continued, "and maybe we can get to the bottom of this quickly." Karl nodded. "First, who else knows about this situation you've got? I'm interested in who you've spoken with in the Church hierarchy."

Karl turned his eyes toward the phone on the desk and said, "Yesterday, I spoke to an old friend and mentor of mine in the Philadelphia archdiocese. He's a parish priest like me, but very, well, let's just say he's 'connected.' Much more of a political climber, you know what I mean?" Kevin nodded and Karl continued, his eyes now fixed on the crucifix over the doorframe behind Kevin and Skip. "Anyway, I described my problem and he said he'd heard about a new outreach ministry that might be helpful. He said he'd call back as soon as he had something for me. Well, I haven't heard from him yet, but a certain Sister Elizabeth Carter called me about ten thirty this morning. She told me a lay minister would be out to assess my situation and to have a car and driver at Lunken Airport at three o'clock, but not to come myself." After a long pause, Karl asked Kevin, "So you're the lay minister?"

Kevin looked Karl in the eye and said, "I guess you could call me that, but really I'm more of an exterminator."

Karl's eyes widened but remained silent as Kevin continued. "Let's start with the basic details. First, I need to know who's walking around despite the fact they are supposed to be dead."

Karl made a slight cough and then said, "He was an older man named Harley Webster. Lived a few blocks from here. About two weeks ago, he died in a hit-skip. The police think he wandered off the sidewalk into the path of a car."

Kevin nodded and asked, "Was he a parishioner? Did you know him well?"

"I guess you could say I knew him," Karl dropped his eyes to the desk and continued, "but he was not a member of the parish. Actually, quite the opposite."

"How do you mean?" Kevin asked.

"When the Church was in the throes of the child abuse scandal some years ago, Mr. Webster and his wife were very outspoken about it. They would come out on Sundays and picket on the sidewalk in front of the church. Anything we did as a parish, they were there to make it hard. At Christmas and Easter, they'd call the city to come and make sure we didn't violate fire code or exceed capacity. You know, things like that."

Skip chimed in, "Well, that's pretty crummy, but I don't see how the death of Mr. Webster becomes your problem."

Karl exhaled. "Mrs. Webster called two days ago, demanding to speak with me. She went on and on, saying somebody in the Church had somehow condemned Harley to walk the earth forever. Probably in revenge for the picketing. So, now I'm stuck dealing with the ghost of a dead man and his widow—who is demanding the parish be held to account for the crimes of persons unknown—who aren't part of this parish, so her husband can finally rest."

Kevin rocked his head back and looked at the ceiling for a moment before leveling his eyes on Karl. "I can't do anything about Mrs. Webster, but if this is what I think it is, I can assure you that the image of old Harley won't be a problem much longer."

"I guess that's good news. So, you can fix things that fast?"

"No, it doesn't work like that. Ol' Harley will probably be replaced by the ghost of somebody else in about a week or so, unless we can intervene and break the cycle. But either way, when Harley is replaced, you can tell Mrs. Webster that her ghostly issues have been resolved and she won't see him again. Then maybe she'll stop being your problem."

"It's not like I'm insensitive to the abuses of the past, but I'm not the one who can resolve these things," Karl explained. "But anyway, what can I do to help the ghost part?"

Skip asked, "Have you seen him? I mean, since he died?"

"I have not," Karl replied, "But apparently Mrs. Webster has."

Kevin scratched his chin and then asked, "Do you think she'll talk to me? She'll be the best source of information about Harley. I also need to know who and when anybody has seen Harley since he died," Kevin said. "I also need as many details as possible about when and where the death occurred. If you can get it, the police report would be helpful too."

Karl shrugged. "I'm pretty sure she'll vent to anybody who will listen. She's that kind of person, you know what I mean?"

"Okay, that's where I'll start. Do you have her contact information?" Kevin asked. Karl nodded and handed him a page from a notepad. Turning to Skip, Kevin said, "I guess I can cut you loose? This may take some time to resolve. Unless you want to stay and see how this turns out."

Skip gave a short laugh and said, "I'm in for tonight, anyway. I'll plan to fly home in the morning."

"Fine," Kevin said. "I'll call a buddy of mine here in town if I need another hand." Turning back to Karl, he asked, "So where can we bunk up for the night?"

"If you don't mind, I'll send you up to our caretaker's house," Karl replied. "He'll look after you. It's just up the street."

"We know where he is," Skip said.

"And the car is for us to use until this is wrapped up?" Kevin asked.

"Yes," Karl replied. "It's Dave's extra car."

"That's fine," Kevin nodded.

"Not many vehicles blend into a parking lot as well as a generic four-door sedan," Skip seconded.

"Thanks again, gentlemen," Karl sighed. "When Sister said she was sending a lay minister, I was expecting some kind of negotiator or lawyer. Maybe broker a deal with Mrs. Webster to get her to be quiet."

"Nothing like that," Kevin reassured Karl. "We're here to solve the physical problem of the animated manifestation of one Mr. Harley Webster, without drawing any more attention to ourselves—or you—than is necessary. In fact, the less we talk about any of this, the happier we'll all be."

Karl nodded and stood up from his chair. Gesturing toward the door, he said, "I'll let Dave know you're staying the night and I look forward to knowing this is resolved."

"We'll be quiet as mice and as quick as we can," Kevin smiled.

The two men exited the house, and walking down the front steps, Skip gave the priest a brief salute before leading the way to the Donham Avenue sidewalk. Turning right and making their way up the hill, Skip asked Kevin, "So what's the procedure and the required resources?"

"Well, I need to make a couple phone calls after we check in with Dave, then I think we need to talk to Mrs. Webster. We need to know where Harley worked, hung out, and anything else like that. That will determine the location and size of the search area. It would be handy to have a photo of Harley, as well."

"Then we canvas the area?" Skip asked.

"Yeah, that's pretty much the plan," Kevin replied.

33

Thursday, October 18

6:02 p.m.

KEVIN AND SKIP sat at Dave's kitchen table, scooping up generous helpings of chili-mac while Dave leaned against the old Delco refrigerator in the corner. Around Dave's kitchen were endless items depicting railroads and railroad history. Magazines and books were stacked on the available horizontal surfaces. On shelves above the windows and cabinets were displays of HO gauge model rail cars and locomotives.

Tipping his engineer's cap up, Dave asked, "Anything else I can get you two?"

Between bites, Kevin responded, "You're a champ Dave. Thanks for the use of your phone, and the chow is just what we needed before heading out."

"It's my pleasure. I haven't had any guests in a while." Stepping forward, Dave held out a brass key on a loop of white string. "If you're out late, you can use this to get in. I'm a pretty heavy sleeper, so I probably won't hear you."

"Great. We'll try to be quiet anyway," Kevin said as he took the key and tucked it into his pocket. After clearing out his bowl of remaining sauce with a slice of white bread, Kevin sat back and asked, "Where would we find Tusculum Avenue?"

"That's pretty easy," Dave grinned. "It's the next street northwest of here. It runs up the hill two blocks from Eastern Avenue to Columbia Parkway, then farther up to Alms Park and St. Ursula school."

Skip looked up from his now empty bowl and asked, "Are the folks around here pretty friendly? I mean, are they going to call the cops when they see a stranger coming up the sidewalk?"

Dave scratched his chin and replied, "Been around here all my life. Everybody knows me, so I can't really say."

Kevin looked from Dave to Skip and said, "I guess we'll let you know what we find."

Dave gave a slight grin, "I guess you will." Then he made his way across the little kitchen, collecting the dishes from the table and setting them in the enameled steel sink. Stepping to the doorway leading into the front room of the house, he looked at his guests and said, "I'll leave you to it."

Looking at Kevin, Skip nodded toward the door and suggested, "Shall we?"

"Right behind you," Kevin agreed.

Exiting the kitchen door at the back of the house, the two men pulled on their jackets. They made their way down the concrete walkway to the street corner where they turned west on Morris Place. Strolling past the century-old houses built along the hillside, Skip commented, "That Dave's a character."

Kevin cracked a slight grin, "Yeah. He loves his trains and his Bengals." After a pause he added, "Not sure how bright his bulb can glow, but you know, I kinda envy people like him."

Skip glanced over at Kevin, "Why's that?"

Kevin looked up at the fading light of the sky, "He's got his thing. It makes him happy. He's not worried about anything. No politics or social upheaval makes it into his model railroad display. His world stopped changing in 1960-something. Maybe he wasn't even out of grade school when his path in life was set, and he never questioned it. Even a stint in the Army working on trains in Europe didn't change that."

Skip responded, "Maybe you're right. There might be something to the simple life." Walking past another couple of houses, he pointed up at the street sign and added, "I think we're in the right place. What's the house number?"

Kevin looked left and right from the corner of Morris and Tusculum. He said, "Three-ten. Probably left," and started down the slight hill. After a few steps, Kevin added, "Keep an eye out for cats."

"Cats," Skip replied. "And homeless folks? Like we did last time we went looking?"

Kevin nodded, "Yeah, them too."

After walking past three houses and counting down the street numbers, Kevin and Skip paused at the entrance to a parking lot on the southeast side of Tusculum Avenue.

Kevin observed, "I think this is where three-ten should be."

"And yet there's no three-ten," Skip agreed. Turning around, he pointed and called out the numbers, "Three-sixteen, three-fourteen here. Three-thirteen and three-eleven over there."

Kevin looked at the piece of paper with *310 Tusculum Avenue* neatly written across it and confirmed to Skip, "It says three-ten. And where three-ten should be, there's a parking lot that serves the building facing Eastern Avenue."

"Now what?" Skip asked.

Kevin looked at Skip with a shrug of his shoulders and replied, "Let's see if we can find a neighbor who knows what's what."

Backtracking up Tusculum Avenue, Kevin and Skip came to a

stop in front of a shamrock-green house with blue gingerbread trim. A tabby cat sat on the front edge of the porch, surveying the street. A dozen steps climbed up to the porch from the sidewalk. Behind the cat, the front door opened, and a middle-age woman padded silently out onto the painted wood.

The woman's dark hair was short, in a spiky buzz cut. She was barefoot and dressed in a thick fuzzy robe. The blue design on the robe mimicked the paint scheme of the house. Walking out to the corner of the porch, she reached into the pockets of the robe and retrieved a pack of cigarettes and a zippo lighter. Paying no attention to the two men standing at the foot of the stairs, she shook out a cigarette and placed it between her lips. Snapping open the lighter, she focused on the flaring of the single tongue of flame and cigarette. She inhaled deeply as the tobacco began to glow, then blew a stream of smoke toward the ceiling of the covered porch. Holding the cigarette between two fingers on her left hand, she slumped back against the low wall surrounding the porch. She dropped the lighter and pack of cigarettes back into the robe pockets. After another drag on the cigarette, she turned her head and looked silently down at the two men while blowing out another stream of smoke.

Kevin smiled and broke the silence, pointing up and down the street, he said, "Excuse me ma'am, can you tell me where I might find three-ten?"

"Please?" the woman replied.

"Three-ten Tusculum Avenue?" Kevin repeated.

"Three-ten?" the woman questioned.

Kevin nodded, "Yes ma'am."

"There isn't a three-ten. I'm afraid you've got a bad address."

Watching the exchange, Skip chuckled. "Figures. Can't be easy, can it?"

Kevin's head bobbed up and down, "Yep." Looking back at the woman, he asked, "Do you know an Arnica Webster?"

A glint of recognition flashed across her face before she said,

"Can't say I do. Why do you want to know?"

Kevin continued. "It's about her recently deceased husband."

The woman's right cheek twitched a moment before she said, "What's it about?"

Kevin paused and quietly let out the words, "A settlement."

"Really," The woman said with squinting eyes. Taking another drag, she turned a little toward them and asked while exhaling smoke, "A financial arrangement?"

Kevin made no expression and said, "We really can't discuss it with anybody but her."

The woman returned her gaze to the ceiling of the porch, and after a long pause, said, "Three-ten Stanley. That's where you'll find Arnica."

Kevin grinned and said, "That's very helpful. Thank you, and since we're not real familiar with the area, which way is it?"

The woman stood up and gestured with her cigarette, "Next block that way. It's a little gray house next to a place painted like this one."

Kevin bobbed his head a little and asked, "Super. And since you're well informed about the neighborhood, can you tell me, are there many feral cats around here? I know it sounds a little off the wall and all."

"You're talking to the neighborhood cat lady."

Kevin and Skip glanced at each other before Kevin continued. "That's fortunate."

She leaned a little forward, looking at the two men, clutching her robe tighter across her chest. "Nobody cares about the cats. Why are you asking?"

"We travel a lot," Kevin gestured toward Skip. "I've got a niece doing feral cat studies. Always looking for more info, you know?"

"Well, I've got two I feed in addition to my five house cats. I'm running a catch-and-release sterilization program. Getting it under control, except for the careless A-holes across the tracks."

"Good to know," Kevin said. "Well, we won't take up anymore of your time. Thanks."

She returned the cigarette to her lips as they turned, then the woman said, "You watch out for that old lady; she's a real bitch."

Skip gave her a casual salute and then whispered to Kevin, "And this young lady is kind of out there."

Kevin glanced at Skip, saying, "I dunno, I thought she was sexy in a Mad Max kind of way."

Skip laughed, saying under his breath, "You spent way too much time with the Marines."

34

Thursday, October 18

6:21 p.m.

KEVIN AND SKIP walked along Morris Place under the dim overcast, chatting about the woman they'd just met. Skip observed, "Any bets on her being an estranged relative of this Arnica lady? I definitely got some familiarity vibe from her."

"You might be right," Kevin offered. "The look on her face when I asked about Arnica suggested more than a passing knowledge. So, to answer your question, no, no bets here."

Skip grinned, "You're no fun, Maloney." After advancing another few feet down the sidewalk, he asked, "Did you have any luck on the phone?"

Kevin nodded, "I left a message back at the house with Uncle Jimmie. That way my brother and Detective Johnston know what's up. Then I called a local buddy of mine. He's going to help me out tomorrow, so you can head back to Philly."

Skip glanced at Kevin, "This buddy is someone you can trust? I mean, I don't want you cutting any corners here. That's how people get hurt."

"Don't worry," Kevin replied. "Abi was my battle buddy in the sandbox. Oh-three-eleven Infantry. He can hold his own in a fight. He also gave us a leg-up figuring out this cat thing. So, yeah, I can trust him."

Skip's eyes looked ahead, but lost focus for a moment until he said, "I like the sound of that. I can leave you here with a clear conscience."

Kevin looked over at Skip and replied, "Yeah. Don't worry about us."

Arriving at the corner of Morris Place and Stanley Avenue, the men came to a stop. Skip pointed to the yellow and green painted building across the street. Lights glowed from inside. "Stanley's. Handy to have a pub on the block."

"Maybe we can check it out later," Kevin agreed. Turning left and heading down a slight incline, Kevin scanned both sides of the street. The fading light created dark pockets between buildings and under the shrubbery. "Empty lot over there, but good places for a cat to hide over here," Kevin observed. Passing the first house on the block, they came to a residence painted much like the one they'd seen on Tusculum Avenue.

Skip commented, "Same color as the intermediate trim on Mad Max's house. But a much simpler style of architecture."

"Good thing we're not making an offer," quipped Kevin.

"Should be the next one," Skip said as he came to a stop on the sidewalk in front of a house marked *310*. "As advertised. Tiny and gray."

Kevin stopped next to him and faced the house. His eyes surveyed the setting. The narrow two-story wood-frame structure was wedged between the much larger green house on the left and a single-story office building and its parking lot on the right. The light-gray siding and white trim were chalky with age and exposure.

Accents that might have been red at one time were bleaching to a dark pink color. Visible through open curtains, a yellow lamp glowed somewhere far back in the room, and a faint flickering of blue light was visible on the ceiling. "Looks like somebody's home," Kevin said in a near whisper.

Skip looked at Kevin, "You got a canned speech, or something, to break the ice?"

"Nope," Kevin acknowledged and stepped forward. "Still figuring it out. I'm winging it." Skip said, "Braver than me," as he watched Kevin climb the nine steps to the front porch. Standing at the door, Kevin knocked three times and then looked back at Skip. "You coming?"

"Yeah, all right," Skip replied as he made his way up the steps.

Turning back to the door, Kevin was greeted by the scowling face of an older woman. She was dressed in blue jeans and an untucked faded flannel shirt. Her long, limp grey hair was pulled back under a red bandana. She growled at the men standing on the porch, "What do you want?"

Kevin said, "Good evening, ma'am, I'm Kevin, and this is Skip." Then he asked, "Are you Arnica Webster? We understand you've recently lost a loved one and we're here to help you find a favorable settlement."

"Who told you?" the woman snarled.

Kevin pressed ahead without answering her question, "May we speak with you about this matter? Maybe inside? We want Harley to rest easy just as much as you."

The woman looked past the two men. She looked left and right, then motioned for them to enter the front room of the house.

Kevin and Skip stood in the tiny foyer, looking at the surroundings. Straight ahead, a stairway ascended to the upper floor. In the front room, sitting on brown carpet, a small sofa with a moss-green geometric pattern occupied the wall under the front window. A matching chair and a wood coffee table filled the rest of the room. The furniture was encased in clear plastic slipcovers. A combination table and floor lamp stood in the corner, topped with a dim glowing light bulb and a cellophane-covered lampshade. The wall leading away and up the stairs was covered in a dull sunflower design wallpaper and was hung with framed concert posters from decades past. The smell of incense, cigarettes, coffee, and stale beer competed to dominate the room. Visible at the back of the house, a small television was playing in the next room, casting a blue hue to the darkening space.

Arms crossed and feet set, the woman asked, "Did anybody see you? Who else knows you've come here? Come on, out with it! Was it that holy roller priest? Huh? Did he send you?"

Kevin replied, "Father Karl asked for our help, but he doesn't mean any ill-will. We came all the way from eastern Pennsylvania to see that Harley is truly at rest. We just want to help," Kevin offered with open hands and a soft, descending voice.

She stared Kevin in the eye for a long moment and then switched her gaze to Skip, who stood motionless and silent. Slowly, her slight shoulders slumped, and she exhaled a long breath, before turning to the stairway. Arnica pivoted and sat on the second step. She covered her eyes with her hands and rested her elbows on her knees. Her pale bare feet projected out from under the bell bottoms of her jeans. They were lined with blue veins in contrast to the chipped yellow toenails.

Kevin and Skip stood still for a long time, looking at Arnica. The room seemed to get dimmer and all that could be heard was the breathing of the three people clustered within arm's reach. Finally, Kevin looked at Skip, shrugged his shoulders and said, "Ma'am?"

Arnica dropped her hands from her face and looked up at Kevin. Her eyes were lined in red, and her cheeks wet from tears. She sucked in a breath, then let it out in a stream of words. "I hated that man, but I couldn't live without him. I miss him something terrible, but I shouldn't. I don't know what I'm going to do."

After a long pause, Kevin held out a hand and said, "Look, Mrs. Webster. We need a little information from you, then we can be on our way."

The woman rubbed her hands on her knees and dropped her gaze to the floor. Under her breath she said, "We were never married."

Kevin dropped to one knee and got to her eye level before saying, "You and Harley were together, right? Just not married?"

"We told each other we didn't believe in marriage. You know, we thought it was a construct of the church and state. Just another way to control the masses, but I . . . deep down wanted to get, you know, make it legal. But now it's too late, and the probate court probably won't recognize me, and now I see him . . ."

Kevin glanced at Skip, who returned a shoulder shrug. Then Kevin said, "So you are Arnica, right?" The woman nodded briefly, and Kevin continued. "And you and Harley have lived here for years? Ten, twenty?" She nodded again and brought a hand up to smooth back the hair flowing out from under the bandana. "Well, I'm no lawyer," Kevin said, "but isn't there some common law marriage thing? You know? You might have to get an attorney, but I doubt all is lost. Did Harley have any relatives, kids, anyone else that could claim inheritance?"

"His parents are long dead, and his older brother died in Vietnam. That's how we got into the protest movement. When we met, you know?"

"Okay, well, don't give up. You might win. But in the meantime, we heard there's somebody that looks like Harley walking around the neighborhood?"

"Yeah, that's right." Arnica asserted. "I'm sure that priest put a curse on me and Harley. Doomed him to haunt the neighborhood."

"Okay," Kevin said, "We're going to look into this for you, and maybe come to some resolution."

The previously silent Skip chimed in, "What day did Harley pass?"

"It was Sunday night, a couple weeks ago. We were over at

Tammy's to watch the game. The damn Browns versus the Bengals. I'm originally from Cleveland and the Dawgs were looking sad. I didn't want to stay to see them lose, so I told Harley he could find his own way home. He was drunk already, and I was sick of him going on about the NFL being fake and nothing but Roman bread and circuses. He was a natural-born contrarian. If I was for it, he had to be against it. That's the way he was."

Skip continued questioning Arnica, "We were told he was hit by a car. Is that right? Where did it happen?"

Arnica gestured over her shoulder, "Right there, in front of the old library on Eastern Avenue."

Kevin asked, "Did the coroner say anything about how he died? Any unusual findings?"

Arnica shrugged, "He was all busted up. That's all I know."

Skip added, "Do you know who found him?"

"No, no. They wouldn't tell me," Arnica shook her head and fell silent.

After a few moments, Kevin asked, "Okay, tell me about seeing this Harley look-alike?"

Arnica became animated and jabbed the air in the direction of Stanley's Pub. She said, "Last Wednesday, he was right there at Stanley's. Stanley's of all places! It was him. I'm sure of it. Been gone two weeks now, but I saw him. The day after he was cremated. Walking through the parking lot like it was nothing. I was so stunned I nearly steered the car into oncoming traffic."

Kevin's brows furrowed, "That's close to home. Is Stanley's significant?"

"Hell, yes. Harley was kicked out of Stanley's for fighting and threatening to take a wrecking bar to the Rumpke Mountain Boys' instruments. He wouldn't shut up. Kept saying they didn't know anything about bluegrass music, and they should take some lessons. The management said they'd call the cops if he ever came in again. Harley had it in for 'em. He was bitter."

"Got it," Kevin nodded. "So, tell me, did Harley look any different when you saw him?"

Arnica gave a questioning look, but Kevin kept going. "Was his hair different? Any changes to his face shape, like fatter or skinnier? How about his clothes?"

Arnica shook her head. "He looked just the same, except his beard was more like a five o'clock shadow. And his hair wasn't long enough to tie back, like it was when he died."

Kevin followed up, "Did he say anything? Or respond to you?"

She crossed her arms and said, "No. Nothing, and I was too shocked to get a word out. Do you think he's haunting Stanley's? Because now that Harley's gone, maybe I can go there again. But not if I'm going to see his ghost hanging out in the parking lot every time."

Kevin made a slight grin at Skip and then turned back to Arnica, "I don't think he's haunting the pub, but you won't have to worry about this too much longer. We'll see what we can find out. Okay?"

"What are you going to do? Are you exorcists? Or ghost hunters? Because I wouldn't have believed you before I saw Harley. I mean he was just as real as you or me."

"Something like that," Kevin said in a softer voice as he stood up again. "I was wondering, Arnica is a unique name. How did you come by that?"

The woman leaned her head back and closed her eyes, "That was the name given to me by Bob Dylan."

Skip did a double take and asked, "*The* Bob Dylan?"

"Yeah. We dated for a while." After a long pause, she opened her eyes wide and said, "That's what he called me. His Arnica. It's a kind of sunflower, you know. I haven't used my given name since. I almost went to a judge to get it legally changed, but I wasn't going to ask the state permission to change my name. They don't have that power over me."

Kevin and Skip looked at each other before Skip asked, "What was Bob Dylan like?"

"I can't really describe him." Arnica took a deep breath and placed a hand on a flower depicted in the wallpaper and caressed it with her fingertips. "He's nothing like what you see in pictures or on TV. Doesn't even look like the same person, especially when you're tripping. But I loved him, and he loved me."

Kevin broke her reverie by saying, "Okay, Arnica. Back to our problem with Harley. We're going to figure out what's going on here, but it would be helpful if we could borrow a couple photos of him."

"Okay, sure," Arnica agreed. "I took a lot of photos of him. Photography was my thing. What kind do you want? I don't need them anymore. They just break my heart."

Kevin replied, "Just snapshots. Maybe a recent one and something from his younger years."

She rose from the steps and walked to the coffee table in the middle of the room. A drawer in the end contained an album from which she extracted three photos. Handing them to Kevin, she pointed at the individual prints and said, "This is last year at a music festival. This one is from when we first started dating; he was about thirty, and this last one is from his grade school." Kevin took the photos and examined them. Arnica asked, "Does that help?"

Kevin nodded, "Yeah, that will be just fine." Turning to Skip he said, "I think we've got all we need."

Dropping the album on the floor, Arnica stepped to the door and opened it to the deep dusk. Cool air rushed in, and she took a deep breath. Turning to look at the two men, she asked, "You never said who told you."

Kevin shrugged, "Who told us? Someone besides Father Karl?"

Arnica replied, "Who told you where I live? I know that papist windbag doesn't know."

Kevin held his finger to his temple and said, "Right. No, he didn't. It was the young lady. On the next street over. In the green gingerbread house."

"Oh, that little witch. Giving me up like that," Arnica half snarled.

"You know her?" Skip asked.

"Yeah, I know her. She's the one reminder I have of my time with Bob. But don't you dare tell her that!"

Making their way out the door, Skip whispered, "Your secret is safe with us, ma'am."

When they were clear of the door, Arnica looked at them with intense eyes, "Will you make that man go away forever?"

Kevin placed his right hand over his heart and said, "If it is Harley, I promise he won't be a problem much longer."

The scowl returned to Arnica's face, and she said, "Good riddance to him!" and slammed the door. The two men looked at each other; Skip shrugged, and they made their way down the steps into the deepening evening.

35

Thursday, October 18

7:12 p.m.

KEVIN AND SKIP walked in silence down the sidewalk to Eastern Avenue. At the intersection, Skip paused under a streetlight and looked at Kevin. Kevin returned the look and said, "I know what you're going to say. You don't even have to go there. Let's just keep walking."

Skip pointed at himself and said, "I wasn't going to say anything about ole Arnica being as steady as an elephant on roller skates."

"Yes, you were. The lady is under a lot of stress, okay?" Kevin replied, then gesturing across the four-way intersection, he changed subjects. "That overpass must be the train tracks Mad Max was talking about. Think we should head over there, or maybe come back with the car?"

"Definitely the car," Skip replied. "We hang a left here and make our way around the block. Complete the circuit back at the church and grab the Camry. We'll attract less attention that way."

Kevin agreed, "Back to the church it is." They followed the sidewalk to the left and made their way southeast along the wide but lightly traveled thoroughfare. Dense foliage lined the far side of the street, masking the railroad tracks. On the left, waist-high stone and concrete retaining walls edged the sidewalk. Set back from the street, the neighborhood's once grand homes were accessed by steps cast into the retaining wall.

After walking in silence for a few minutes, Kevin spoke up. "I thought she was sweet. A little hot and cold, but sweet."

Skip grinned, "Sure, she was sweet, like a can of honey-roasted mixed nuts!"

"So, you doubted her Dylan story?" Kevin asked.

"You believed it?"

Kevin shrugged, "I guess not, but I mean, she's old enough to have a love child with him. Dylan probably hooked up with any girl he wanted. Maybe her story has an air of plausibility."

"Not buying it," Skip stated as they stopped to wait for traffic before crossing Tusculum Avenue. "She probably got knocked up at some music festival, and when she came home, she had to have a story to make it palatable to herself and her folks. What's better than saying you had a go with old Robert Allen Zimmerman himself?"

"Damn, Skip, you're sounding a little jealous. Like you wish it'd been you. Hell, you even know Dylan's real name!"

Redirecting the conversation, Skip declared, "I'm an American music aficionado. I know this stuff. Especially when it comes to the music from the Vietnam era. You're not old enough to appreciate it."

Continuing their walk along Eastern Avenue, Kevin claimed, "I know some of the songs. Like, 'Purple Haze' by Jimmie Hendrix." Kevin hastily added, "I've seen *Apocalypse Now*."

"You're a real historian, aren't you." Skip laughed. "Go do some research and then we'll talk."

Walking the length of a block in silence, Kevin said, "Skip, you asked a question earlier that kinda caught my ear."

"Yeah?" Skip replied.

"If it's not too personal," Kevin stopped speaking for a couple of steps and sighed before continuing, "I was wondering what you meant when you asked about my buddy and leaving me here with a clear conscience."

"Huh," Skip exhaled. "That made an impression?"

"Yes," Kevin replied.

"I'm not much for touchy-feely stuff," Skip claimed and then went silent. After turning left up Donham Avenue, he resumed speaking. "It's like this. Riding around, doing tactical airlift, you eventually end up putting people in dangerous places, with angry neighbors and little or no means of support. When we come back, after the shooting stops, we're just hoping there's something left to take home. That weighs on you after a while."

"I never thought of air crews caring like that," Kevin admitted.

"Well, a lot can happen between stepping off the C-130's ramp and coming back up again."

Kevin glanced over at Skip as they walked. "That's very true, but speaking for the guys on the ground, somebody's got to ride to the rescue. Anybody can face their worst fears once, but that coming back again and again? Hanging it all out there in a big paper-thin aluminum tube? That takes nerves of steel."

Skip sighed. "It's not that big of a deal. Ain't like I'm riding a medevac helicopter in a hot LZ or something. Let's just say I care about people and leave it there."

"Okay, we'll leave it there, but it's still nice to know you care."

36

Friday, October 19

9:00 a.m.

KEVIN AND SKIP descended the steps from Dave's house to Morris Place, carrying their bags. As they arrived at the car, Kevin used the remote fob to unlock the doors. "I never had one of these remotes. Pretty handy," Kevin commented.

Skip scoffed, "Really? Welcome to the nineteen nineties."

"Kind of pointless on a Jeep," Kevin defended as they opened the doors, tossing their bags in the back.

After they were seated, Skip said, "Okay. I'll concede that point. Now take me to the airport. The forecast is calling for some precipitation in an hour. I'd like to be gone when it gets here."

Kevin chuckled, "Aye, aye, skipper."

Kevin started the car, shifted it into gear and started down Morris Place. Skip and Kevin looked at the surroundings as they drove. Skip commented, "Not a bad neighborhood. A little buffing up, and this place will be worth something."

"Is that your expert analysis?" Kevin said, laughing.

Skip said. "Compared to your experience couch-surfing and sleeping in the dirt, I'd say I know something about real estate. For example, that old Carnegie Library there by the church. If an entrepreneur with some imagination could get their hands on that place, they could make something of it. Maybe a restaurant or reception hall. It'd be nice to have a renovated historical building in the neighborhood."

Turning onto Eastern Avenue and heading southeast, the car blended with the morning traffic. Changing subjects, Skip said, "Too bad we didn't find any clues on last night's drive."

"I didn't expect to see anything, but I'm starting to get the measure of the land," Kevin said as he steered onto Airport Road. "Thanks for your help on this. Abi and I will check out the local establishments. Somebody else knows something. There's a lot of empty space in the story."

When Kevin turned into the parking lot of Signature Flight Support, Skip directed, "You can just drop me off at the door."

Stopped outside the glass building, Kevin said, "Have a good flight."

With a serious look, Skip advised, "And you be careful subduing this cat."

With a straight face, Kevin replied, "Roger, careful."

As Skip disappeared into the building, Kevin pulled away from the door and made his way back to Morris Place.

Kevin parallel parked on the street in front of the rectory and waited, occasionally scanning the rearview mirrors. It wasn't long until he noticed a sleek and angular silver car turned onto the street behind him, its tailpipes emitting a bubbling bass note. The front license plate displayed a military medal and had a title across the bottom that indicated Combat Action. The large blue letters spelled *A STAN*. Kevin grinned as he exited the sedan.

Kevin watched the car come to a stop in the next parking space. The engine fell silent, and the driver's door opened. A tall, muscular Black man stepped out, closed the door, and approached Kevin. The men embraced and pounded each other's back. Abi said, "It's good to see you man!"

Kevin responded, "You too, pal." Stepping back from the embrace, he said, "Come on. Let's get to work. Lots to catch up on and lots of places I want to check out this morning."

37

Friday, October 19

11:04 a.m.

FOLLOWING KEVIN AS he walked uphill on Stanley Avenue, and swinging left into the parking lot of the neighborhood baseball diamond, Abi offered, "Now that we've hiked the river side of the railroad tracks, how about I show you some more attractive parts of the Queen City of the Midwest?"

Dropping into the passenger seat of Abi's car, Kevin grinned back and replied, "Based on what I've already seen, I can't imagine what the rest looks like."

Abi said from the driver's side, "It's Porkopolis! It's all of middle America squashed into one place."

"Okay," Kevin consented. "You've got our lunch break to show me the essential city. Then we've got to get back to work showing off photos of Harley and asking the hard questions."

"Aye aye," Abi grinned. Twisting the key to the right, the engine cranked to life, creating a low vibration and rumble throughout the interior of the car.

"Couldn't help yourself, could you? Had to get a Dodge Challenger, just like everybody else?" Kevin asked.

Abi glanced at Kevin, "You talking about my car?"

Kevin replied, "Yeah."

"Every combat Marine needs a Hemi V-8. Frankly, I was disappointed to learn they don't hand them out at boot camp graduation, but like most gear, there is what they issue and what you want."

"Right." Kevin laughed. "So where are you taking me?"

Abi idled away from the parking lot. "Downtown," he said.

At Stanley Avenue, he turned uphill and drove two blocks to Columbia Parkway, where he turned west. After passing two more traffic lights, the four-lane road built on the side of the hill overlooking the Ohio River was unobstructed, with no sharp turns. Abi pressed hard on the gas pedal. The transmission downshifted and the tailpipes roared. The rear tires chirped, and Abi and Kevin were pressed back into the black leather seats.

Blasting past slower traffic, Kevin grinned at Abi and yelled above the engine's roar, "Very impressive. Maybe you should be in the drag-racing business."

Letting off the gas pedal as the speedometer reached eighty, Abi slapped the steering wheel with his hand and exclaimed, "That never gets old!"

Kevin asked, "How many tickets have you gotten so far?"

"A couple," Abi admitted. "But it's worth it. Makes you feel alive, and in the dead-people business, that's very important."

Coasting back down to a more restrained speed, Abi followed the Columbia Parkway as it parallelled the westward flow of the Ohio River. Across the river valley, green bluffs rose from the waterway, reaching up to a sky full of deep blue-gray clouds and rain showers.

Kevin asked, "What's on the other side of the river?"

"That's Kentucky. Mostly residential. Ahead of us is downtown. You'll see it here in a minute." As the road bent left from west to southwest, the tops of riverfront buildings on both sides came into view above the trees lining the parkway. Abi added, "You know that old movie *Rain Man*? With Tom Cruise and Dustin Hoffman?"

"Yeah," Kevin replied.

"You know the scene in the old convertible where Rain Man keeps saying '97X, Bam! The future of rock and roll!'? That was filmed right here, on this road."

"Cool," Kevin agreed in a flat voice, then said, "You know that series of hit movies with Sly Stallone called *Rocky*? That was filmed all over Philly."

Abi glanced over at Kevin in the passenger seat and responded, "Really? One little bit of movie trivia, and it's out with the 'Philly is better than everything else' routine."

After an awkward long pause, Kevin began laughing, "Got you!"

Abi groaned, "I've only been in mortician training for a couple months, and I've already met several dead people with better jokes than you."

The parkway bent to the right again passing the Mount Adams exit. Rounding the curve, the cityscape and sports stadiums came into view. From the now descending freeway, exit ramps peeled off from both sides as they crossed over Interstate 71. Abi followed a swooping road to the right that dropped into the street level of downtown.

The car coasted to the intersection of Sixth Street and Broadway just as large rain drops started plopping on the windshield. Pointing left toward a double-towered office complex, Abi said, "The Dolly Parton building. Home of Tide detergent, Pampers diapers, Charmin toilet paper, and too many other brand names for me to remember."

Kevin asked, "Like P&G? The makers of Pringles chips? I love those."

"The same company," Abi confirmed as he switched the windshield wipers on. "But I'll have you know; your favorite processed potato crisp was sold last summer to another company."

Kevin made an exaggerated gasp, "Shut up. No, they didn't. Who would be dumb enough to sell a brand like Pringles? It's only one of the most iconic foods ever. That would be like Nestlé selling their Crunch Bar."

When the green traffic light changed, Abi gently accelerated the car and said, "Yeah, I agree, but they sold it to the Battle Creek breakfast mafia."

Halfway down the block, Kevin asked, "How'd you get so brand conscious?"

Abi shrugged, "After they're done with the hit-and-miss sports teams and insulting each other's high schools, that's all they talk about in this town."

At the next intersection, Abi turned south on Sycamore Street, idling along with traffic in a building downpour. Dominating the view at the south end of the brick and concrete canyon was an insurance company's high-rise headquarters building. Topped with an open grid semielliptical dome, the building had a distinctly phallic form. Kevin asked with a smirking laugh, "What's that supposed to be? I mean, come on, that's kind of awkward. Who thought that was a good idea?"

Abi guffawed, "Don't look at me. I didn't design it."

Crossing Fourth Street, the road angled down toward the baseball stadium and the Ohio River. Halfway along the block Abi turned left into a parking garage built into the lower floors of the insurance company's shiny silver building. Abi explained, "I was going to park down by the river, but I'm not walking back up here in the rain."

"Mighty thoughtful of you," Kevin acknowledged.

"Not really." Abi added with a chuckle, "You're paying for it."

38

Friday, October 19

11:29 a.m.

A TALL MIDDLE-AGED WOMAN with a blond ponytail stopped at the table where Kevin and Abi were seated. Dressed in a royal blue company logo shirt, black slacks, and sneakers, she placed two small bowls of hexagonal shaped crackers on the table and said, "Welcome to Skyline, my name is Maddie. Can I start you off with a drink?"

Kevin looked up, but before he could speak, Abi ordered without looking at the menu, "Two sweet teas, two three ways and four cheese coneys."

Maddie repeated the order back to Abi.

"That's it," Abi confirmed.

"Coming right up, honey," she said to Abi and then looked at Kevin, "First time? You'll like it," and disappeared into the mass of business-attired people coming and going in the restaurant.

Kevin watched the other servers carrying out plates of food to the nearby tables. Across the aisle, two middle-aged men, both dressed in coats and neckties, tied plastic bibs around their necks and draped them carefully over their clothes. Looking back at Abi, Kevin asked, "What kind of hazmat is this? Don't you think the bibs are a little ridiculous?"

"Not really," Abi explained as he started popping the six-sided oyster crackers into his mouth. "This stuff is good, I promise, but the chili wants, and I mean *really* wants, to stain your clothes. It's like wearing your best uniform to the chow hall and ordering spaghetti. You just can't take the chance."

"I get that, but I'm not doing the bib," Kevin asserted.

"Your call," Abi said with a shrug. "Now tell me what you know about this cat we're looking for. We haven't talked about them since you went pro, so I want to make sure I understand the whole situation."

Kevin asked, "So as to not waste time, are we talking cats in general, or this one?"

Abi replied, "Start with the big picture." Then after crunching another cracker, he said, "In fact, I'll summarize what I know, and you fill in the deets."

"Deets?" Kevin asked.

"Come on man, get with the lingo! It's short for details," Abi laughed. Kevin rolled his eyes and Abi began, "So, we got these cats roaming around. They look like regular house cats, or feral cats, or what have you. They hang out with the old, the sick, or the vulnerable, waiting for them to die. When the person kicks off, the cat consumes some aspect of the deceased that allows it to transform into an image of that person. The cat can appear in either form and can transform at will. It's usually working an interval of three weeks between victims, give or take a few days."

Kevin bobbed his head and said, "So far, so good, and that jibes with what Uncle Matt and Protodeacon Stepan have discovered."

Abi continued. "These cats have some decent capabilities not known in your average street cat. They have a serious scratch with an anticlotting agent of some sort. Touching the human form causes subsequent damage to the skin at the point of contact. They seem to be able to find their antagonist with some sort of super-cat sense.

"Were you taking notes all along?" Kevin asked.

"Shush. I'm on a roll here," Abi said. "The weaknesses of these cats are a need to feed on a pretty regular schedule. They also don't like water. They seek shelter in the rain and dissolve into a cloud of bubbles if submerged." Abi finished his description just as Maddie returned to the table with a tray.

She said, "Here you go, gentlemen," as she placed glasses of tea on the table followed by four white oval-shaped plates of food. "Hot sauce and napkins are on the table. Anything else I can get for you?"

Kevin surveyed the table and looked up at Maddie with a smile. "Forks."

Maddie shifted her hips, placed a hand on Kevin's shoulder and said, "I'm so sorry honey. I'll be right back."

Kevin replied, "That's all right—I'm not sure what I'm looking at anyway," referring to the food. Maddie disappeared into the crowd and Kevin turned his attention back to Abi. "Pretty good brief. Need a few more bits though."

Abi asked, "What did I miss?"

"We've never seen them eat anything," Kevin described, "or found a witness who's been able to get them to eat, despite offering all the usual cat favorites like milk and canned tuna. They also don't seem to be functional if forced below ground in human form, for example in a basement stairwell or underpass, and similarly, they become inanimate at sunrise for a minute or so. In both cases, they just go limp."

Maddie walked up behind Kevin and placed two forks on the table, then said, "So, who goes limp at sunrise? Because that sounds like an old boyfriend of mine."

Abi and Kevin laughed a little before Kevin said, "Just a zoology project. We're studying a certain cat condition."

Maddie sneered. "Cats, huh. Well, you can have 'em. I've got no love for the filthy beasts."

Kevin shook his head. "Yeah, well, we don't either to be honest, but it comes with the territory."

Maddie touched Kevin's shoulder again. "Honey, if you ask me, you should consider a different territory."

Kevin grinned and said, "Noted," as Maddie spun away from the table and disappeared again.

Abi leaned in over the table and said, "She seems to be interested in you."

Kevin blurted, "No way. Oldest waitress trick in the book. Just fishing for a bigger tip."

Abi picked up the red plastic bottle of hot sauce and squeezed a few drops onto his food, then said, "Take a bite before you add hot sauce. Try the coney first. A hot dog nestled in chili and cheese can't be wrong, right?" Kevin picked up the coney as suggested and took a mouthful while Abi continued talking. "This Stepan guy. Tell me about him. He's up to speed on the cats?"

Kevin nodded until he swallowed, "Yeah, he's the Old World, bad-ass Ukrainian fixer that Uncle Matt brought in. He goes back to the days of the Red Army in Afghanistan. In fact, that's where he first encountered them."

"You and I were in Afghanistan for six months. We didn't see any cats," Abi objected.

"The cats are up north. I found a photo of one. It's a small ball of fur with stubby ears that eats rats and mice. Perfect for the mountains. Besides, what wild animals did you expect to see in the freaking desert of Helmand Province?"

"Yeah, okay. Aside from a couple birds and a herd of camels coming through, I guess, but there was that one guy in Kandahar that got bit by the snake." After a thoughtful pause, Abi added, "Anyway, you're right." Abi then began devouring his coney dogs.

Kevin followed Abi's lead and they ate in silence for a couple minutes. When Abi had finished his meal, he looked at Kevin and asked, "Not bad, right?"

Kevin nodded, "Yeah, I could get those again. Maybe skip the onion next time."

Abi pointed to the plate of spaghetti noodles covered in chili and cheese. "Maybe the three-way will be more to your liking. Try a dab of hot sauce."

Kevin did as Abi instructed and forked a mouthful.

While Kevin ate, Abi asked, "Speaking of hot sauce, how's your old boss down on the ship? Daisy? She seemed to know a good thing when she saw it. Namely me."

Kevin responded between bites, "What did I just tell you about the oldest waitress trick in the book? Besides, I haven't seen her for a while. Maybe you'll have to come back to Philly and find out for yourself."

Abi grinned and scratched his chin like a movie character. "Maybe I'll just do that."

Kevin smiled. "And you can check out the new place."

Abi said, "Right on. Maybe at my next long weekend break."

Kevin finished chewing and wiped his mouth with a napkin. "That could be fun. But I wouldn't get my hopes up with Daisy."

39

Friday, October 19

6:26 p.m.

THE SUN WAS below the rooftops and trees to the west when the Dodge Challenger idled to a stop across from Stanley's Pub. The engine fell silent, and the headlights blinked out. Abi and Kevin exited the car and made their way across the street. They paused on the sidewalk in front of the pub's green door. The front window had red curtains over the lower half, but the warm yellow interior lights were visible above them. To the left of the door, the window was covered with a sheet of green-painted plywood. A flyer tacked to it advertised the coming entertainment.

Kevin pointed to the listing. "Too bad it's not Saturday—we could catch the Rumpke Mountain Boys."

Abi asked, "I've heard of the landfill called Rumpke Mountain, but a music group?"

Kevin replied, "It's the band that Harley argued with. It got him thrown out."

"Got it. Well, tonight's supposed to be the Licking Pike Ramblers," Abi said as he reached for the door handle. "Come on. Let's see if this place has something to recommend it." Walking in with Kevin behind him, Abi took three steps to the corner of the bar. The bar top stretched nearly the length of the right side of the room, with a dozen bar stools pushed up to the front. A half-dozen tables and booths occupied the left side of the space. The floor was covered in the original tiny white hexagonal tile from a century before. On an ankle-high platform opposite the front corner of the bar was an array of musical instruments and sound equipment. Hanging from the ceiling were various spotlights pointed toward the performance stage. The room was empty except for a solitary figure dressed in a black shirt and dark pants standing in a shadow at the far end of the bar. The person was looking down at a magazine and had a lit cigarette perched in one hand while flipping the pages with the other.

At the sound of the door closing against the jamb, the sole occupant looked up at the new arrivals. Abi and Kevin paused to survey the surroundings. Kevin's eyes settled at the far end of the bar and said, "Kind of quiet, eh?"

Returning to the magazine, the reader said in a gravelly contralto voice, "It's early."

Abi asked, "What time does the band start?"

"Usually about nine," was the reply.

Kevin advanced down the bar at a meandering pace. After passing half the chairs he asked, "I was wondering if you could help us with something a bit unusual."

"Don't do weird shit. I'll serve you a drink and put up a bowl of pretzels, but that's about it."

Kevin glanced back at Abi before saying, "Let me rephrase. We're trying to find somebody. Would you mind looking at a couple photos?"

The person looked up at Kevin, closed the magazine, stepped behind the bar into the light, and in a brighter voice asked, "Didn't you come down my street yesterday looking for Arnica?"

"You're the cat lady from the green house," Kevin acknowledged. He pointed two fingers at his own eyes, then turned them toward the woman behind the bar. "I didn't recognize you in the shadows there."

The woman glanced at Abi then back to Kevin. "Where's the other guy? The short one you were with before."

Kevin replied, "Oh, you mean Skip. He had to fly." Gesturing with his thumb toward Abi, he said, "This is Abi. I'm Kevin."

"Okay, Kevin and Abi, did you find Arnica?" she asked.

"We did." Kevin nodded. "Um, I mean Skip and I did."

The woman asked, "How was your meeting with her?"

Kevin replied as he turned to the bar, "Productive."

"Then what else do you want from me?" the woman asked as she dropped her smoldering cigarette into a glass of water behind the bar.

"I didn't catch your name last night," Kevin said.

"Didn't offer it," she replied.

Kevin then pointed at a photo taped to the mirror behind the bar. In the snapshot, the same woman was surrounded by several men mugging for the camera. It was labeled in black marker, *Happy Birthday, Carly!* Kevin said, "That's you, right?"

Looking back at the photo, she said, "Yeah," as she pulled it down and dropped it in the trash.

Kevin smiled, "Nice to meet you, Carly."

"Likewise," she replied.

Kevin laid the three photos Arnica had supplied on the bar. "Can you shed some light on who he is?"

"That's Harley Webster," Carly declared. "Arnica's now deceased live-in boyfriend."

"And you're certain he's dead," Kevin said.

Carly let out a long sigh and replied, "I was the first person the police called. So, I'm sure." Running her hand up the back of her closely cropped head, then letting it drop to the bar, she explained in a distressed voice, "Arnica isn't easy to get a hold of." Carly made air quotes with two fingers on each hand. "She's been 'hiding' from the Feds since the nineteen seventies." Carly then shuffled the photos around with one finger, barely touching them. "Between you and me, I don't think there is anybody looking for her, but that's why you got a bad address. On top of that, she's pretty unreliable. The type that might or might not make it to her own funeral."

Stepping up to the bar next to Kevin, Abi said, "You seem to know Arnica well."

Carly agreed, "Yeah, you could say that."

Abi asked, "Is she a regular here, or maybe she's a relative?"

"She's my mother," Carly admitted.

Abi's eyes widened at the statement. Then he said, "Okay. That makes sense."

"Makes perfect sense. Explains a lot, don't it," Carly said as she fished around under the bar and removed a pack of cigarettes and a lighter. Then she continued. "But don't get the idea that Harley was my father, because he wasn't. He was just a regular old jackass. I even had to throw him out of here once."

Kevin said, "Arnica told us about that." Then Kevin looked up at the bottles arrayed behind the bar for a moment before looking back at Carly. He continued. "Do you have any siblings?"

"No, hell no." Carly let out. "Well, not that I know of, anyway."

Kevin hesitantly offered, "I don't want this to sound odd. I mean, Arnica seemed to indicate she had a child with Bob Dylan, and I thought that sounded, well . . ."

Carly laughed. "She's so full of crap. I could blame it on all the drugs she did, but I suspect she was like that before she dropped acid." Lighting a cigarette and blowing out a long stream of smoke toward the ceiling, she said, "I did one of those new genetic tests. My father was most likely a guy named Rob Dunham. He was a roadie for hippie bands until he got arrested on his third-strike felony."

Kevin said, "I'm sorry. That's a little less romantic than the Dylan story."

Carly agreed. "Yeah, that's Arnica." After another drag on the cigarette, Carly said, "My sperm donor daddy recently died in a California prison. I never met him, and thankfully I never will."

Abi waited a moment, watching Carly take a couple more drags from her cigarette before asking, "I know this will sound off the wall, but is there a chance there's somebody around the neighborhood, or comes in here, who looks like Harley? Maybe a relative?"

Carly looked at the far end of the bar for a moment, then gestured toward Abi with her cigarette. "You know . . . maybe."

"Really?" Kevin asked.

Carly offered, "There's a guy, I don't know his real name, but they call him Bud. He's been in here a couple of times. Pays his tab from a wad of wrinkled up ones and likes the thrash-grass bands. Up close, I don't think he looks all that much like him, but you know, there is some resemblance to the younger Harley in that old photo."

Kevin asked, "Has he been in since Harley died?"

Carly said, "Last Wednesday. Same night the Rumpke Mountain Boys were playing."

Abi and Kevin looked at each other before Abi said, "Wow."

Kevin agreed, "Damn right, wow. Lines up perfectly with the timeline Arnica gave me."

Carly interjected, "What timeline?"

"Arnica must have seen Bud in the parking lot," Kevin concluded.

Carly tapped the ashes off the end of her cigarette into the glass of water with an old butt floating in it. Then she said, "Okay, I see. She's got a good view from her front steps, so that's possible. But why is that important?"

Kevin asked, "Has she mentioned anything to you about seeing Harley's ghost?"

"We don't really talk," Carly stated. "I usually only hear from her when she needs cash. Although, she occasionally tells me about off-the-wall stuff." After another puff of smoke toward the ceiling, she asked, "So she said she saw his ghost, huh? Serves her right. That jerk Harley has been haunting me my whole life, so payback would be just fine in my book, but I'm sorry to say, Bud isn't a ghost. He's just another beer-swilling redneck who leaves crappy tips."

Kevin asked, "Is there any chance Bud might be back again tomorrow? The flyer out front indicates the same band is playing."

Carly shrugged her shoulders, "Maybe. But you never know. I got some real regulars. You see them like clockwork, but this Bud guy, who knows?"

Kevin nodded, "Tell you what, we'll come back tomorrow and hopefully get a chance to meet him. In the meantime, I'm willing to bet Arnica saw Bud, and our ghost story ends with him."

Carly chuffed, "Arnica is off her rocker most of the time. You're going to have to drag Bud to her front doorstep so she can see and touch him before she'll let go of it."

Abi slapped Kevin on the back and said, "Then that's just what we'll do. Kind of like Doubting Thomas, huh? Way better than naked cat wrestling in the river."

Carly shot Abi a concerned look, but Kevin cut it short by asking, "Can I give you a phone number to call if Bud happens to show up before tomorrow, or you come across any more details about him?" Carly tore a corner off a page in the magazine and fished a pen from a cup on the bar. Kevin printed Dave's numbers in neat handwriting and said, "I'm not far away, so any time. Just leave a message if I'm not there." When he was finished writing, he slid the paper and pen across the bar to Carly and asked, "Do you work tomorrow?"

Rubbing a hand across her buzz haircut, Carly said, "I'm here most nights, and I'll ask around. Arnica has enough delusions going on; God knows I don't need her chasing ghosts too."

Kevin concluded, "Great. Then we're all set. We'll be back tomorrow, if I don't hear from you before." Turning to Abi, Kevin directed, "Let's leave this lady alone."

Abi agreed, "Right behind you," as Kevin led the way out the door. They stepped out to the sidewalk and Abi waived at Carly through the slowly closing door, saying, "Thanks. Good night."

Kevin took a deep breath of the cool night air. Letting it out, he said, "I forgot what one cigarette can do in a closed space, let alone three or four."

Sniffing at his shirt sleeve, Abi agreed, "Yeah. We're stuck with it. But in the meantime, I think we're closing in on an answer here, huh?"

"Yeah, I might be able to get out of here quicker than I thought. That would be a lucky break, because I have a real cat back in Philly that I need to close out." Looking Abi in the eye, Kevin asked, "But hey, can you do me a favor?"

Abi replied, "Sure."

Kevin looked back at the door and gestured with his chin, "How 'bout not mentioning the naked-river-cat-wrestling next time in front of the civilians. It isn't good for business, and I don't really want to try to explain something I can't really explain myself."

40

Saturday, October 20

7:00 a.m.

A SMALL WINDOW, CENTERED on the southeast wall of the house, admitted a stream of light that illuminated Kevin's face. His right eye fluttered momentarily before closing tight again. His arms and legs shifted under a blanket until he rolled onto his side. Kevin's face cringed at the sound of steel bed springs creaking under the twin size mattress in the tiny second bedroom of Dave's house. Once he was still again and the bed was quiet, Kevin's eyes opened one at a time, making erratic blinks until they stayed open. He let out a long sigh. "I gotta get out of here."

With a heave of his legs, Kevin partially emerged from under the blanket. He pushed upright to a chorus of squeaks and groans from the bed springs. Talking to himself while running his hand over his stubble-covered chin, he said, "Maybe today." The bed protested with metallic screeches while Kevin donned a pair of jeans. He then slipped into a rumpled dark-blue T-shirt with yellow letters spelling *NAVY* across the chest. Then Kevin made his way down the narrow hall to the tiny bathroom, closing the door quietly.

Moments after the door closed, Dave, dressed in denim overalls and a flannel shirt, came from the kitchen at the other end of the house. Knocking on the bathroom door, he said, "I'm making S-O-S for breakfast. Can I interest you in some?"

From the other side of the door, Kevin's voice could be heard over the shower water turning on, "Yeah. Give me fifteen minutes."

"Okay, great." Dave smiled and returned the way he came.

Kevin emerged from the bathroom, dressed in a clean pair of blue jeans and a gray and white checkered button-down shirt. With his pack in one hand and a pair of shoes and socks in the other, he padded down the hall to the kitchen.

Dave stood at the stove, his hands busy manipulating a cast iron skillet and a whisk. "Good morning to ya," he said with his back to Kevin.

"Morning," Kevin acknowledged. "Smells good. Like the galley on a ship."

Dave, still with his back to Kevin, said, "I like to think of it more like caboose cooking, but thanks."

"Hope I didn't wake you when I came in last night. Has anybody called for me?" Kevin asked as he sat at the little table, slipping on his socks and shoes.

Dave answered, "Nah, I was awake anyway. No calls, not yet." Still working the white liquid in the skillet, Dave asked, "Mind stoking up the toaster?"

Kevin replied, "Sure." He turned his attention to the loaf of store brand wheat bread and the well-used Sunbeam two-slot toaster sitting in the middle of the table.

Dave turned around and set two plates on the table with a small, serrated knife. "When you've got four slices, cut 'em into two on the diagonal and stagger them out to make the shingles. I'll be ready to serve here shortly." Returning to the skillet, Dave prattled on. "This dish is known as a military food, but the train men used to make this while riding the rails too. They had these little pot-belly stoves in the caboose for heating and cooking."

Kevin replied, "I had no idea," as the first two slices of toast popped up. He quickly replaced the bread and pushed the plunger back down. Kevin watched the wires in the toaster turn from black to orange before speaking again. "If everything goes as planned, I should be able to finish up today."

"Whoa, how about that! You move pretty fast," Dave said.

Kevin shrugged. "Mostly got a lucky break, but if a woman named Carly calls, I gotta know right away."

"Sure thing." Dave then asked, "You going to tell the padre?"

Kevin replied, "I was thinking about doing that first thing this morning. Should I call ahead, or just drop in on him?"

"He's an early riser," Dave declared just as the last slices of toast popped up. "You can probably just go down after breakfast."

Kevin cut the bread on an angle and divided it between plates. Then he carried them to the counter next to the stove. "Shingles ready to go."

Dave pointed with his elbow toward the refrigerator. "Get yourself some milk or juice. I'm sorry I don't have any coffee."

Kevin opened the door and removed a pitcher of orange juice, saying, "I'm not really a coffee guy. Juice for you?"

"Yep. Glasses by the sink," Dave said as he ladled out the white gravy filled with chunks of chipped beef. He carefully covered the triangles of toast and let it pool on the plate. "Looking good," he commended himself. After completing the second plate, the two men sat down. Dave made the sign of the cross, and Kevin, following his lead, did the same. Dave unintelligibly mumbled a prayer and then crossed himself again.

"Amen," Kevin added before crossing himself. Then picking up a fork, he asked, "So, I'm going to have a few hours to kill this afternoon.

Any recommendations on Cincinnati sights I need to see?"

Dave's eyes lit up like a child. "Oh sure. I highly recommend the Union Terminal museums."

Kevin listened and ate as Dave described the complex in detail. "Dome with art deco interior ... it was completed in 1933 and served seven different railroads ... now it's just Amtrak, but the offices on the back of the building have a great view of the freight lines."

When Dave let up to take a bite, Kevin said, "That'll be great. I love museums. How about I call you periodically to see if there are any messages. Hopefully, I can stay out of everybody's way until Abi is done with classes."

"Hold on, I've got a better idea," Dave offered. Getting up from the table, he disappeared into the next room. Dave returned a moment later with a black hand-size box. "The padre gave me this a while back, and I don't use it. How about you take it, and I can call you if something comes up." Sliding the box across the table as he sat down, Dave added, "I'm no futuristic techno guy. It just confuses me, so this thing just sits there."

Kevin picked up the box and opened the top flap. Inside was a black Nokia cellular flip phone and accessories. Kevin asked, "You sure?"

"Yeah." Dave gestured with his fork. "I keep it charged and the padre says it has a prepaid calling plan, so it can call anywhere. The number's on a piece of tape on the inside of the battery."

Kevin said, "Well if it isn't a problem. Sure. We'll give it a try." Flipping the phone open, Kevin pressed the power button and watched the screen light up. A small row of dots marched across the screen and the word *WELCOME* appeared. Kevin closed the phone and set it on the table. "Thanks. It'll be handy for today."

Dave stood up again and disappeared into the other room again. Shortly after, the cell phone began making an electronic chime sound. Kevin flipped the phone open and held it to his ear saying, "Hello?" before snapping it closed again.

Dave reappeared from the other room. "That problem is solved."

"That's great," Kevin added as he finished up his S-O-S and chugged down his glass of juice. Standing up from the table, Kevin organized his dishes and carried them to the sink.

Dave said, "I'll wash up. You should get down to see the padre before he gets distracted with something else."

Kevin slipped the phone into his pocket, shoved the phone box into his pack, and said, "Thanks again, Dave. You're a real champ."

Dave smiled, and said, "Just trying to help," as Kevin shouldered his pack and walked out the kitchen door.

Kevin descended the walkway and steps to the corner of Morris Place and Donham Avenue. After passing Dave's car parked on the curb, Kevin turned up the walk to the rectory building. At the door, he pressed the doorbell button and watched for movement inside the windows. A light came on and Father Karl Myers came walking down the long central hall.

Opening the door, the priest said, "Top of the morning, Kevin. Good of you to stop by. Come on in." Kevin stepped into the doorway as Karl stepped back. "Follow me—I was just having breakfast. Are you hungry? Maybe a cup of coffee?"

After closing the door, the priest led the way down the hall. Kevin followed, saying, "I'm good. Dave is feeding me well." At the far end of the passageway was a spacious eat-in kitchen. A table with four chairs was placed by the southeast window, in the morning sun. A single place was set with a bowl and a box of raisin bran cereal. Kevin was directed to a chair, where he sat down and placed his pack on the floor.

Karl commented as he sat, "I've heard he's a good cook, but that his repertoire is very limited."

Kevin replied, "His chili-mac is decent and the S-O-S was spot on."

Karl made a slight chuckle and declared, "Then you may have had all of the dishes for which he is known."

"Well, I for one," Kevin asserted, "am not going to complain about the food. The squeaky springs on the bed, however, are a serious piece of medieval torture gear, and I'm happy to report I hope to be finished with them tonight."

Karl's eyes widened, "Already?"

Kevin nodded, "We got a lucky break. It seems that Arnica isn't seeing a ghost, but rather somebody who looks like Harley Webster. Once confirmed, and I convince Arnica that the ghost is an actual living person, I'll be able to head home."

"That's great news," agreed Karl. "I hope it isn't premature, but congratulations."

"Thanks," Kevin replied. "Now, if you don't have anything else that needs my attention, I'll be out and about on the town, seeing the sights, until it is time to find our look-alike."

"Very well. I assume Dave knows how to reach you if there are any difficulties."

Kevin rose from his chair and shouldered his pack, saying, "He does."

"Very good, very good," Karl puffed. "I hope you have a productive day, and I'll be anxious to hear how it all turns out."

41

Saturday, October 20

4:10 p.m.

KEVIN STOOD IN the entrance to a small, red-roofed pagoda at the Cincinnati Zoo. He was intently reading a plaque when a grade-school-age kid snapped his focus. "Hey mister, your phone's ringing. Will you please answer it, and make that lame ringtone stop?"

His head jerked toward the kid and Kevin stammered, "Yeah, yeah." He patted the pockets of his jeans and finally pulled the phone out. He stepped outside and flipped it open. Holding it to his ear, he exhaled, "Yo."

After listening for a moment, he responded, "Yeah, it's been a good day. I tried to go to the Union Terminal like you said, but it was closed. So, I came to the zoo. I mean, who doesn't like seeing the animals, right? Anyway, I'll check in with Abi. Yeah. Thanks, Dave. Yeah, I did—I saw the white tigers. Yeah, okay, bye."

Snapping the phone shut, Kevin shoved it in his front pocket. From his hip pocket he retrieved a folded map of the zoo and opened it to the panel indicating the Passenger Pigeon Memorial. With a finger on his location, Kevin said, "Past the reptile house and the shops, bear right and back across the footbridge to the lot." He refolded the map and began walking at a brisk pace toward the exit.

Once back at the car, Kevin opened the door and sat on the edge of the driver's seat with his feet still on the ground. He extracted the flip phone once more, opened it, and entered a number. After a short pause, a voice said, "Hello?"

"Hey, Abi, it's Kevin."

The voice on the phone replied, "I didn't recognize the number. And you sound weird. Am I on speaker?"

Kevin explained, "Yeah, Dave at the church lent me his cell phone so we could all keep in touch."

"Okay. I'm finished with the school thing and headed toward Tusculum. Where are you?"

Kevin answered, "I'm at the zoo, enjoying a beautiful sunny day."

"The zoo? What? And a cell phone?"

"Yeah, what about it?" Kevin defended. "I can do technology and like animals at the same time."

"I'll have to think about that," Abi said. "In fact, I might need some therapy after this is over."

"Give me a break," Kevin remarked. "I'm leaving as soon as we hang up. We should arrive about the same time. Park by the church and we'll stake out Stanley's in Dave's car."

"See you there—if it is in fact you," Abi's voice trailed off before the phone went silent.

Kevin climbed in the car, dropped the phone into its original box, and slipped it into the glove compartment. He then drove out of the lot onto Vine Street, headed south toward Martin Luther King Drive and an on-ramp to the interstate.

42

Saturday, October 20

4:53 p.m.

KEVIN STEERED THE sedan onto Donham Avenue and brought it to rest behind the silver Challenger. He watched as Abi exited the car and walked to the passenger door of the Camry. Dropping into the seat and shutting the door, he said to Kevin, "The zoo, huh?"

"I think you're a little envious," Kevin replied. "You've never been to the world-famous Cincinnati Zoo and Botanical Garden, and now, just because I have, you want to go."

Abi rolled his eyes. "You're right, I haven't been, but I think I'll save it for when I've got a wife and kids."

"You know they have white tigers? You'd like the white tigers."

"Bro, how do you know what kind of animals I like?" Abi asked. "Besides, you got work to do. How about instead of talking about albino tigers, let's get down to the pub and see if we can catch an undead cat-man named Bud."

Kevin said, "Okay, but they aren't albino," and started the car. Pulling away from the curb, Kevin turned left on Morris Place and proceeded two blocks to the Stanley Avenue intersection. He parked on the left side of the one-way street facing the front of Stanley's Pub. The position at the intersection gave them a view of the sidewalk leading down to Arnica's steps, the parking lot on the left side of the pub, and the three buildings to the right. Abi said, "Good spot. This will be a piece of cake."

Kevin sighed, "I've heard that before." After a few moments of watching cars pass by on Stanley Avenue, Kevin said, "I had a great time at the zoo."

Abi groaned, "Really?"

"Perfect weather and I got to look at the animals I wanted to see. Not like a school trip where the teacher has to act all smart and show you the stuff they think is important. I even got to try some more of your local cuisine."

Abi looked at Kevin. "What was that?"

Kevin declared, "LaRosa's pizza. Have you had it?"

"I have—it's a fair pie," Abi agreed, "but I'm a fan of their spaghetti-a-plenty nights. Can't go wrong with the all-you-can-eat option."

Kevin nodded. "Right on."

Abi took a deep breath and let it out abruptly before saying, "You had to go talking about food. I haven't had anything since this morning. You got anything to eat in here?"

Pointing to the right, Kevin replied, "No, but you can walk over there to the Tusculum Market."

Abi looked over at the storefront, almost obscured behind untended shrubbery. Exiting the car, he looked back at Kevin and said, "I will be right back."

"I'll be here," Kevin said as he began drumming on the bottom of the steering wheel with his fingers.

Kevin watched several cars go past the intersection and then a flat black Econoline van turned into the parking lot next to the pub. It backed up to a parking space close to the front door. Two bearded middle-aged men exited the van and walked into the pub. After the men had been inside long enough for Kevin's attention to wander, Abi returned from the market. He opened the passenger-side door, tossed a plastic bag of snacks into Kevin's lap, and slid into the seat. Holding up two bottles of Coke, Abi asked, "Did I miss anything?"

Kevin began rummaging in the bag and said, "A couple of beards just got out of the black van and went into the pub. Otherwise, no."

Setting the bottles in the center console cup holders, Abi said, "Finally, some action. And don't get any ideas about that bag of jerky. That's mine."

Kevin tossed the package of jerky back at Abi and pulled out a Payday candy bar. "Is this fair game?"

Abi nodded while ripping into the jerky bag. "Made for you, dude."

Kevin said, "Thanks, man," as he resumed his watch of the pub's front door. After a couple bites of the candy bar, he alerted Abi, "Here we go. The beards are back outside." The two men opened the back doors of the van and began unloading large black cases and boxes.

Abi said, "Drums and sound gear. Must be the band."

Kevin agreed, "Excellent. Hopefully patrons will follow."

When the van was empty, one of the men came back out and drove it to the back of the parking lot. After closing and locking the doors, he re-entered the bar through the backdoor. Abi leaned his head back and slouched in his seat. Rubbing his eyes, he offered, "The early drinkers will roll in here soon. I wonder how many of them walk down from the local neighborhood?"

Kevin stretched and yawned in response. "Good question for our bartender."

As the sun got lower in the sky, more vehicles trickled into the parking lot. A small knot of middle-aged people walked past the car and crossed the street to the pub. A few couples wandered in on foot from the surrounding area. With the sun finally gone behind the buildings, Kevin announced, "Looks like nine customers and two band guys so far, but no sign of Bud."

Abi asked, "Are you sure we'll recognize him when he arrives?"

Kevin's voice dropped. "Nope."

At least we have that going for us," Abi concluded. "Think one of us should walk over there and take a look inside?"

Kevin ran his hand over his close-cut red hair, then said, "Not yet. It's only seven fifteen. If we haven't seen him by eight, we'll go look. Okay?"

Abi responded, "Sure, okay." Then, after scratching his chin, he added, "You know, we saw that band guy go in the back way. Maybe Bud went that way too. We might just be wasting our time out here watching for somebody that's already inside."

Kevin yawned again. "You're right. He might be in there, but we'll wait until eight."

43

Saturday, October 20

8:00 p.m.

WHEN THE SKY was fully dark and streetlights illuminated the intersection in a pale greenish white light, Kevin reached over and poked Abi's shoulder. "Come on, let's go see if the guy is here."

Abi's eye's popped open and he grabbed for the door handle, saying, "I was just resting my eyes."

"No shame in that," Kevin replied, "or in taking a nap. A man's got to rest some time." Standing up in the street next to the car, Abi and Kevin both yawned and stretched. Kevin looked at Abi. "Ready?"

"Oorah, Devil Dog!" Abi chanted under his breath.

Kevin laughed at Abi's response. "No fighting tonight, amigo. Hopefully just trying to get some answers."

The two men strolled across the street to the pub's front walk. The sound of music and the chatter of people was audible through the door. Kevin observed, "I may have underestimated the number of folks that came in the back door."

Abi offered, "How about we do a little three-sixty recon, so we don't get caught by surprise?" Kevin nodded and followed Abi down the left side of the building. At the far end was a fenced-in patio. Several tables were tucked under an awning that extended off the back wall. A string of white lightbulbs encircled the edge of the patio, illuminating a door that led into the building. Abi paused at the gate from the parking lot.

"Good call, partner," Kevin acknowledged as he continued along the fence toward a group of people smoking cigarettes in the back corner. Catching the attention of a woman facing his direction, Kevin asked, "Hey, can you help me? I'm trying to find a guy named Bud. I guess he comes around here now and again."

The woman pushed some strands of long black hair out of her eyes and said, "I don't know anybody named Bud." Looking around at the others, she asked them, "Do any of you know a guy named Bud?" There was a chorus of negative answers and heads shaking in response.

A bearded pear-shaped man a head shorter than Kevin asked, "What's it about?"

Kevin shrugged. "I'm told we have a mutual friend."

Leaning forward against the fence, the man came back at Kevin, "Who says so?"

Kevin paused, drew back slightly and then smiled back. "I'm not sure why it matters, but it was Carly's mom."

The pear-shaped man began laughing. "You know Arnica? Well, good luck with that one."

Kevin responded, "So you know her?"

"Only by reputation," the man replied, still laughing.

Kevin stepped back, waved, and said, "Okay, thanks." Turning to Abi, he gestured toward the gate and said, "Shall we?" Abi proceeded without response and led the way across the patio to the back door.

He pulled it open and stepped aside to follow Kevin.

Inside, Kevin stopped in a dim hallway. On the left was a line of empty liquor boxes, on the right were two small restrooms. "I feel like I'm back on the *Moshulu*," he said over his shoulder to Abi. Pushing ahead, they entered the saloon where they'd met Carly. A handful of people sat at the bar. A few more were seated at tables on the opposite wall. The two men from the van were arranging sound equipment on an ankle-high stage. Rock music from the 1970s played over the PA system.

Abi, raising his voice to be heard over the music, said, "I don't see him."

Kevin responded, "I don't see Carly either." Tilting his head in the direction of the tables, Kevin suggested, "Let's hole up back here in the corner."

Abi nodded, followed him to a table, and sat down.

"Godfather seat," Abi commented. "Good call."

The room slowly filled with people. The two men from the van began opening instrument cases and setting out the contents on stands.

Abi observed, "Banjo and Mandolin. I guess they weren't kidding about the trash-grass style."

Kevin nodded, still watching for new faces in the room. Looking back to Abi, Kevin asked, "Want a beverage?"

Abi replied, "Not really."

Kevin remarked, "Good, because it's been ten minutes, and we still don't have a bartender."

Abi pointed to the front door as it swung open and Carly stepped into the room. "Don't get in a huff. Here she comes."

Kevin relaxed back into his seat and said, "I hope Bud isn't far behind."

Carly walked down the front of the bar and looped back behind it at the end farthest from the door. After washing her hands in the sink, she said in a loud voice, "Okay, the bar is open again. Thanks for your patience." Several customers quickly clustered around her, ordering drinks. In between ringing up and taking the next drink order, she looked across the room and made a curt wave at Kevin and Abi. After she served all the immediate customers, Carly walked over to the back corner table. "Imagine seeing you two here again."

Abi smiled a big toothy grin and Kevin said, "Hello," before asking, "Any news about Bud?"

"As a matter of fact, yes. His real name is Chris Case. He's from a little holler way down past Alexandria, Kentucky. He's kind of like a groupie for bluegrass but doesn't really have a posse or anything."

Kevin's eyebrow raised, "What do you mean by posse?"

Abi laughed at Kevin and slapped his shoulder. "Come on man, she means a group of friends."

Kevin said, "Oh yeah, I knew that."

Abi continued laughing. "You did not. You are so not hip to the language."

Carly interrupted, "So that's all I know about him. I guess you're going to wait and see if he shows?"

Kevin replied, "I guess so, if that isn't a problem for you."

Carly declared as she turned toward the bar, "Nope. As long as you're not disruptive and you buy something. Just so you know, I just came from Arnica's. She'll be in for the night."

Kevin and Abi watched her walk away. Abi spoke first, "I like the buzz haircut. It's like Eighties-cutting edge. Like Annie Lennox."

"Really?" Kevin asked. "I'm a little more partial to the girly-girl type," he said as they watched her pour a glass of white wine for a customer. Turning his attention to his watch, Kevin called out, "It's closing in on nine. If Bud's a big fan, he'll be here soon; if he wants a decent vantage point, anyway."

Abi offered, "Maybe we should check out back again?"

Kevin agreed, "Good thinking." Standing up from his seat, Kevin said, "I'm going to visit the men's room, then I'll sneak a peek out the back door."

Abi leaned back in his chair and said, "I'll be right here."

Kevin made his way to the back hallway and disappeared into the bathroom. Upon re-emerging a few moments later, he continued toward the back of the building and opened the door onto the patio. Several people were still gathered under the awning. Among them was a new arrival who had his back to Kevin. The man had shoulder length brown hair and some heft to his build. He wore a faded black hoodie, and a mesh-backed trucker style cap. Kevin watched him for a moment. He whispered to himself, "Come on dude, turn this way so I can see your face," but the man was fixed in position. Finally, Kevin exited the door onto the patio and walked up behind him. Lightly touching his shoulder with one finger, Kevin said in a falling soft voice while moving back a half step, "Excuse me?"

The face spun into view quickly, and his eyes zeroed in on Kevin. The man said, "Can I help you?"

Kevin held out a hand and said, "It's Bud, right?" No change of expression crossed the face of the middle-aged man while they shook hands, "I'm Kevin." The round face of the man still didn't come to life with recognition, but Kevin persisted. "We met here a couple weeks ago. Same band?"

Finally, Bud spoke, "Okay, if you say so, but I'm sure I'd remember you. What did you say your name was?"

"My name's Kevin. You were going to tell me about some business opportunity?"

"Did I say that? I mean, I only had like three or four beers that night, not like I blacked out or nothing. I think I pretty much remember all of it." The man removed his hat and scratched his balding head before putting it back on again. "I suppose it's possible I might have said something about my machines." Looking Kevin in the eye, he squinted for a moment and then cocked his head to the side. "I just don't remember. But hey, old friend, new friend, just the same to me." The man extended his hand back to Kevin.

They shook hands again and Kevin asked, "What kind of

machines did you say you have?"

"I got some Polyvends and a bunch of Vendovue machines. Mostly selling snacks and sodas. Seventeen total."

Kevin smiled back at Bud. "Yeah, right. I wanna hear all about it."

"I'm sure you'll want to get into the business," Bud said. "It's easy work and decent money."

Kevin held his hand up and said, "Hold on just a sec. I want to get my buddy out here. He's the one that wants to do it. I mean, I'd just be an investor." Kevin backed away to the door and said again, "Wait one sec," then disappeared inside.

After a moment, Kevin came back out the door followed by Abi. Bud gave a slight nod as Kevin gestured between them and said, "Bud, this is my friend Abi. Abi this is Bud."

Abi said, "Nice to meet you."

Bud replied, "Likewise."

Kevin said looking at Abi, "Bud was telling me about his vending machines and the great business opportunity they present."

Abi said, "Really? I could get into that. I used to service machines for my old boss."

Bud asked, "Where was that?"

Kevin interrupted Abi as he started to speak. "Hey, before you talk about that"—he turned to Bud and asked, "do you know Carly, the barmaid?"

"Uh, yeah," Bud answered. "Anybody who's been here more than once knows Carly. She's way more sophisticated than the women back home."

Kevin smiled back. "Cool, listen, Abi and I are trying to do her a favor, and you might be just the guy to help."

Bud said, "I'd do anything for Carly."

Kevin continued his pitch, "I figured you might say that. You know about refrigeration, what with running vending machines, right? Anyway, me and Abi don't really know much more than how to open and close the door."

Bud stammered, "I know a little bit."

Kevin put his hand on Bud's shoulder and eased him toward the gate to the parking lot, saying, "It is so great of you to help, man. Look, we're going to walk over to Carly's mom's place right over there and see if we can get her fridge working again." Looking at Abi and winking, Kevin asked, "Which one is it again?"

Abi smiled back and made a big gesture pointing at Arnica's house. "That one."

Kevin kept a little pressure on Bud's shoulder and guided him in the direction Abi pointed. "Abi, why don't you run ahead and let Arnica know Bud and I are coming."

As Abi trotted away across the street, Bud offered, "It could be a breaker, or dirty coils, but that's about all I know."

Kevin said, "Well, that makes you a freaking expert compared to us. I'm sure Carly will have something nice to say for doing this for her."

"Is that really where her mom lives?" Bud asked.

Kevin assured him, "Sure as shooting. I met her last night. She's a pistol."

With quick steps, Abi soon bounded onto the front porch of the gray house, knocking on the door. "Miss Arnica? Are you home?"

44

Saturday, October 20

9:08 p.m.

KEVIN AND ABI stood on either side of Bud, facing the open door of the gray house. Dressed in a long green kimono decorated with flowers, Arnica looked out at the three men on the front porch. Her eyes were locked on Bud. She trembled slightly when she lifted her hand to her face and said, "I can't. I can't believe my eyes. You're surely a phantasm."

Bud looked back in confusion. "Uh. I'm just a guy. Here to look at your refrigerator?"

Kevin gently reached forward and took Arnica's hand, "It's okay. He's not a ghost. He's as real as you and me." Kevin gently eased Bud a half step forward and said, "Arnica, you can touch him. See for yourself." Arnica let Kevin place her hand on Bud's shoulder, then Kevin withdrew his own hand. "He's just a guy. The same one you saw in the parking lot across the street last week."

Arnica's eyes watered up as she slid her hand down Bud's arm to take his hand. Bud looked back and forth at Abi and Kevin, his mouth moving but not making any noise. Arnica took Bud's fist in both of her hands and said, "I'm at a loss for words. I never thought God would be so cruel as to make two of them, and yet, here he is."

Bud's mouth finally managed a squeak. "I don't know what's going on here."

Kevin patted him on the back and explained, "Arnica's man recently passed away, and she saw you in the parking lot last week. She mistook you for the ghost of Harley Webster."

Bud nodded and said, "I'm real sure I'm not a ghost."

Arnica, still looking at Bud, said, "You look just like Harley when we first met." Reaching up, she removed Bud's cap with one hand and then placed her other palm on Bud's cheek. "Look at you," she whispered. "You're too warm to be a ghost." Then she handed his cap back to him and asked, "What's your family name and where are you from?"

Bud replaced the cap on his head and answered, "Case, Christopher Case is my real name. I grew up on Twelve Mile Creek, down in Peach Grove, Kentucky."

Arnica's eyes widened and she made a slight gasp. "Harley's kinfolk was from Mentor, Kentucky. Is that near Peach Grove?"

Bud stood a little straighter and clasped his hands together, "It's the next place down the road toward the river from Peach Grove."

Arnica's face reddened and she began to fan herself while asking, "What are your folks' names?"

Bud recited in a matter-of-fact tone, "Pa was Jefferson Case. He died in September, a year back. Ma was called Sissy, but I don't remember her much. She passed when I was little. She was married to a soldier that died in Vietnam and then she married again to Pa."

Arnica's eyes began flowing with tears. She pulled herself close to Bud and wrapped him in a hug. "A child should know his mother. I'm so sorry for you, honey." Bud stood still with his arms pinned to his side by Arnica's embrace. When Arnica finally let go of Bud, she asked, "Do you know the name of the soldier your mother was married to?"

Bud looked to his left and right at Abi and Kevin, then back at Arnica, "I don't really know, but heard the name George mentioned once or twice when Pa was talking to relatives. I always imagined that was his name."

Kevin looked at Bud, "Was anybody else in your family named George?" Bud shook his head in response as Arnica stepped backward from the door and slumped to a seated position on the steps. Kevin followed her into the house and asked, "Are you okay?"

Arnica looked up at Bud, "How old are you?"

Bud replied, "Forty-five this year."

Kevin looked back and forth between Abi, Bud, and Arnica in silence and then said, "Why don't you two come in here and we'll close the door." The two men on the doorstep followed the suggestion while Kevin knelt down in front of Arnica. She had both hands covering her face and sobbed quietly. He asked, "What is it, Arnica?"

She wiped her tears away with the back of her hands and looked up at Bud. "Your daddy was Harley's older brother; that's why you look so much like him."

Bud shook his head, "But my Pa didn't have any brothers. Just sisters."

Arnica nodded. "I know you were told Jefferson Case was your father, but I don't think he was. Jefferson was the man who raised you, but George Webster was your father."

Bud was silent for a long while and swayed slightly from side to side. Abi put a hand on his shoulder and said, "Let's step out and get some fresh air. Maybe sit on the front steps for a moment." Bud pivoted and followed Abi's guidance back out the front door.

Kevin asked Arnica, "Did you know Sissy or George?"

Arnica nodded. "No. That was long before I ever met Harley. He never really talked about his family. Wouldn't even go to a funeral. What I know came from obituaries in the paper."

Kevin leaned in to hug Arnica, but she pushed him back. "No, no. I'm okay." Wiping her eyes dry, she instructed Kevin, "Take Bud back to the pub. I know that Harley is really gone. I was seeing things from a place of fear."

Kevin responded as he stood up, "Are you sure you're fine?"

Arnica glanced at him and said, "Better than fine." Arnica stood up, straightened her kimono, and pulled the belt tight. "I'm totally free, for the first time in my life. Nobody needs me, nobody wants to control me."

Kevin nodded. "That's good." Backing toward the door, he said, "I'll be leaving for Philly as soon as I can square up with Father Myers." Kevin added, "Good luck with the probate court and settling the affairs."

Arnica took his hand in hers and said, "I owe Father Myers an apology." Then, letting go, she went to the door and said to the two men sitting on the front step. "Thank you, Abi." Addressing Bud, she said, "Good luck to you, but I can't bear the sight of Harley's likeness right now, so please go back to Jefferson's kin. Trust me; live like this night never happened."

After Kevin stepped outside, Arnica closed the door behind him. The sound of a deadbolt clicking home was audible through the wood. "I guess that's it," Kevin said. "Let's get out of here."

Bud led the way back to the street, "You boys have given me the strangest night of my life, and I think because of that, y'all owe me a drink."

Abi nodded and said, "You know Bud, I think that's the least we can do for you."

45

Sunday, October 21

12:38 p.m.

KEVIN WALKED OUT the automatic doors from the Philadelphia International Airport Terminal F baggage claim and stood near the curb of the arrivals-level driveway. He scratched the beard stubble on his chin, and after rubbing his eyes, leaned against a concrete pillar and watched the approaching vehicles. Scattered around him, people stood with their baggage, chatting among themselves, or craning their necks to see what cars were entering the tunnel-like pick-up area. Drivers positioned their cars at angles to secure a place at the curb and occasionally accentuated the maneuver with a honk of the horn.

Kevin watched a green rent-a-car shuttle bus come to a stop in front of him. Its forward progress was blocked by a Ford Aerostar minivan that straddled two lanes while trying to wedge into a short piece of curb. A group of women wearing matching

Las Vegas–themed attire surrounded the minivan and tossed bags in the back. After slamming the rear hatch closed, they began loading through the side door. While the women jostled for seats, a silver sedan came to a stop behind the shuttle bus. The dark-haired driver of the sedan leaned left and right, trying to see around the traffic jam. When the bus didn't move, she laid on the horn in a long, dissonant honk. The sound attracted Kevin's attention, and he walked to the curb. The driver let up on the horn and lowered the window, yelling out, "Maloney!"

Kevin stepped to the car and waved at the driver. After dropping into the front passenger seat, Johnston said to Kevin, "Nice to see you, sailor," and then turned her attention to the other vehicles. "Too bad these jerks don't know how to drive, otherwise we'd be moving already."

"Hey there," Kevin said with a smile. "Thanks for coming to get me."

Johnston declared, "Yeah, well if I didn't volunteer, I probably wouldn't get to see you for another week."

Kevin asked, "Has it been just a week? I feel like I've been gone a month."

Johnston revised, "Well, five days since the party. So almost a week."

Kevin leaned his head back on the seat and let out a sigh. "Damn, and I was only in Cincinnati for three days. What a journey that was."

The minivan began moving and the bus began creeping forward. Detective Johnston matched the crawling speed until she found a gap to the left and accelerated around the blockage. When the car was out from under the parking garages and moving at speed down the ramp toward the highway, Johnston reached over to Kevin and patted his leg. "It'll be okay after you get a little rest in your own bed."

Kevin caught her hand and held it for a moment. "Yeah, it'll be back to normal tomorrow." Kevin let go of Johnston's hand and turned to look at the passing scenery as she steered the car around the curving off-ramp to Island Drive. The sky was overcast and the leaves of the few trees around the airport were brown and half fallen. "Looks like I missed the best of the fall colors."

Johnston replied, "Not really. It just looks bad down here. When you get out of the city a little, there's still some good colors."

Kevin nodded in reply. He turned to look at her and said, "I'm not sure my skin is thick enough for this job. I'm afraid I'm not going to last."

Johnston looked at him and gave a slight smile, "It'll come. Unfortunately, it'll come."

"I was afraid of that," Kevin sighed.

Johnston asked, "Want to talk about it, or let it simmer for a bit?"

Kevin shrugged as the sedan snaked up the Cobbs Creek Parkway. "It's been simmering all morning. I guess I should just start bitching and dump it in your lap."

"I'm all ears," Johnston replied with a quick glance across the car toward Kevin.

Kevin held up a single finger, counting. "First up, I got waylaid on this whole thing. Nobody asked me what I thought, they just laid it on and expected me to be good with flying out on zero notice."

Johnston nodded and Kevin continued by adding another finger. "Second, there was no intel when Skip and I got there. They dropped us into this operation cold. Thankfully, the situation wasn't complicated, but nobody did any homework or asked any questions. I had to develop my own leads on the fly."

Johnston commented, "Seems like you came out of it okay. Better than last summer."

Kevin continued. "Only because there was no cat. It was a case of, I don't know, mistaken identity? But meanwhile, I have a real case here, a real, confirmed cat running loose in North Philly." Kevin fell silent and looked out the window while Johnston kept driving.

After turning on Sixty Third and crossing Market Street, Johnston broke the silence, "Listen Kevin, I think you're putting yourself in the wrong frame of mind here. You've got a job that defies description, and you're still figuring out how to do it, and do it right."

Kevin replied, "It's frustrating, you know?"

Johnston stopped for a traffic light at Haverford Avenue. She looked over at Kevin and in a lower, softer tone said, "You'll get it. There's no manual yet because you are still writing it. So, just talk it out, and let your grievances be lessons."

When the car started rolling forward again, Kevin took a deep breath and let it out slowly. He sat up straighter in the seat and said, "Okay. I've got to learn the lessons and not get upset. I'm the only dude doing this job, and I get to figure out the best way to do it."

Johnston agreed, "That's right."

"Triage," Kevin said firmly. Then he said it again, "Triage, like the docs at medical units do. I need to think up a way to manage multiple cases, because it'll happen again."

Johnston nodded. "We get multiple homicides, and your brother gets multiple problems on the same call. So yeah, sit down and think it through. Maybe a flow chart."

Kevin broke a slight smile and said, "Maybe I need to get back to the bat cave? Ask myself, *What would Uncle Matt do*?"

Johnston then prompted, "Then write it down. For Pete's sake, please write it down."

Kevin nodded while saying, "And write it down."

At the intersection of Sixty Third and Lancaster Avenue, Johnston made a slight left on Lancaster and proceeded northwest to City Avenue. Kevin looked up at the tall white cross and blue sign on the opposite side of the street that announced St. Charles Seminary and said, "Don't you want to turn here?"

"Nope," Johnston said. "You've got a new way home, now."

Kevin asked, "What do you mean?" but Johnston remained silent as she drove across the intersection and followed the slight curve of Lancaster Avenue. The roofs of the seminary buildings were visible over the tall shrubbery and nearly bare trees. A sign on the right advertised "Welcome to Historic Montgomery County." To the left were the red brick buildings of a large apartment complex followed by a stoplight at the entrance to the Lankenau Hospital.

The neat shrubs surrounding the seminary gave way to an overgrown wrought iron fence backed by old trees. After a quarter mile, the trees thinned out and left a gap in the foliage overgrowing the fence. Here was a black iron gate set against two heavy concrete pylons. The vines and grass around it were freshly cut back, and a shiny hydraulic arm was attached to the back of both sides of the gate.

Slowing down for the turn-off, Johnston pressed a remote control clipped to her purse. The gates opened, allowing the car to pass onto the seminary grounds. Kevin's jaw dropped. He looked out the back window and watched the closing gates as Johnston drove slowly up the hill toward the old farmhouse. He said, "Well, kiss my grits! That was fast. I didn't really expect to get access for another year!"

Johnston pulled into the drive, set the shift lever in park, and shut off the engine. She turned to Kevin and said, "I think your brother helped it along. He said he knew a guy who does that kind of stuff."

Kevin smiled and said, "Well, good work, Brian—and Mr. Warren for letting him do it." Exiting the car, Kevin retrieved his pack and walked around the front of the car.

Johnston met him there and leaned against the front fender. She said, "I need to go back to work, but I think I can be done in time for dinner."

Kevin dropped his pack on the ground, took Johnston in his arms and said, "Pick me up?"

Johnston pulled him in closer and kissed his lips. When she

released him, she replied, "Sure, I can do that. I'll give you a jingle when I'm on my way. Now, I'll kiss you once more before I must get in the car. Otherwise, you might get ideas."

Kevin grinned, "No ideas here, officer. Just want to get a load of laundry going and maybe take a nap."

46

Sunday, October 21

17:55 p.m.

BRIAN MALONEY ENTERED the kitchen and let the screen door slam behind him. He flipped the light switch and tossed his keys and duffle bag on the kitchen table, then diverted right to the refrigerator. Opening the door, he bent over and nearly inserted his head into the appliance. Rummaging around among the contents, he came out with a green bottle of beer. Standing up, he bumped the door closed with his hip and faced the center of the room. "Hello Brian," Detective Johnston said from the chair on the opposite side of the kitchen table.

Brian flinched and stepped back against the refrigerator. "Whoa, I didn't see you there."

Johnston grinned. "I know you didn't. Good thing I outgrew my dream of being a serial killer."

Brian stepped forward and placed the bottle on the table. "You don't have to give it up. Some of the best arsonists are firefighters. Why not a killer-cop?"

She responded, "You make an excellent point."

"Beverage?" Brian asked as he reached for the handle of the refrigerator.

"Got a soda in there?"

Brian said, "I think I saw one," as he pulled the door open and ducked his head for a better view. After shuffling several items around he stood up and closed the door again. "Birch Beer work for you?"

Johnston nodded and he placed the brown bottle on her side of the table. She twisted off the top and held it up in toast saying, "Here's to the psycho-killers." Brian tipped his bottle forward and clinked it against hers.

As Johnston lifted the bottle to her lips, Brian said, "How's things downtown?"

Johnston finished a long sip from the bottle and then answered, "Same as it ever was."

"I hear you," Brian said with a nod and sat down at the table. "I take it you have plans with Kev?"

Johnston made a slight toss of her hair. "I suppose so, but when I got here, he was sound asleep on the couch. I sent him for a shower and a change of clothes."

Brian chuckled. "Keeping a lady waiting like that. That's first class."

Johnston took another sip of beer and replied, "Yeah, but it's okay. He probably needed the rest. Besides, it's no fun hanging out with grumps."

Brian smiled. "And yet, here you are having a beer with Grumble Claus himself."

"Yes, but you wear it well," Johnston complimented, giving a little salute with the bottle.

Brian took a long swallow and rocked the chair back on two

legs. "So, did he say anything about his trip?"

Johnston replied, "A little. He said there wasn't a cat. More like some kind of mistaken identity. He wasn't happy about being dragged away from an active case." As she finished speaking, thumping footfalls could be heard on the steps. Brian pivoted to look at the passage from the dark living room. Kevin emerged into the light of the kitchen wearing fresh clothes, clean shaven, and smelling of soap.

Kevin looked at the two seated at the table and remarked, "Talking about me?"

Brian said, "Some—and welcome home, little brother."

"Thanks," Kevin replied as he dropped into an open chair at the table. "Looks like you've been busy while I was gone. I like the new gate and really like that Jimmie's van isn't parked in our driveway."

Brian smiled and said, "He's moved on to his next gig, so we won't be seeing him for a while, but it almost didn't happen."

Kevin cocked his head. "What do you mean?"

Brian gestured up the hill with his beer bottle. "Mr. Warren was asking him if he wanted a job here running a mower—but don't worry, I took care of it."

"Yeah? How'd you manage that?"

Brian answered, "First, I told Mr. Warren how much Uncle Jimmie likes the bottle, then I offered to do some grass cutting on my off days. That pretty much sealed the deal."

Johnston laughed. "Free grass cutting to get rid of a squatter in your house? That's some firehouse logic for you."

Brian squinted at Johnston. "Who said anything about free? I'll be on the payroll."

Kevin patted Brian's shoulder. "That's fine work, and Uncle Jimmie parks his van somewhere else. That's what really matters. So did anything else happen while I was gone?"

Brian tipped back his beer again and set it on the table before answering, "Yeah, as a matter of fact. I heard from your team in Rome."

Kevin's eyes lit up and he asked, "Did you talk to Uncle Matt? What did he say?"

Brian stood up and retrieved a notepad tucked behind the top of the wall phone. "Let's see here," he said as he resumed his seat and laid the pad on the table. "They were in Rome for a couple days. They'd been out to see all the sights while they waited for a research librarian to find what they needed." Kevin nodded in response and Brian continued. "Matt really liked the catacombs and Coliseum, and he said there were feral cats everywhere. Stepan was interested in the food. They had to stop twice a day for gelato, and dinners lasted from seven in the evening until midnight."

Kevin grinned and asked, "I'm glad they're having a good time, but did they say anything about the research?"

Brian sniffed. "Not really, but Matt did say something about getting kicked out of the Vatican Library and that they were going to head up to Florence to some zoology place."

Johnston said, "Sounds like two kids on a hall pass."

Kevin shook his head. "Okay. Well, let's hope they have better results after their trip to Florence than I did in Cincinnati."

Brian commented, "You seem to have a bee in your bonnet about that."

Kevin replied, "I have a real cat here, and they send me off to look for a ghost that turned out to be a long-lost nephew."

Brian nodded. "Kinda burns your behind, doesn't it? Well, if I may offer a thought?"

Kevin rolled his eyes and said, "Yeah, go ahead, oh wise one."

Brian asked, "Did anything good come of it? Did you fix something that needed fixing?"

Kevin nodded. "Yeah, I guess so, and I got to hang out with Skip and Abi for a day."

"Okay," Brian said. "Start there. You know, firefighters often feel the same way, like when we're hauling a noncritical patient to the ER while the rest of the house is fighting a three-alarm blaze. You know you're missing all the action, but you're still doing an important job."

Looking down at his hands, Kevin agreed, "Okay, I think I get what you're saying."

Brian wadded up the note paper and said, "Might as well get over it. It's part of the job." Then, standing up, Brian added, "Well, you kids have a good dinner. I'll be here on the couch if you need anything." After dropping the wad in the trash can, he shuffled into the dark living room.

Kevin and Johnston pushed back from the table and stood up. As they headed for the door, Johnston called after Brian, "See you later."

From the other room came a grunted "Yup."

47

Sunday, October 21

7:49 p.m.

KEVIN HELD THE door for Detective Johnston as they exited Barnaby's Restaurant. Walking across the parking lot to the silver police sedan, Kevin asked, "What did you think of that place?"

"It was fine," Johnston replied.

Kevin added, "Mom and Dad used to bring us to Barnaby's for special occasions."

As they opened the car doors, Johnston called across the roof from the driver's side, "What do you want to do next, sailor? Call it a night?"

Kevin looked back and shrugged as he let himself slide down into the seat. After the doors were closed, he said, "I know I said I'd pick up the search tomorrow, but I don't know. I hate to waste a minute of time."

Johnston looked at him as she buckled her seatbelt and said, "You want to go make a pass through the neighborhood, don't you?"

Kevin replied as he buckled in, "Yes, I think so, and I'd appreciate the backup."

Johnston turned her attention to starting the car. When the motor was running, and the headlight beams illuminated the blacktop, she asked, "I know this is important, but whose life can we save if we go over there tonight?"

Kevin remained silent and stared straight ahead as Johnston dropped the car into gear and maneuvered out of the parking lot. Turning onto West Chester Pike and heading east, Johnston looked back over at Kevin, who returned the glance. In a quiet voice, he said, "Mine."

Johnston returned her attention to the roadway and said, "Okay. I'll give you until nine thirty. Then I'm taking you home."

Kevin nearly whispered, "Thank you."

Johnston expertly maneuvered the sedan to avoid traffic slowdowns along West Chester Pike. Reaching City Avenue, she turned left and proceeded northeast to join Lancaster Avenue and the familiar route across West Girard Avenue.

The two remained silent until they crossed the Schuylkill River, when Johnston said, "Aside from the lost time, I sense you're not at ease with this case."

Kevin admitted, "Yeah. It's a real mixed bag, you know?"

Johnston patted his hand quickly before returning it to the steering wheel. "Okay. Let it out. One thing at a time."

Kevin took a deep breath and blew it out slowly. "There's that kid, Seven."

Johnston nodded and said, "Yep. Kinda sucks, but that's water under the bridge. Got to let him go. Be satisfied that you're doing right by his family."

"Okay," then Kevin added after a long pause, "but there's also Johnny Squares."

Johnston brought the sedan to a stop at a traffic light, then looked at Kevin and said, "You're scared of him and his crew."

Kevin agreed, "Yes, I am." Looking out the window as the car began moving again, he said, "I got off with a simple beatdown the first time, then the last time I was saved by the lucky appearance of Borys and the Ukrainian super friends."

Johnston concluded, "And you don't want 'luck' to be the most important part of your survival plan."

"In a nutshell," Kevin confirmed.

Johnston steered the car across Broad Street on Girard Avenue, slowing as much as traffic would allow. Kevin lowered the window and began scanning the sidewalks. Turning north on Thirteenth Street, the traffic diminished. Johnston idled the car at a walking pace. She said, "Tell me what we're looking for."

"The cat is small, mostly black, with a white face and mittens," Kevin described.

Johnston replied, "That'll be tough to see in the dark."

Kevin said, "I know. Hopefully it'll be in human form and out in the open."

"Surrounded by a moat would be helpful," Johnston added.

Kevin smirked, "Yeah, like that."

For two blocks, the left side of the one-way street was occupied by modern academic buildings fully illuminated by floodlights mounted on towering utility poles. The backscatter from the floods illuminated the opposite side of the street and the array of brick two-story apartment buildings that faded into the darkness.

Johnston commented, "Getting cool out. If you don't mind, I'm going to crank up the heat while you've got the window open."

Kevin looked back at her and said, "Sure," and then returned his attention to the street.

Johnston continued north on Thirteenth, leaving the bright floodlights behind. The regular streetlights were widely spaced and were only installed along the right sidewalk. Their weak yellow illumination cast the left side into patchy darkness under the trees growing along the pavement. "In a couple blocks we can cut over into Seven's neighborhood. What do you think?" Johnston asked.

Kevin replied, "Swing past the SEPTA station on Berks. Maybe we can find some local folks who know something about Seven, or maybe the cat."

Johnston continued north into the center of the student housing area of Temple University. Concrete dormitories and modern apartment buildings lined the streets. She turned right on Montgomery Avenue and proceeded east through empty lots being prepared for construction. At Warnock Street, she turned north, passing between an industrial building with a tall chimney, and an empty lot being used to store construction materials. At the next intersection, she turned right and slowed to a crawl under the railroad overpass and SEPTA commuter rail station. Johnston said, "There's a parking lot on the other side." Kevin nodded and raised the window as she maneuvered the car into the lot and pulled into a parking space.

Exiting the car, Kevin looked up at the elevated train station. Johnston came alongside and commented, "Seven's home is just a couple blocks up Ninth Street from here."

Kevin nodded and said, "Okay," then he led the way toward the deep shadows under the overhead rail structure that crossed Berks Street. Johnston followed, unzipping her jacket, and looking around in all directions. The massive steel and concrete bridge formed a roof over the steps leading to the platforms above. Pale greenish-white light filtered down the stairway from the platform level. Fencing boxed in the bottom of the steps with a gap for turnstiles. A metal and glass security booth overlooked the area. There was a dim solitary light over the door, but the booth was unoccupied.

On the west side of the fencing, barely visible in a deep shadow, a yellow pedal reflector gave away the shape of a white bicycle leaning against the metal mesh. On the ground next to it, was a dark pile of stuffed trash bags, only discernible by the sheen of the plastic. Kevin approached slowly and called out, "Anybody there?"

The pile of trash bags rustled, and one rolled off to the side. A gruff voice responded, "What do you want?"

Kevin froze in place and watched as a dark human head and torso emerged from the pile. "Yo, sir, sorry to disturb you," Kevin apologized. "I'm looking for a young man and a cat. I was wondering if you'd seen either one."

"Hmph," the dark shape replied.

Kevin said, "The cat is small and black. White on its face and paws. The kid's name is Seven. You might have seen him. He's from around here and worked at the grocery store."

The voice replied, "I knew him, but he's dead."

Kevin added, "Have you seen the cat?"

The shape dissolved into the shadows with a faint acknowledgment. "Hmm. It followed me a couple days until I swatted it. Bad luck."

Kevin asked again, "When did you see it last?" but no sound was forthcoming from the inky black. Kevin backed out slowly into the light cast by the fixture on the booth. He called out once more, "Thanks," and then pivoted back toward Johnston.

Johnston asked, "What did he say?"

"Not much really," Kevin said. "He's seen it. Then he said cats are bad luck. Like I need any reminding of that fact."

Johnston turned and led the way back toward the sedan, saying, "Next time, don't get out of the car until I have my damn flashlight. You have a way of finding the darkest places in the city."

"Yeah, I should have mine too," Kevin replied. "You know, if I were riding the train, I think I would avoid this black-hole station after dark."

Johnston remarked, "Perhaps you should lodge a complaint. Then maybe somebody would fix the lighting." Arriving back at the car, they climbed in and looked at each other in the glow of the dashboard lights. Johnston tapped her watch and said, "You've got about ten more minutes before I am driving you home."

Kevin's voice started strong and then tailed off, "Yeah, okay. Take me past Seven's house and then back down Tenth Street. If I were a cat or a misappropriated soul, I guess that's where I'd go."

Johnston patted Kevin's shoulder after dropping the car into gear. "Buck up, sailor. Tonight isn't a complete bust. You talked to a guy living under a bridge and had a date with me."

Kevin half smiled. "I can't believe you just put those two things together in a single declaration of success, but I'll take what I can get."

48

Sunday, October 21

10:33 p.m.

BRIAN RECLINED ON the leather couch, bathed in the blue light of the television on the far side of the room. When Kevin entered from the kitchen, Brian's eyes flicked open and he said, "Hey bro," before slowly lifting himself to a seated position.

Kevin nodded toward the television. "Yo, what are you watching?"

Brian glanced at the screen. "Don't know. Looks like some kind of weather disaster documentary." Brian pointed at the television. The image was of a woman and child wading in waist deep water. At the bottom of the screen, scrolling text described Tropical Depression 18 as being located thirty miles south of Jamaica. Brian added, "Man, can you imagine flooding like that here? Anyway, I was watching a game, and when it ended, I went looking for the West Coast games, but I guess I fell asleep in the middle of changing channels."

"Sure," Kevin said, smirking, "we'll go with falling asleep while flipping through the channels."

Brian changed the subject and asked, "How was the cat chasing tonight? Any luck?"

"Not really. We came across an urban outdoorsman who knew the last victim and saw a similar cat sometime in the past." Kevin dropped onto the vacated end of the sofa and sighed, "Didn't seem like a reliable sighting, so not much help."

"Right, I know the feeling," Brian replied. Then he added, "Have you checked the messages recently? There was one from Michele Fields at St. Malachy. She left a number. I wrote it down."

Kevin let his head fall back against the couch and said, "Crap. I forgot about checking in with her. I need to call first thing tomorrow. She'll be relieved to hear that her mother isn't roaming the streets anymore."

Brian asked, "You're pretty sure of that? The cat has moved on?"

Nodding, Kevin said, "Unless there are two cats working the area, yes. I'm willing to say that the cat has moved on to Seven, and I'm running out of time before it flips to somebody new."

"If it helps, I'll get in touch with her for you. I mean, we seemed to be on the same wavelength and all."

Kevin looked at Brian. "If you really want to."

Brian shrugged. "Yeah, I'll do it.

"All right, bro, I'll leave it to you."

49

Monday, October 22

11:04 a.m.

THE DISSONANT CLATTER of the ringing telephone penetrated every room of the dead quiet house. Kevin jerked upright from his bed, where he was reading his book on cats. He bounded down the stairs and hooked a turn around the newel post at the bottom of the banister. Dashing into the kitchen, he caught the phone's handset on the fourth ring and spoke into the microphone, "Hello?"

A voice crackled on the speaker. "Father Matt!" Kevin exclaimed. While he listened, Kevin stretched the cord far enough to sit at the kitchen table. When there was a break in the speaking, Kevin said, "That's great. So, you're going to get access to everything they've got?" Father Matt continued and Kevin listened intently. After a long discourse, Kevin replied, "Yeah, I'm working one now. I know what the cat looks like, and I even met the most recent victim before he died. I'm trying to get this wrapped before it can change again." He paused while Uncle Matt responded and then followed up with, "Right. Well, good luck tomorrow. I hope you're having a good time. Goodbye."

Kevin stood up, replaced the handset on the wall phone's cradle, then slipped on a jacket from the peg board by the door. Stepping outside, he quickly walked up the hill to the maintenance building. Inside he was met by Mr. Warren who was carrying a cup of coffee from the kitchenette to his office. "Hey Kevin, how's it shaking?"

Kevin smiled in return. "Pretty good. Glad to be back from my little trip."

"Yeah, how was it? Riding in that little airplane?" Mr. Warren asked. "I'd be too scared to do that."

Kevin replied in a casual voice, "It was fine. We flew right into Cincinnati in just a couple hours. Skipped the whole baggage claim and airport rigamarole."

Mr. Warren asked, "So it wasn't scary?"

"No, no," Kevin waved his hand. "I've done stuff way more intimidating than that, and the pilot was great. It turns out I know him. He and his partner in the airplane built it themselves. The partner is somehow connected to the archbishop through a law firm or something. Anyway, he was repaying a favor by flying me out there."

Leading the way into the office, Mr. Warren said, "Well, I'm glad you're back in one piece." Taking his seat, he asked, "Now that I've got your brother learning the Toro, how can I help you?"

"I'm in over my head a little on the current project," Kevin began.

Mr. Warren frowned a little and said, "How so? I mean you got the lights on my truck busted, and I've seen the scrapes on your face, but other than that?"

"Yeah, well, what I need is somebody to watch my six while I'm doing my thing."

"I'm not sure how I can . . ." Mr. Warren tapered off.

"I want to try taking Fast Eddie with me to keep a lookout." Kevin added, "He's got some street smarts, I hope. Maybe he can help me steer clear of sketchy situations?"

Mr. Warren took a sip of coffee and then swiveled back and forth in his chair while looking up at the light fixture on the ceiling. "Maybe I can spare him when he's not busy fixing equipment. And I gotta figure out how to get him paid for it, but I might be able to work something out." Looking back at Kevin, he asked, "How many hours are we talking?"

Kevin replied, "Right now, I just want to try him out. It'll be less than a full workday."

Mr. Warren nodded and said, "Talk to Eddie about it. Whatever you're doing isn't part of his job description, so I'm going to leave it up to him. If he's game, I can see if Father Tucker will chip in."

Kevin smiled. "Cool. I'll go chat with him right now. Where is he?"

Mr. Warren gestured with his thumb. "In the garage, fixing the lights on the truck."

50

Tuesday, October 23

1:41 p.m.

A LOW-SLUNG HONDA CIVIC descended the road from the seminary maintenance building toward the farmhouse, its wide-open tailpipe emitting a popping growl. It turned into the driveway just as Kevin exited the kitchen door carrying his backpack. Kevin raised his hand and the hatchback's white eight-spoke wheels came to an instant stop. The engine sound dropped to a soft idle and the black-tinted driver window lowered slightly. Fast Eddie sat behind the wheel, smiling at Kevin. "Hey, mister man, since I can get mileage for this, mind if I drive?"

Kevin grinned and looked over the car. Air dams nearly scraped the pavement, and its bright metallic orange paint contrasted with the gray sky and expanse of green grass behind it. "I didn't know this was your ride. Sure, Eddie, we'll blend in well where we're going."

Eddie gave a thumbs-up and said, "Cool, hop in."

Kevin ran his hand along the black oversized carbon-fiber rear spoiler as he walked around the back of the car. After reaching for a nonexistent passenger door handle, he rapped on the window. The door emitted a snap as it unlatched. Kevin pulled it open by the window glass and looked inside. The door had no interior panel, and a pair of locking pliers were clamped to a metal rod. "Saving weight?" Kevin asked.

Fast Eddie replied, "Yeah, man, I removed the right door handle and smoothed over the hole for aerodynamics. Then I took out all the interior panels, most of the dashboard, and the back seat. These are actual race car seats with five-point harnesses. And there's a cross brace in the back if we roll over."

"And the vice-grip is my door handle?" Kevin remarked.

Fast Eddie smiled. "You got it."

Kevin shoved his pack in the back and maneuvered into the passenger seat. Once in place, Eddie demonstrated how to use the harness and Kevin secured himself to the seat. Looking left, Kevin said, "You know North Philly at all? Around Temple?"

Fast Eddie shifted the car into reverse while saying, "Shoot man, I had an uncle around there. Of course, I know it."

Kevin replied, "Then let's get going."

Eddie eased out the clutch and revved the engine to back out of the drive. Cutting the wheel left, the car responded quickly and came to a stop pointed up the hill toward the maintenance buildings. Eddie said, "I'd burn it out for you, but it might get me fired."

Kevin laughed. "Save it for another time; besides, I've smelled plenty of tire smoke in my short time on this planet."

The car idled forward and made its way toward the main gate. At the entrance, the uniformed guard waved as they passed. Eddie gave the horn button a tap, causing it to emit a short beep. Turning right onto Lancaster Avenue, Eddie gunned the engine. The front tires squealed for half a heartbeat, then he eased off the gas pedal and let the now racing engine drop back to an easy purr.

Kevin looked across at Eddie and said, "Does that move get results with the ladies?"

Eddie laughed. "Naw, mister man. But it's still fun!"

Making their way east and south toward the city, Eddie drove and talked nonstop about his uncle from North Philadelphia. Kevin nodded along and watched the buildings as they passed. When they were within a few blocks of Broadway, Kevin interrupted. "Do you save up this stuff all week, or is your brain just going this fast all the time?"

"Uh, sorry. I guess I'm kinda nervous," Eddie replied.

Kevin asked, "About what?"

Eddie's head twitched as he formed new words. "Well. It's like, um, you got something, you know, weird going on, and . . . nobody exactly knows what."

Kevin snickered, "Well, okay. I get that." Kevin looked at Eddie again and continued. "What do you want to know?"

Eddie slapped his left hand in a fast rhythm on the steering wheel and made jerky glances toward Kevin. He asked, "So are you some kind of spy?"

Kevin snorted, "Whoa. That's a good one. Who says that?"

"People," Eddie shrugged.

"No, I'm not a spy."

Eddie said, "I also heard you're an exorcist, and you hunt demons and stuff."

Kevin exhaled and said, "Naw. Not demons."

Eddie's eyes went wide. "So it's the occult, huh? Satanic covens doing ritualistic sacrifice?"

Kevin chuckled. "Nope, no. Nothing like that, Eddie. I'm just here to make sure dead people are really dead, and their bodies aren't being mistreated."

Eddie slowed the car for a traffic light and then looked hard at Kevin. Then he said, "Yeah, I heard about that necrophilia stuff in school, but I didn't never believe some sick bastard would actually, you know, make it with a dead chick."

Kevin shook his head and said, "No, no, that's not what I mean."

Eddie gasped. "So people don't actually do that. Right?"

Kevin looked up at the top of the car's cabin. "I don't, no, I mean, maybe. If they have a name for it, then somebody's done it, or tried it, but that's not my thing either."

Eddie looked at Kevin again and said, "Oh," before accelerating the car back up to speed.

Kevin then explained, "You see, it's like this. When some people die, their body gets corrupted, and its physical form gets . . . taken over by some other thing. And my job is to find the corrupted bodies and see that they get disposed of properly."

Eddie then asked, "So if this is a thing, why do you keep it a secret and not tell anybody what you're doing?"

"That's a bigger question," Kevin acknowledged. After rubbing his eyes and letting out a long breath, he said, "People tend to overreact. Know what I mean?"

Eddie laughed quietly. "Yeah, like my grandma. Whenever I'd fail a grammar test or something, she'd go crazy. And I didn't see what the big deal was. Cars and machines don't care if I can diagram a sentence or spell *thesaurus*."

Kevin smiled. "Yeah, okay, like that. But what I really mean is something bigger. You see, people often screw up when faced with a problem they don't understand. They feel like they have to do something, even if it's the wrong thing. So that's why I don't tell people about what I'm doing, because they will pretty much panic and make my job harder."

Eddie nodded. "Yeah, I get that. It's kinda like running from the cops when all you've done is roll through a traffic light."

Kevin looked at Eddie and said, "Good example. Let me guess; you've tried that?"

Eyeing the rearview mirror, Eddie replied, "No, but I want to."

"Oh, are we going to get pulled?" Kevin asked, craning his neck to get a view behind the high-backed race car seats.

Eddie depressed the clutch and coasted to the right side of the street while he said, "I think so."

He came to a stop next to the curb. The amber hazard lights on the corners of the orange car's fenders began flashing in a slow and steady rhythm, and the driver-side window lowered a hand-span. A moment later, a Philadelphia police cruiser pulled up behind Eddie's car. Police officers exited both front doors. The officer from the passenger side stood behind the orange car, while the other officer walked up along the rear fender and cocked her head to see into the open window.

Eddie sat with his hands on his thighs, eyes straight ahead, and asked the uniformed woman, "Yo, what's up?" while Kevin still craned his neck to see the area behind the car.

The officer droned, "Can you lower the window all the way, please?"

Eddie said, "That's as far as it goes."

"Really?" she asked. Then turning to the other officer, she said, "The driver says the window only goes down about four inches. Can you believe that?"

The male officer standing behind the car replied, "Maybe you should use your baton to open it all the way."

"No, no, you don't need to do that," Eddie pleaded. "I'll get out if that would help."

The officer replied, "Stay where you are and just give me your license and registration."

Eddie slowly reached his right hand across the car to the glove compartment." Popping the door open, Eddie retrieved a piece of folded paper, closed the glove box door, and then passed the paper over his shoulder to the officer. He then slowly slipped his right hand to his pocket and retrieved a black nylon Velcro-closure wallet. Ripping the velcro apart, Eddie unfolded the wallet and plucked a laminated card from a slot. "Here you go," he said as he handed it out to the officer.

The officer said, "Stay put. I'll be right back."

Eddie sighed and asked, "Do they ever not come back? I mean, maybe they could get a call and just leave?"

Kevin smiled as he unbuckled his seatbelt, "I doubt it's ever that easy, but if I can get a good look, I might know that cop." Kevin worked his butt loose from the confining seat and turned sideways in the cockpit of the cramped car. Looking between the seats and cross-checking in the mirrors, Kevin said, "Yeah, that's Hertz. If I can get the lady cop to let me talk to him, we might get on the road again."

"Okay, mister man. do your thing. My insurance company will probably drop me if I get another ticket."

The female officer returned to the side of Eddie's car and handed the documents back through the window. Kevin looked at the officer and asked, "Is that Officer Hertz? Can you tell him Kevin Maloney says hello?"

The woman made a surprised face and called back to the other officer. "There's a guy in here named Kevin Maloney. Says hello."

The male officer standing behind the car replied, "You gotta be kidding me," and walked up the passenger side of the orange car and knocked on the black tinted glass. "If you're in there Maloney, why don't you step out here." Kevin followed the instruction and pulled up on the locking-pliers door handle, popping the door catch loose. Officer Hertz pulled the door open, and Kevin unfolded himself from the seat and stepped out onto the curb.

"Nice to see you again, Officer Hertz," Kevin said with a grin.

Hertz asked, "Are you working a case, and what the hell are you doing in a low-riding piece of tuner crap? Think you're going to blend in with the neighborhood?"

Kevin smiled. "Just by chance, my coworker and I are indeed on a case. We're looking for that kid Seven. Haven't seen him by any chance, have you?"

Hertz shook his head. "No. Not since we saw his dead body hauled out of that yard."

"Yeah, okay." Kevin then asked, "How about a young, smallish black cat with white feet and facial markings? Maybe hanging around with street people?"

Hertz looked at the female officer and asked, "We haven't seen any lost pussy cats, have we? Kevin here seems to be missing his."

The female officer shook her head and Officer Hertz looked back at Kevin. "So, I'm going to have my trainee let you clear out of here with a warning. I don't want to get involved in whatever you're doing but tell your punk driver there that his car isn't street legal, and if he comes around here again, I'll have it impounded."

Kevin gave a curt half salute and said, "Thanks, and it was nice to see you again." He slipped back into the car and closed the door while the police officers returned to their patrol car.

Eddie looked at Kevin and said, "You got us out of a citation? Well, ain't that the shiz, mister man."

"The officer said don't come back into his patrol area, or he'll have your car impounded."

Eddie asked, "What for?"

Kevin shrugged his shoulders, "Beats me. He just said your car wasn't street legal."

Eddie laughed. "Aw hell, he's just bustin' chops and letting us know he thinks he's the boss of this neighborhood. Jus' cop BS, and he knows it."

Kevin looked at Eddie and asked, "So if the cops aren't it, who is the boss of this neighborhood?"

Eddie started the car and said, "Everybody knows Johnny Squares runs this hood." Then he asked, "Now that the police work is done, where to, mister man?"

Kevin sighed and retrieved a small notebook from his backpack. After flipping it open to a dog-eared page, he said, "Twenty-one twenty-eight North Ninth Street, where we'll hopefully find a cat."

51

Tuesday, October 23

3:14 p.m.

THE ORANGE HONDA snaked between two parked cars on North Ninth Street and then jerked to a stop next to the curb. Kevin surveyed the block of row houses and said, "This might take a few minutes, so wait here and keep an eye out. If you see anybody who might be capable of dishing out the pain, honk twice."

Eddie said, "I got your back, mister man." He then cut the engine, lowered the driver side window as far as it would go, and watched Kevin step up to the front door of a row house.

Kevin rapped on the heavy wooden door and then shuffled back toward the sidewalk. The door opened a hand width to a dark room and a pair of wide eyes peered out. Kevin smiled and said, "Hi, my name is Kevin Maloney. Is Mrs. Mason home? I'm here about Seven?"

The eyes behind the door shifted and the door opened a little wider. The diffused gray light revealed a young woman wearing a tracksuit and hair pulled back into a bundle of cornrows. She said, "I'll get her."

Kevin replied, "Okay," as the door closed in front of him. He examined the faded green paint for a moment and then glanced back toward the car. Fast Eddie wasn't visible behind the dark windows. The creaking sound of heavy footfalls on an old wood floor was audible from the front step, and Kevin returned his attention to the door. The sound grew louder and then stopped, followed by the door clicking open again.

The round face and sad eyes of Mrs. Mason appeared in the widening gap between the doorframe and the door, half a head higher than Kevin. She said in a low, gruff voice, "May I help you?"

Kevin looked her in the eyes and then looked down at his feet, "Uh, ma'am, my name is Kevin Maloney. I, ahh, work with the police and the survivors of the deceased, you know, following up on cases." Kevin looked back up at her face. "Are you okay?" he asked. The woman's expression was unchanged, absent of emotion except for sad, watery eyes.

Mrs. Mason stepped forward out the door, her breath labored. Kevin backed down to the sidewalk and made room for her as she lowered herself onto the steps. "Let me tell you something, honey," she said wearily. "Mommas are never okay. They are always worried about something from the time they get old enough to be a woman." She looked up at Kevin and patted the concrete step next to her. "My heart can't take standing too long, so you might as well have a seat with me." Kevin sat next to her and folded his hands in his lap. Mrs. Mason glanced sideways at Kevin, took a deep breath, and said, "You're the first person to come asking about me. I do appreciate it, but why so long? Why does it take so long?"

Kevin unfolded his hands and rubbed his knees. "Yeah, I'm sorry about that. I really am. I got sent to Cincinnati and couldn't get back to you until today. Please understand and forgive me."

"What did they send you to Cincinnati for?" Mrs. Mason asked.

Kevin replied, "A case like yours, I'm afraid."

"Was it a child, like my boy?" she asked.

Kevin explained in a soft voice, "An older man—his name was Harley. He passed in a traffic accident. His widow, her name was Arnica, she told me she'd been seeing his ghost wandering the street. She wasn't sure if he'd passed on or not. Very unsettled."

Mrs. Mason was quiet for a while, then she asked, "Do a lot of folks see the lost souls after they've gone?"

Kevin shrugged. "Sometimes. It can be wishful thoughts as part of the grieving process. It can also be something else. That's why I'm here. In case it's something else."

Mrs. Mason reached across to Kevin and took his hand in hers. Squeezing it, she said, "I see him everywhere."

Kevin folded his free hand over hers. "I know, and I'm sorry." After a moment he said, "I met your son at the grocery store. He helped me when I needed it. I hope I can return the good deed by helping you."

Mrs. Mason's voice cracked slightly. "I appreciate it, Kevin, but what can you do? You can't bring him back."

Kevin smiled slightly and said, "No, I can't, but maybe I can help everybody move on."

Mrs. Mason let go of Kevin's hands and breathed in. Letting it out in a long slow exhale, she said, "So how do I start moving on?"

"Listen, I need some specific information," Kevin said, "And I know it'll sound odd when I ask you."

Mrs. Mason said, "Go ahead, honey."

"When did you last see your boy?"

Mrs. Mason was quiet, looking up and down the block, then at Kevin. Finally, she said, "The night before last, I looked out the window and I swear he was walking down the street." She pointed to where the orange car was parked. "Right there. As plain as you and me."

"Okay. That's fine. By any chance," Kevin asked, "have you seen any stray cats around?"

"We got all kinds of stray cats around here," she replied.

Kevin prompted, "Specifically, a small black-and-white cat?"

"I wonder if you're talking about Felix?"

Kevin's eyes widened and he continued. "Felix? Like the old cartoon?"

"My daughter Lizzy needed something to hold, so I didn't say no when she let it in the house."

Kevin's head spun toward the door and gestured with his thumb, "Mostly black with white mittens and face markings? Is the cat in there now?"

Mrs. Mason puffed, "I guess that's right. I don't think it is there now. It comes and goes. Felix likes to curl up in my lap sometimes, but mostly it likes to be outside."

Kevin looked at Mrs. Mason, "Okay. Look, that cat is part of letting Seven pass on." She nodded as Kevin continued. "I need you to call me the next time the cat is around. Can you do that?"

"I ain't got a phone, but I'll have somebody call."

Kevin explained, "When you call me, if you can keep it in the house, that would be helpful, but don't corner it. It has crazy sharp claws, and I don't want you to get scratched. Take it from me, the scratches take forever to stop bleeding." He then retrieved his card from his pocket. "Take this. Let me know when you next see the cat, okay?"

Mrs. Mason nodded and said, "Okay."

"Any time of day. Don't wait." Kevin then asked, "Are you seeing a doctor for your shortness of breath and heart?"

Mrs. Mason nodded and said, "I'm taking pills, but I don't know if they're helping."

"How about diabetes?" Kevin asked.

"I don't know about that."

Kevin stood up and said, "Okay, keep taking your meds, and

maybe think about seeing a doctor. I need you to be strong, mentally and physically."

Mrs. Mason said, "Thank you, Kevin."

Kevin helped Mrs. Mason up from the step and saw her safely back into the house. The young woman who had answered the door was just inside the room and Kevin said to her, "Look after your momma, and if you see that Felix cat again, please call me. She's got my number." The young woman nodded but didn't say a word. After closing the door, Kevin stepped out to the sidewalk and crossed to the orange car. Just as he arrived, the passenger door popped open, and Kevin slipped inside.

Eddie, slouched behind the steering wheel, asked, "Is that what you do? Console people?"

"It goes with the job. Mrs. Mason will call me when it's time for the next step," Kevin replied.

Eddie asked, "Where to next?"

"We'll make our way along the train tracks down to the Ben Franklin Parkway. If we don't see anything, then it's back to the shop." Kevin then added, "I'm sorry you're not getting much overtime today, but on the bright side, you will be home in time for supper."

Eddie started the engine. He said, "You got it, mister man," as he maneuvered away from the curb and accelerated up North Ninth Street.

52

Thursday, October 25

7:02 a.m.

BRIAN SAT IN the kitchen, dressed in the seminary's green groundskeeper uniform, with a cup of coffee and the manual for the Toro bat-wing lawn mower spread out on the table. When Kevin entered from the living room, Brian said, "Morning, Kev. Long time no see."

Kevin grunted in reply and diverted to the refrigerator, where he retrieved a pitcher of orange juice and a carton of milk. He placed them on the table and turned back to the cabinets. Adding a box of cereal and bowl to his collection of breakfast items, he parked across from Brian and said, "Good reading material?"

Brian replied, "I'm getting the blindfold cockpit test today on the biggest mower in the shop. Thought I'd brush up on the specs and limitations."

Kevin's eyebrows pitched up when he said, "I didn't think Mr.

Warren let anybody else drive that mower."

Brian grinned and said, "John the Baptist is allowed to use it, but he doesn't like the enclosed cabin. So, when I make the grade, it'll be my ride."

"Right on, brother," Kevin said as he began assembling his breakfast. When he was finished pouring milk on his cereal, he asked, "You really like it in that shop, cutting the grass and stuff?"

Brian sipped from his coffee and then said, "Yeah, it's a good side gig. Might even make a decent retirement job, if I can make it closer to the top of the pecking order." Kevin nodded in response, then Brian added, "Speaking of pecking order, I asked Mr. Warren about another phone for upstairs. He said there isn't a jack up there, but he did snag a new desk phone for us. It's on the floor next to the couch, so I figured you hadn't seen it yet."

"Oh yeah?" Kevin responded in surprise. "That's great."

Brian went on. "It's got the usual stuff like a hold button and speaker. I think it's a good get."

"Just need a nice side-table for it," Kevin added casually.

Brian laughed and said, "Look at you, thinking like an interior decorator!" Kevin ignored the comment and returned to eating his cereal. Brian changed topics by asking, "So you took yesterday off; what did you do?"

Kevin replied, "I took Mom to mass at St. Denis, then we met up with Mark Francini and his folks for lunch. Kind of a spur-of-the-moment thing when we ran into them in the parking lot."

Brian responded, "I'll bet she liked that."

Kevin nodded and said, "We both did. It was good to catch up. It's only been a month since I saw Mark last, but it feels like forever. His wife Jessica is big as a house. She's going to pop any day now. Can't believe they're going to be parents soon."

Brian inquired, "Boy or a girl?"

Kevin shrugged. "If they know, they aren't saying. Kind of old school."

Brian said, "I can respect that."

Kevin added, "We might go out with them again. Might become a regular thing." Then Kevin asked, "Speaking of things, did you catch up with Michele Fields?"

Brian made a half grin gesture and then said, "I did. You will be glad to know that Michele feels very reassured knowing she'll not be encountering her dead mother wandering the sidewalks of the neighborhood."

"I'm glad, and thanks for taking the time."

"Happy to do it. I think Michele really needed to connect with somebody outside her usual circle."

Kevin asked, "Why do you say that?"

Brian replied, "We're going to get coffee next week. You know, kind of a progress check. Follow-up."

Kevin's eyes narrowed to a squint as he looked at his brother, but he didn't say anything.

Brian continued. "And you? Making progress with Seven?"

"I met with his mom. I suspect she's been marked as a target. Mrs. Mason is in bad shape health-wise, and her daughter has been friendly with a little black-and-white stray that matches the description I gave them. It wasn't around when I stopped in, but I told her to call me if she lays eyes on it again. Given Mrs. Mason's condition, it won't be long until it comes back."

"So now you're just waiting for a phone call from Mrs. Mason," Brian observed.

Kevin agreed, "Yeah. I'm going to use today to catch up on chores. Then back out tomorrow morning."

Brian grinned again, saying, "And Detective Johnston?"

Kevin cocked his head and said, "We'll see. She's got a lot going on right now, but I'm hoping to hear from her soon about a DNA test from the Eastern State body I looked at a few weeks back. I'd like to scratch that from my list of problems."

Brian tipped back the last of his coffee and stood up from the table. "I'm glad you're making progress."

Kevin nodded and said, "Yeah, I'm getting there. Good luck on the Toro."

"Thanks," Brian acknowledged as he deposited his coffee cup in the sink.

"See you later," Kevin offered. As Brian reached the door, the wall phone began ringing. Kevin and Brian both turned to look at it.

Brian said, "Stay put; I'll get it," and crossed the room to the phone. He lifted the handset to his ear and said, "Hello?" After a moment he said, "I'm great. Just fine. Hey, Uncle Matt—hold on a sec. Let me get you on the speaker phone so Kevin can hear."

Kevin stood up from the table and stepped into the living room. He picked up the new phone from the floor and placed it on the arm of the sofa. He then pressed a button on the face and said, "Can you hear me?"

A slightly muffled voice replied, "I can hear you, Kevin. How are you doing?"

Kevin gave Brian a thumbs-up, grinned, and replied, "Good, good. You called at the perfect time, since both of us are here." Brian replaced the wall phone handset on its hook and joined Kevin on the living room couch.

"Wonderful. It's good to hear your voices," came Uncle Matt's voice from the speaker.

Kevin asked, "So have you been enjoying yourself in Florence?"

"Oh yes. Lovely town. So much history here. It's like somebody froze it in time, but I want you to know, we've not been messing around with tourist stuff. We're all business over here. Stepan and I got to work in the archives of the zoological museum right away."

Kevin replied, "I didn't know they had such a thing in Florence. I thought it was all old churches full of frescos and art museums."

"Oh, yes, there is plenty of that, but La Specola has been here since the late seventeen hundreds. The staff claim it is the oldest science museum in Europe. It is filled with thousands of taxidermies and beautiful waxes of the human anatomy. Simply fantastic."

"So, what do they know about our specific animal?" Kevin asked.

"The curator of the collection has us in touch with a library associated with the museum, and they have an extensive collection. Some of which might be exactly what we seek."

"Have you seen any of it yet?" Brian asked.

"We have begun reviewing the manuscripts. They are old and not so well preserved, with no translations, so it is slow going, but our work has borne fruit already."

Kevin looked at Brian while listening to the phone. Then he said, "How's that?"

Uncle Matt explained, "There is an index of the materials and a letter from a Borgia family accountant explaining that these materials were accumulated while evaluating the lethality of certain creatures."

Brian chuckled quietly, "That sounds Machiavellian."

"Good, good. That's just it," replied the voice with a slight coughing laugh. After a brief silence, another voice came on the line and more coughing could be heard in the background. In his Ukrainian accent, Stepan said, "There are many pages and even a book on cats. One is very old and labeled *Egyptian Cat*. Call it a hunch, but we are going to look at that tomorrow with the help of a local translator."

Kevin's eyes widened and he said, "The Egyptians were pretty much obsessed with all things dead. Sounds like a good start to me."

Brian then asked, "Is Uncle Matt okay?"

Stepan replied, "He's an old man and tires easily. You know how it can be—short of breath after walking much. We've been walking a lot here. The coughing started today after looking at very old boxes of materials. Maybe dust?"

Brian looked at Kevin and then asked, "Any other symptoms?"

"Not so much. He said his shoulder was sore from sleeping on a lumpy hotel mattress. I don't know what he was talking about. His mattress was just like mine."

Brian said, "Don't let him work himself sick. Tell him to take the day off if he's not feeling well. Maybe even go see a doctor."

"You know your uncle—he wants to see everything for himself. But if he's not so good tomorrow, I will insist he stay in bed for the day."

Kevin said, "Thanks, Stepan. Good luck with the search. Let us know what you find tomorrow."

"Is not a problem; have a good day," Stepan replied and then the phone clicked. A dial tone buzzed from the speaker of the phone until Kevin pressed a button.

Brian said, "I'm concerned Uncle Matt is overdoing it."

Kevin agreed, "Yeah, but he wouldn't miss this for the world."

53

Sunday, October 28

4:06 a.m.

KEVIN UNCONSCIOUSLY MUMBLED in his sleep, rolling left and right in his bed. He then sat up abruptly, wide awake. Damp sheets clung to his skin as he looked over at the red digital numbers of the nightstand alarm clock. "Damn, it's too early, but I might as well," he muttered. Casting his feet over the edge of the bed, his toes extended and found the cool wood floor. Once upright, he gathered some clothes and carried them down the stairs to the bathroom.

Dressed and wandering through the dark kitchen, Kevin stopped to look out the window. The overcast sky reflected the surrounding lights, silhouetting the tree line behind the house in a deep, impenetrable black. He stared at it for several heartbeats before reaching over to a light switch next to the door. With a plastic click, two exterior floodlights cast a pale yellow light over the driveway. The white of the Jeep Wrangler nearly glowed, but the red of Brian's more distant vehicle seemed to absorb the light. A dark animal form, roughly the size of a cat, scampered away from the trash cans outside the door and into the tree line.

Kevin switched off the floods and switched on the light over the kitchen table. He crossed the room to the phone, where he retrieved the notepad and pen. Scrawling out a note, he left it on the table. With his keys and backpack in hand, Kevin walked out the door with only the slightest sound.

Moments later, the white Jeep coasted down the driveway to the back gate. While the gate hummed open, the engine growled to life and the lights flicked on. After the Jeep turned left, the gate closed with a gentle clank.

54

Sunday, October 28

10:56 a.m.

DRESSED IN JEANS and a fire department sweatshirt, Brian reclined on the couch, scrolling through the television program guide. A small window on the screen showed a satellite view of the Atlantic Ocean. A voice issued from the speaker saying, "The Category two hurricane left widespread power outages and flooding in the Bahamas last night..."

A knocking at the exterior of the kitchen door caught Brian's attention. He leaned around the corner and looked at the door's four-pane window. After switching off the television, he came to an upright standing position and said, "Just a second."

Brian shuffled across the kitchen and opened the door to a waiting Mr. Warren. He asked, "What's up? Why are you here on a Sunday?"

Mr. Warren pointed at Brian's bare feet and said, "Some news has come in from Italy. Put some shoes on. I need to get you back to the shop."

Brian said, "Okay," and slipped into a pair of sneakers from a collection of shoes next to the door. Outside, Brian saw the green 6x4 Gator utility vehicle Mr. Warren used to inspect the grounds. They took seats in the cab and began driving up the hill.

As the Gator bounced across the lawn toward the driveway, Mr. Warren glanced at Brian and said, "Any idea where Kevin is?"

"No, he and his Jeep were gone when I woke up this morning. I guess he's working the Seven case. Why? Is there something wrong?"

"I don't know, but Father Tucker called me into the office, wanting to talk to Kevin."

"Should I know Father Tucker?"

"No, not really, but he's way above me in the pecking order where Kevin's concerned."

Brian responded, "I hope everything's okay."

Mr. Warren added, "We'll soon find out," as he steered the vehicle through the parking lot and brought it to a stop next to the equipment service garage. The two men dismounted and walked into the open bay. Mr. Warren directed Brian to the door leading into the break room. "You go ahead; Father Tucker is in my office."

Brian nodded and entered the door.

Mr. Warren's office door was open, and Brian stopped just outside. A man dressed in priestly black sat at the desk. He was reading from a sheaf of papers and made no indication that he knew Brian was there. Brian rapped on the doorframe twice and said, "Father Tucker?"

The man looked up from the papers and remained silent for several heartbeats as he looked over the figure in the doorway. Finally, he spoke, "Yes. You're Brian?"

"I am. You wanted to see me?"

"I did. I was hoping to find Kevin as well."

"I'm sorry; I don't know where he is." Brian shrugged. "He was gone by the time I got up this morning."

Father Tucker leaned back in the chair and said, "Well, I guess we'll proceed without him." Gesturing to the empty chair in the corner of the office, he said, "Why don't you have a seat."

After Brian lowered himself into the chair, he placed his feet flat on the floor and laced his fingers together on his lap.

Father Tucker slipped the papers he was reading into a folder and secured it with a large rubber band. When he was done, he looked up at Brian again but remained silent.

Brian asked, "Do you want to wait for Kevin? I mean, it could be a while before he gets back."

Father Tucker's face crinkled slightly and then relaxed again as he exhaled. "No, we can't wait. I guess I'm just going to get this out there, and I'm sorry I'm not very good at this sort of thing. Most of my career has been administrative and I haven't dealt with adversities very much."

Brian asked, "What adversity? Just say it. It doesn't get easier by trying to sugarcoat it."

"All right," Father Tucker sighed. He folded and unfolded his hands before saying, "It seems your uncle, Father Matthew O'Conner, passed away this morning."

Brian sat in silence. While his face was unmoving, his hands balled up into fists one finger at a time, knuckles creaking and cracking as they folded. He then took a deep breath, held it for a moment, then blew it out in one slow, controlled stream. The fingers relaxed and his hands came to rest, palms down on his thighs. When his breathing returned to normal, he looked at Father Tucker and asked, "Is Stepan okay?"

"He's fine." Father Tucker then quickly added, "He called me with the news earlier this morning."

Brian asked, "We just spoke to them a couple of days ago. Did Stepan say anything about the circumstances?"

Father Tucker explained, "He said when they got up this morning, Matthew was not feeling well. Stepan wanted to take him to the hospital, but Matthew decided to stay in the hotel to rest. He told Stepan to go ahead without him." Father Tucker paused and gathered his breath before continuing. "When Stepan came back at lunchtime, your uncle was unresponsive. He was rushed to the hospital, but there was nothing that could be done. Stepan said it was most likely a heart attack."

The two men sat in silence. The only sound came from the ticking of a clock somewhere in the break room. They remained that way until the distant sharp metallic ring of a tool hitting the floor in the garage disturbed them.

Father Tucker said, "The staff will make the arrangements, so don't worry about that. I guess my question for you is . . . would you like me to tell Kevin and your mother?"

Brian half whispered, "No. I'll tell them. It should come from family."

55

Sunday, October 28

2:14 p.m.

KEVIN MANEUVERED THE Jeep through the Lancaster Avenue gate, then stopped to watch in the rearview mirror as the mechanism pushed the gate back into place. When it clicked shut, Kevin eased out the clutch and proceeded up the hill with the engine emitting its usual high-pitched first-gear whine. Turning into the driveway to the house, Brian's red Cherokee and two other vehicles came into view.

Kevin muttered quietly, "I wonder what's up?" and jerked the steering wheel right, diverting the Jeep's motion toward the grass. With all four tires off the pavement, he killed the motor, set the parking brake, and bailed out the door. He quickly rounded the corner of the house and leaped to the top step at the back door. Brian was standing just inside and opened it for him.

Kevin inquired, "What's going on?"

Brian's face was fixed, expressing nothing, when he said, "It's Uncle Matt." Kevin locked his eyes on his brother until Brian finally said, "He passed away this morning."

Kevin didn't make a sound but slightly shuffled his feet as he reflexively closed the door behind him. When the latch clicked into place, he took a deep breath and then exhaled slowly saying, "Yeah, okay, but I thought we'd have more time."

Kevin crossed to the living room where several other people were gathered. The first person he encountered was his mother, who stood by the doorframe holding out her arms. Kevin walked into her embrace. Mrs. Maloney's head barely reached Kevin's shoulder and she laid it against his chest, where her silent tears wet the fabric of his shirt. Kevin kissed the top of his mother's head and whispered, "He was a good and faithful servant."

She replied, "He was a good brother too," and then fell silent.

The long quiet in the room was broken when Brian maneuvered around his brother and mother and said, "Mom, you're looking a bit wobbly. Why don't you sit down here on the couch." Without a word, she complied with Brian and Kevin's guiding hands.

Detective Johnston, who'd been leaning against the stairway newel post, moved to sit next to her. "Can I get you anything? Some water?"

Mrs. Maloney nodded and looked up at her two boys.

Kevin said, "Tell me the rest."

Brian repeated what Father Tucker had said earlier about the circumstances and then added, "The Seminary will make all the arrangements to get him home. The only trick is that it might take a little while. I understand there is a lot of paperwork involved."

Kevin asked, "Has Stepan called?"

"Not yet," Brian said while shaking his head. "I imagine he's pretty busy right now."

Kevin nodded and sat down next to Johnston, filling the last space on the couch. He then looked over at Mr. Warren. "Thanks for coming down. I'm sure this isn't in the job description."

Mr. Warren said, "You two are part of my team. If there's anything I can do, just say the word." He turned toward the kitchen, scanned the occupants of the room, and added, "Now that Kevin's back, I'll be heading up to the shop."

Mrs. Maloney murmured, "Thank you," and Mr. Warren nodded to her as he departed. When the kitchen door closed, Brian retrieved a chair from the table and brought it into the living room. He positioned himself on the chair opposite the sofa.

Mrs. Maloney then asked nobody in particular, "Was Matt doing the work he loved?"

Kevin said, "Yes, Mom. I think he was."

Brian chimed in. "He was also having a good time in Italy. Whenever he called, he sounded like an eighth grader on a field trip. He and Stepan had been to see all the monuments and ruins in Rome and had been eating gelato twice every day."

Mrs. Maloney said in a recovering voice, "His inner child was never far below the surface, that's for sure."

56

Sunday, October 28

7:57 p.m.

KEVIN HUGGED HIS mother then released her to Brian's waiting hand. She said, "Thank you Kevin, and thank you Della."

"Anything you need, just call me," Johnston replied as Brian guided his mother out the kitchen door and down the steps.

Kevin and Johnston watched the red Cherokee drive away before closing the door. In the new quiet of the kitchen, Kevin silently gathered the remains of a pizza box and paper plates and deposited them in a trash bag. Johnston returned to the living room and dropped onto the couch. She clicked on the television and scanned through the channels, stopping on channel 29. The muted TV displayed a beer commercial before giving way to a scene from Tiger Stadium in Detroit. All the seats were full and the fans were vigorously waving white towels over their heads. A graphic overlay spelling out *World Series* floated across the screen and dissolved to show a male announcer.

Kevin walked in and asked, "What's on?"

Johnston replied, "Game four of the World Series."

Kevin dropped onto the cushion next to her. He said, "I guess I pretty much forgot what the rest of the world is doing. Who's playing?"

"Giants and Tigers," Johnston recited.

Kevin exhaled. "Huh."

Johnston took Kevin's hand in her own and said, "Games don't seem very significant anymore, do they?"

Kevin instructed, "Turn on the sound. Maybe we could use the distraction."

The speaker came to life with the announcer saying, "Here tonight, the Giants start play three games up on the Tigers . . ." Kevin and Johnston sat in silence as the first announcer was joined by another who described the setup for the baseball game.

While the man with the microphone talked about the pitchers for the night, Kevin turned to Johnston. "Maybe it will get more interesting later."

Johnston nodded and looked at Kevin. "It might be a while before life gets back to normal enough to watch a baseball game."

Kevin looked at the screen again. The Tiger's pitcher was warming up on the mound, a graphic overlay describing his record. "I think you're right. It might be that guy's biggest game ever, but it's not life or death, is it?"

Johnston, still holding Kevin's hand, kissed him on the side of his head and said, "Tell you what, we haven't caught up on your case in a while. Why don't you fill me in on the latest?"

Kevin agreed, "Yeah, it might help to talk it out." After shifting himself on the couch to a position that faced Johnston more directly, she turned down the sound. He began, "I went out this morning. Real early. Mostly because I couldn't sleep. Something nagging me, you know?" Johnston quietly nodded. "Anyway, I scooted over to Seven's neighborhood before the sun was up. I started by watching over the street where his family lives. Did you know there's a lot going on at dawn? You know what I mean?"

Johnston nodded. "When I worked nights on patrol, I only saw it as the end of the day, so I didn't pay as much attention as I should have."

"I get that. I was surprised by how much you can see when you sit real still. I also saw the one thing I wanted to see."

"What was that?"

"I watched the little black-and-white cat stroll right up to the Mason's house. I got visual confirmation that the cat I'm looking for was the same one visiting the house."

"So what's your next move?"

"I've got to get it fixed in place, then I guess I'm going to get ready for a catch," Kevin said. "I don't want a repeat of the last battle, but I can see it being something like that."

"Yeah," Johnston exhaled. "You're still healing from that one."

"Tell me about it." Kevin leaned his head against the back of the couch and continued. "Wrestling a naked dude and then ending up in the river wasn't optimal."

Johnston asked, "So what's the new plan?"

"I'm envisioning a catch near water, or if not that, at least a pit or basement. I think I can make a safe catch if I can get the cat knocked out first before trying to get it into the reinforced cage."

"You're not thinking about doing it by yourself, are you?" Johnston inquired.

"I'd rather not," Kevin replied, "but if it comes down to it, I will. Cornering it in a lockable dumpster isn't going to happen every time."

"Yeah, but if you did get that lucky, next time call the fire department and have them fill the dumpster with water."

"Oh, you are a genius." Kevin chuckled. "If only we'd known back then that the cats are water soluble."

"You could have skipped the whole dead skin and unstoppable

bleeding thing too," Johnston added.

"*Now* you tell me," Kevin sighed. Glancing back at the TV screen, Kevin said, "Look at that." A crawling text graphic covered the bottom of the screen. "The New Jersey shore and Delaware Bay are under a flood watch from a hurricane? Since when do we get hurricanes this far north?"

"Hurricane Sandy? Well, isn't that something?" Johnston added. "I hope my mother knows. I'm sure she does. She watches the Weather Channel all the time. Can't get enough of that Jim guy who's always standing out in the storms."

"There's a joke about how that storm-chaser guy is like an ex-wife."

Johnston asked, "How's that?"

Kevin answered, "When he shows up, you're going to lose everything."

"Cute," she said with a smirk. "Speaking of weather, do you hear that?"

Kevin cocked his head and looked toward the ceiling, saying, "Heavy rain shower. I'm sure it isn't part of the hurricane."

Johnston nodded and said, "So I'm not working tomorrow. I was thinking you might want some help."

"Yeah, that would be great. I'm getting close. Tomorrow might be the day," Kevin declared.

57

Monday, October 29

11:05 a.m.

HEAVY BANDS OF gray clouds scudded across the urban landscape of northern Philadelphia. Leaves and trash picked up by random wind currents tumbled through the unusually warm and humid air. Buffeted by the same gusts, the seminary's white Chevy 4x4 pickup truck idled east on Jefferson Street, splashing through puddles along the curb. In the bed was the heavy-duty metal cage and a pair of catch-all poles for snaring animals. After passing under the elevated quadruple rail tracks running north from downtown, Kevin turned the truck left onto Ninth Street. On the east side of the roadway, every other lot was choked with weeds or was paved with the concrete floor of a building that used to stand on the site. The remaining row houses were either abandoned or in a pathetic state of disrepair. On the next block north, a newer eight-story apartment building was surrounded by trees that shed a flurry of leaves as they rocked in the wind gusts. From the cab of the truck, Kevin and Johnston observed the deteriorating conditions.

Kevin shook his head and said, "I swear this area looks more run-down every time I come over here."

Johnston replied just as a wind gust plastered the truck with water drops, "I'd say I agree, but this time I think it's the weather. Could it be any grimmer?"

Kevin remarked, "I can't imagine the cat would show itself on a day like today."

Johnston asked, "Think it will be seeking shelter in somebody's house?"

Just as a curtain of rain swept over the street, Kevin answered, "Probably. Of course, if it just melted in the rain, that would be okay too." Kevin switched on the wipers to the high-speed setting and leaned forward toward the windshield. "Let's check in on the Masons."

The truck stopped at the intersection with Berks Street. Kevin peered to his left, looking under the elevated SEPTA commuter station, and observed, "No sign of the bicycle man I talked with the other night."

The adjacent parking lot was largely empty and a handful of pedestrians sheltering under umbrellas were making their way out of the station toward the few parked cars. Johnston nodded and said, "Not too many folks around today. I guess that storm coming up the coast is keeping people at home."

The truck rolled forward from the stop sign and before it traveled the length of the block, the rain abated. Kevin switched off the wipers, relaxed his grip on the steering wheel, and sat back in the seat. On the right there were a few remaining row houses, but most of the block was an open grass field. North of the Norris Street intersection, the right side was a continuous wall of brick-faced row houses. Cars were parked bumper-to-bumper on the curb. The building fronts looked west over the street and a retaining wall topped with a chain-link fence and a parking lot. Beyond that, the elevated railroad tracks defined the street-level horizon.

Kevin remarked, "From here it's just another block to the north."

Johnston nodded and said, "I see the *BEER TO GO* sign on the corner of the Masons' block."

As they approached the intersection of Diamond Street, Kevin admitted, "I've been over here several times and never noticed that."

"Really? You're kidding. A giant sign sticking out from the corner of the building?"

Kevin shrugged, "I guess I've been looking down at street level. You know, where cats hang out."

Johnston explained, "Good excuse, but if you're going to survive the streets, you're going to have to keep your wits about you and think in three dimensions."

"Point taken," Kevin replied.

Crossing the intersection, Kevin looked at the old storefront of The Diamond Deli. The metal roller shutters were down, and the door was obstructed with debris. Continuing farther up the block and stopping in front of the Masons' row house, Kevin said, "We're here. Let's hope we get lucky."

Kevin and Johnston opened the doors and splashed their feet into the thin layer of water standing on the pavement. Crossing the street to the sidewalk in front of Mrs. Mason's row house, Johnston said, "It'll be raining when we come back out. We should have brought umbrellas."

"I think you're right," Kevin added as he knocked on the door. "We might have underestimated the severity of this Sandy storm."

58

Monday, October 29

11:49 a.m.

"WHAT ARE YOU doing out there? Don't you know there's a hurricane coming?" Mrs. Mason asked as she opened the door to Kevin and Detective Johnston. "Get in here," she commanded.

Kevin led Johnston into the dim front room of the nearly century-old building. The air was heavy with humidity and carried a faint musty smell, mixed with the scent of old cooking oil. The front window was covered with a heavy curtain, and the only light came from a single bulb floor lamp that stood next to a brown three cushion couch. A frayed lime-green wingback chair was opposite, and a small television sat on a table next to the back hallway. Mrs. Mason eased into the chair and gestured to the couch. "Sit down; sit down."

Kevin smiled and said, "Thank you, Mrs. Mason, and this is a friend of mine, Detective Johnston. She helps me from time to time."

Johnston stepped forward and took Mrs. Mason's hand in hers and said, "It's nice to meet you." When she stepped back, she and Kevin sat on the front edge of the couch, leaning forward.

Kevin patted his hand over his heart. "How are you doing? Feeling any better?"

"About the same as last time, maybe a bit better." Mrs. Mason sighed. "Another week has gone by without my boy, but I'm still here."

Kevin nodded and said, "I know a little bit about that feeling. My Uncle passed away since I saw you last. It hurts down deep, doesn't it?"

Mrs. Mason exhaled, "Well ain't that the business. I'm sorry for you, sugar. What was his name?"

"Father Matthew O'Conner," Kevin replied. "He was a seminary professor."

Mrs. Mason exclaimed, "Oh, a man of the cloth! We need to pray for him." She then bowed her head and spread her arms wide, palms up toward the ceiling. In a forceful voice, she proclaimed, "Dear Lord, God Almighty, we pray for the soul of Uncle Matthew. Accept him into your heavenly army. Let his good deeds reinforce the battalions of angels, so that they might smite the evil doers and demons that plague our earthly state. In Jesus's name we pray, Amen."

"Amen," Kevin and Johnston said in small voices.

After making the sign of the cross, Kevin said, "Thank you for that."

Mrs. Mason continued in a soft but accusing tone, "So now, tell me. You two aren't coworkers, are you?" Kevin and Johnston glanced at each other and then back at Mrs. Mason.

Johnston explained, "I work homicide, ma'am. Some of my cases require Kevin's special skills."

Mrs. Mason smiled. "I'm sure they do, but don't you fool with me. You two got feelings for each other. How long have you been dating?"

Kevin smiled back. "Is it that obvious?"

Mrs. Mason asserted, "Yes, it is. And since I know all about how precious life is, and just how short it can be, I think you should get it together, know what I mean? Make it official."

Johnston stammered slightly and said, "We've only been dating a couple of months."

Mrs. Mason said, "That doesn't matter, honey. A woman your age needs to get busy making babies."

Johnston recoiled slightly and looked at Kevin with wide eyes.

Kevin returned the look and changed the subject. "Thank you, Mrs. Mason. I'm sure we'll talk about that someday, but today we've got a job to do. Have you seen Seven or the cat since we talked last week?"

Mrs. Mason leaned forward and whispered, "Lizzy didn't want me to know when the cat was here. She thought she was keeping it a secret from me, but I saw her with it outside. I tried to call you a couple times, but it ran off before I could let you know."

Johnston's lips eased into a soft smile. "Does Lizzy have any health issues, like Seven did?"

Mrs. Mason nodded and said, "She stays with me because she gets the seizures from time to time. The doctor doesn't think she's going to die or nothing, but it really looks scary when she locks up and shakes. I got to tell the kids to stay out of the way. Stay out of the way!"

Kevin and Johnston looked at each other and then back to Mrs. Mason. Kevin asked, "Any idea where the cat is now?"

"I saw it just this morning, before the rain and wind started," Mrs. Mason patted the arm of her chair and then exclaimed, "That cat done run off and followed old Ten Speed down the street. Apparently, he and the cat don't know about that mean old Sandy coming around."

Johnston asked, "I think we've met him. Is he the old guy with the bags tied to his bike? Do you have any idea where he stays?"

Mrs. Mason answered, "That's him, and he's a lazy

good-for-nothing. Always thieving and begging money or cigarettes or booze. He's usually down by the SEPTA station, but Seven told me he sometimes stays in an empty house down on Darien Street by the city garage."

Kevin asked, "Does he have any medical conditions you might know about?"

Mrs. Mason puffed, "You mean besides being hooked on the bottle? I don't know. I do know he never worked a proper job more than three days in a row, and he only made it that far because the second day was a holiday!"

Johnston suppressed a snicker and said in a level voice, "You seem to know Ten Speed pretty well."

"Unfortunately, I know him real well," Mrs. Mason admitted with a growl in her voice. "He's my late husband's half-brother. When Donald passed, God rest his soul, old Ten Speed came sniffing around here for money and tried to snake the car from me. Damn near broke up the family." Mrs. Mason leaned forward in her chair and clenched her fists and snarled, "Ever since then, when I see him on my block, I yell at the top of my voice for him to get away. We don't want his kind around here. Then Ten Speed yells back about it being a public street. Then I remind him the taxpayers own the street and he's never paid a cent in taxes his whole life."

Johnston asked, "Does he have a name? I mean, other than Ten Speed?"

Mrs. Mason snarled, "Damon."

"Damon Mason?"

Mrs. Mason said, "Damon Jones. After Donald's father died, his mother got in a bad way with Ten Speed's daddy, Edmond Jones. I can tell you the son learned everything he knows about sloth from his daddy."

Johnston said, "Okay, got it. Clearly a sore subject."

Mrs. Mason added, "And it figures he'd make off with the one thing that makes my Lizzy happy."

Kevin and Johnston looked at each other for a moment before he interjected, "Don't fret over the cat. You don't want that thing around here."

"The good Lord knows," Mrs. Mason exhaled. "It's just like Ten Speed to wreck something good that might come this family's way."

Kevin looked down at his hands, then over to Johnston, before looking back at Mrs. Mason. He took a breath and then said, "I really need you to understand that this cat isn't good. It's not something you want around your house. It's trouble of the worst kind. It is the reason you see your son walking down the street. His soul won't rest until it is gone. And if something should happen to Ten Speed, he'll be the next one, and I'm pretty sure you don't want him haunting you for the next month, either."

"Okay," Mrs. Mason whispered as she sank back into her chair. "The good Lord sent you to help me, and I need to be humble enough to accept it. Thank you, Kevin."

"Think nothing of it, Mrs. Mason—and thanks for understanding."

Johnston stood up from the couch, placed a hand on Kevin's shoulder and said, "I think it's starting to rain again. We'd better get moving." Looking at Mrs. Mason, she added, "You be safe during the storm."

"I will," Mrs. Mason replied. Holding up a scolding finger, she said, "And you two need to take each other seriously, and don't go getting in trouble out in that storm."

"Yes, ma'am," Kevin acknowledged. Stepping to the front of the room, he fished the truck keys from his pocket and opened the door. A blast of wind pushed it from his grip and banged the doorknob against the wall. Immediately, wind-driven rain spotted his face and the front of his clothes. Taking a half step back, he looked at Johnston and said, "Ready?" She nodded and he added, "I'll give you a thumbs-up when the passenger door is unlocked."

Out on the street, rain poured from the ragged low clouds,

and wind gusts rippled the water puddles accumulating along the curb. Kevin positioned the truck's door key in his right hand and said, "Let's go!" as he dashed from the front door of the row house. He skipped the top step and sprinted across the street, nearly slipping as he came to a stop at the driver's door. Fumbling with the key in the door lock, he eventually managed to insert it in the slot and unlock the door. He quickly jumped in, slamming the door closed behind him. Reaching across the cab, he pulled up the passenger door lock knob. Kevin looked back at the house and gave a thumbs-up to Johnston. She departed the dry safety of Mrs. Mason's doorway, sprinting to the truck. Water streaming from his head and torso, Kevin pulled the latch and pushed the door open just as she arrived. She piled into the cab, sprawling headfirst onto the bench seat. Kevin laughed and said, "You were right about the rain and umbrellas."

Johnston, hair wet and shirt soaked, grinned at Kevin from the level of the seatbelt latches and replied, "Damn straight I was." Then she reached up with her left hand and pulled Kevin's face down to hers, kissing him briefly in an awkward upside-down mismatch.

Returning to a more upright position, Kevin asked in a surprised voice, "That caught me off guard a little. What happened to no PDA while on business?"

"I'm taking you seriously, and this isn't police business, is it?" Johnston laughed. "Now let's get out of here and find Ten Speed—and that damned cat."

59

Monday, October 29

1:51 p.m.

KEVIN STARTED THE truck, switched on the headlights, and selected the high setting for the windshield wipers. Even standing still, the wipers were minimally effective at keeping the windshield clear of the downpour. When he switched on the snowplow auxiliary headlights, the beams were diffused by the cascade of water, reducing forward visibility. Kevin said, "That doesn't help," and switched them off. "Buckle up," he said, then asked, "What's the best way to Darien Street?"

Johnston replied, "Go up the block and make a left. Susquehanna is one way westbound, then back down the next street."

Kevin nodded and dropped the truck into gear. Pulling away from the curb, the tires made a wave in the standing water that sloshed onto the sidewalk.

At the end of the block, the truck turned left on Susquehanna

Avenue just as the sky became dark enough to trigger the streetlights to turn on. After just a moment driving west, the truck made its way south on Percy Street. Scattered cars were parked up on the sidewalks next to the few occupied dwellings. Farther along, after passing several empty buildings on the narrow side street, Kevin commented, "This is going to be a wet and memorable afternoon."

Johnston nodded and replied, "Yeah," and pointed ahead at the row of utility poles on the left side of the pavement. "The streetlights just went out."

Kevin half grimaced, "That'll make cat hunting easier." Passing the back side of Mrs. Mason's row house, he pointed ahead to the empty lot where Seven's body had been discovered. A mature tree on the corner was now bare of leaves and the naked branches swayed in the wind gusts. Kevin muttered, "That's kind of depressing."

Johnston remained silent as they passed.

At the end of Percy Street, Johnston pointed left, and Kevin steered the truck past the red doors of the Deliverance Church onto Diamond Street. At several low points in the pavement, water was topping the curb and creeping up the sidewalks. Johnston said, "Look at the puddles. The drains are either blocked or they are already overwhelmed by the rainfall."

"Maybe both," Kevin acknowledged.

At the intersection with Ninth Street, the stoplight wasn't working, and no lights were visible in windows. Mid-afternoon was already as dark as evening. Splashing through the increasing puddles, the truck rolled slowly past the intersection with Darien Street. Johnston said, "It's one way northbound, so go to the next block and we'll come back at it from the south end." She peered down its length as they passed and said, "Nothing moving, as far as I can see." At Eighth Street, Kevin turned right, slowing to follow the only other vehicle they saw driving, a rust-eaten black Honda CRV. It crept along at a walking pace until it pulled into a gap on the left side of the street, inching through a growing reservoir of standing water. It stopped on the sidewalk with the left door over visible concrete. The driver quickly exited the car with his jacket pulled up over his head. Running up the front steps of a row house, he disappeared into the darkness behind the front door.

With the street now empty, Johnston said, "Pretty dark and desolate."

Kevin gestured to the backpack on the floor next to Johnston's feet. He said, "There's a few things in there that will help."

Johnston pulled it up onto the seat and said, "What do you want out of here?"

Kevin said, "Hold on a second," as he inched the truck between two poorly parked cars and then said, "I think I've got a plan on how to do this search."

Kevin resumed the slightly faster second-gear drive and asked, "You okay driving this thing?" Johnston let out a slight huff sound, and Kevin resumed speaking, "Got it. I insulted you by even asking."

The flooded gutters on Eighth Street were beginning to top the curbs onto the sidewalks. The truck was making waves that washed up to the walls of the row houses. "As soon as I find enough dry land to stop, we'll switch seats. You drive, and I'll do the door knocks and poking around. That way only one of us gets soaked to the bone."

Johnston said, "Deal," as Kevin brought the truck to a stop in the middle of the next intersection.

Kevin looked left and right down the graying and rain obscured Norris Street and said, "This is as good a place as any." He unbuckled his seatbelt and looked outside again. Looking at Johnston, he suggested, "Maybe we can switch seats without getting wet?"

Johnston chuckled and said, "So you want me to crawl over you in some embarrassing comedy-movie awkwardness?"

Kevin smiled. "I guess you could call it that. But if you don't want to slide over me, I can work my way over your lap."

Johnston shook her head. "That kind of undignified movement is not going to happen on my watch, sailor boy."

"Fine. How about I slide halfway toward you, and you just slide across my lap into the driver's seat."

Johnston agreed, "Fine, but hands to yourself."

"Okay," Kevin said, laughing.

When Johnston managed to switch places, she wiggled behind the steering wheel of the truck. "How do I adjust this seat?"

"There's a lever under the front, between your legs," Kevin said, gesturing with his left hand.

She smacked his fingers, saying, "I got it," and then found the lever. After moving the seat forward, she adjusted the interior rearview mirror. Looking at the exterior mirrors, she said, "I'm not putting the windows down to fix them."

Kevin laughed then said, "I don't blame you. I'll get them when I get out." Johnston nodded and dropped the shift lever into gear and eased the truck forward at a walking pace. They continued south to Berks Street where Johnston turned right and took another right on Darien Street. Johnston stopped the truck facing north, between the empty lots on both sides of the street. A rowhouse stood on the next lot to the right. The window glass was broken out and the door was boarded over. A condemned building notice was nailed to the front. The rusted hulk of a car was pulled up on the sidewalk at the bottom of the front step.

"It's all you," Johnston said. "I'll hang out here where I can see a couple sides of the building."

Kevin unzipped the backpack and began pulling things out. He placed a military rain poncho on the seat, then a Leatherman multi-tool, and his high-powered flashlight. He slipped the poncho over his head and aligned the hood. He extracted his wallet from his pocket and replaced it with the multi-tool. Opening the glove box, Kevin removed a crumpled black Toro Equipment trucker-style cap and replaced it with his wallet.

Johnston asked, "You think that hat is going to keep you dry?"

Kevin chuckled and said, "Are you kidding? I just hope it keeps the rain out of my eyes for half a second." Then he instructed, "Honk twice if you need me. If I don't come out after five minutes, call for help." Leaning over to Johnston, he kissed her on the cheek and said, "Wish me luck."

Johnston said, "Good luck," and Kevin, slipping on the cap and drawing the hood over it, quickly exited the truck cab. Slamming the door behind him, Kevin walked around the rear of the truck and adjusted the left mirror slowly until Johnston gave him a thumbs-up. He did the same on the right side and then walked away toward the first abandoned row house.

60

Monday, October 29

2:20 p.m.

KEVIN CAUTIOUSLY WALKED along the south wall of the condemned row house. There were no windows or doors on what used to be a common wall with another house. At the far end, weeds and shrubs obscured the rear of the structure, denying access to the back door. Kevin reversed course and returned to the front of the house.

Standing close to the hole that was once the street-level front window, Kevin looked at the frame edged in broken glass. Black charred wood was visible inside. He raised his flashlight to eye level and directed the beam into the bowels of the house. The floor was partially caved in by burnt timbers that had fallen from the second story and smashed into the floor below. Kevin looked back at Johnston in the truck, gestured to move forward, and he turned up the street.

Kevin walked past three empty lots, the wind plastering the green poncho to his body. Ahead, the next building had a boarded-over window, with the front door standing ajar. Kevin climbed to the top step and pushed on the door, but it didn't move. Pushing harder, the door gave way and ground across a debris-strewn floor. "Hello?" he called out, but the only sound was the wind swirling through the building.

Kevin brought up his flashlight and played the beam around the room. The white glare revealed smoke stains on the ceiling and upper walls. In the center of the room, a circle of red bricks hemmed in the remains of a small fire. The odor of wood smoke was carried on the air. A mattress and tattered blanket lay next to the left wall. Farther back in the house, water could be heard trickling from somewhere above the main floor.

Kevin stepped into the room and bent down next to the remains of the fire. A paper *Condemned* notice lay half burned on the pile of charred wood bits, which was cold to the touch. Moving carefully along the wall, Kevin peeked into what had once been a kitchen. The flashlight's beam reflected from a small stream of water dribbling from the ceiling and puddling in the center of the sagging floor. Pulling the poncho hood from his head, Kevin cupped a hand behind his ear and slowly pivoted back toward the front room. After standing perfectly still for a moment scanning the surroundings, he worked his way out the front door, pulling it mostly closed behind him.

Once again on the sidewalk, Kevin pulled the hood back over his head and waved Johnston forward. Another half block up the street, the last two row houses on the left side attracted Kevin's attention. The facade of the matched pair was red brick with two symmetrical windows on the second floor, and a mirror-image single window and door on opposite sides of the common wall. A small rectangular window just above the sidewalk indicated there was a basement. The windows were unbroken, but the gray front door of the right unit was shattered and pushed in. A mangled white bicycle lay on the sidewalk.

Kevin stood in the rain, whipped by wind gusts, studying the house from directly across the street. No movement showed through the open door, and after watching for a long time, he dropped off the curb into the ankle-deep street. After sloshing through the water, Kevin stepped up to the sidewalk and then to the front door. He knocked on the doorframe and called into the front room, "Hello? Anybody here?" After a pause, he pushed the remains of the gray door aside and entered the house.

61

Monday, October 29

4:33 p.m.

THE RAIN DIFFUSED flashing blue lights reflected in the rearview mirror, catching Johnston's attention. She looked up and saw the lights grow brighter as they approached from behind. Johnston pulled the truck off to the right side of the narrow street, driving the passenger side tires up onto the sidewalk opposite the house Kevin had just entered. Soon a Philadelphia Police car came to a stop several car lengths behind the truck. Johnston watched it in the center mirror and mumbled to herself, "What is going on here? Surely you have something else to do in this weather." Soon she became impatient and rolled down the window halfway and waved the police car forward.

The cruiser splashed through the wind tossed river of rainwater, throwing off a wake that rolled across the sidewalk and washed the walls of the remaining row houses. Johnston watched it come to a stop next to the truck. The side window partially lowered, revealing the profile of an officer seated in the passenger seat. Johnston swore under her breath, "Aw, hell. Not today."

"Is that you Johnston?" a voice called across the gap between the vehicles.

"Yes. What on earth are you doing, Hertz?"

"Are you aware the mayor declared a state of emergency? Wants everybody to stay home. That's why I got a call about looters at 1954 Darien Street," Hertz yelled over the wind noise. "That wouldn't be you and your boy toy, would it?"

Johnston replied, "I wasn't aware of the mayor's orders, but we're working here. So, why don't you go serve some other citizens."

Hertz asked, "Aw, that's okay. Maybe I can help."

"I doubt it," Johnston groaned.

Hertz persisted. "Who or what are you looking for?"

Johnston called back, "We're trying to find a local character that goes by the name Ten Speed. We got word he sometimes camps out in one of these condemned houses." Hertz laughed, and Johnston threw her hands up and said, "What?"

Hertz said, "Ten Speed, huh? Well, I doubt you'll find him here, today. He's probably down with his girlfriend. She's got a place that isn't condemned yet and might stand up to this storm."

Johnston asked, "Where is it?"

"Eighth and Brown," Hertz said. "I'll lead you down there when your boyfriend vacates this property."

Johnston squinted at Hertz and said, "Fine." She closed the window and then laid on the truck's horn in two long blasts. The dark figure of Kevin in the poncho appeared in the doorway of the house a moment later. He then dashed across the street to the passenger side of the truck.

Piling into the cab and slamming the door behind him, Kevin said, "What's up?"

Johnston, recoiling from the very wet poncho dripping water

everywhere, said, "New development. Officer Hertz over there, along with his trainee of the day, are going to show us where to find Ten Speed."

Kevin replied, "That's handy. Especially since I wasn't making much progress in the condemned houses of Darien Street."

Johnston picked up the near corner of the poncho. She held it high enough to form a channel that drained water onto the floor of the truck before saying, "Yeah, but Hertz is the last person I want anywhere near this."

Kevin lifted the hood and hat off his head and said from under the wet rubber-coated nylon fabric. "I get it, but sometimes you take what you can get. Today he can take us right where we want to go, so we go."

Johnston sighed. "Yeah, okay."

Kevin folded the wet outer surface of the poncho onto itself and rolled it into a compact ball and set it on the floor. Tossing the hat onto the dashboard, he ran his hand over his wet hair and wiped the water off on the seat fabric next to him. When he was settled and buckled up, he pointed at the police car and said, "I'm ready. Tell them to lead the way."

Johnston cracked the window and yelled, "After you!"

Officer Hertz gave a thumbs-up and the police car pulled away.

Johnston dropped the truck into gear and followed the flashing blue lights into the curtain of relentless rain.

62

Monday, October 29

5:52 p.m.

THE POLICE CAR led the truck south on the blacked-out Eighth Street. In the deepening gloom of evening, the headlights revealed wind-driven rain blowing sideways. Swirling gusts rocked the vehicles as they passed the gaps between buildings. Trees and vegetation whipped back and forth in the vigorous blasts. The streets were wind-rippled rivers that flowed toward the south and east, fed by pools that formed in any open space.

Two blocks south of where Kevin and Johnston had started the search for Ten Speed, the vehicles approached Oxford Street, where a mature tree was down. It had uprooted several segments of the concrete sidewalk and crushed a gold Dodge Intrepid sedan. The cruiser maneuvered to the right and up onto the curb to get around the tree's canopy. Johnston guided the truck along the same path. Kevin grimaced at the sound of tree branches scraping along the side of the fenders and door as it cleared the obstacle.

"I saw you cringe. It couldn't be helped," Johnston declared from behind the wheel.

"Yeah, I know," Kevin groaned. "It's just that I've damaged this poor truck enough already. I'm really going to catch hell when I get it back to the garage."

Johnston grinned and said, "Don't get too concerned with the cosmetics yet, sailor, the night is still young."

Advancing at a little more than jogging pace, the two vehicles made slow progress down the congested street. Cars were parked on both sides of the street and water reached the undercarriage of many of them. There was just enough room for the cruiser and truck to pass, waves and spray flying from their wheels as they went.

Looking ahead, Johnston called out, "Looks like flashing yellow lights up in front of us. Some kind of service vehicle at the intersection."

Kevin asked, "Think we can get through?"

"Not to worry. We'll get around it if Hertz has any influence on the matter. After spending two minutes in his presence, they'll be fully motivated to get rid of him."

At Poplar Street, a damaged delivery van was resting against a utility pole on the southwest corner of the intersection. An electric company bucket truck sat diagonally in the street, yellow beacons flashing a disorienting sequence in the relentless rain. Its roof-mounted spotlight was trained on the pole fractured by the van. It was splintered just above the point where the delivery van had hit it, but it was still held upright by the tangle of utility wires coming from every direction. The police cruiser turned left, using the sidewalk as an alternate roadway to make room to pass. Johnston matched the path and headed east on Poplar Street. Soon she made a right turn, trailing the cruiser onto the mostly empty Franklin Street.

Kevin peered out into the near blackness of the early evening and said, "The lights are on at the Ukrainian Cathedral. I can see the gold dome shining in the dark."

Johnston said, "Huh. Must have a backup generator."

Kevin smirked as they passed the illuminated cathedral. "Or they never lost power. That would be just like those guys."

At the end of the block, the cruiser ignored the one-way traffic signs and turned right on Brown Street. It then promptly made a left back onto Eighth Street, where it pulled up to the right curb and stopped. Johnston followed the maneuvers and parked just ahead of the cruiser. A solitary two-story row house sat in an otherwise empty block. Behind it was the hulking blackness of the SEPTA railroad viaduct. She looked out to the right at the building, nearly invisible except for the reflection of the blue flashing lights of the cruiser and said, "Typical of a place I'd rather not visit on a dark rainy night."

Kevin looked at her and replied, "And yet, here we are."

63

Monday, October 29

6:27 p.m.

KEVIN STOOD NEXT to the passenger side of the police cruiser. The green poncho was plastered to his body by the wind and the bill of the Toro hat projected from under the hood. He leaned into the side of the car and conversed with Officer Hertz through the narrow gap at the top of the window. Yelling over the howl of the wind, Kevin asked, "I'm going to see if anybody is home; care to join me?"

Hertz replied, "The boss would have something to say about it, if I left this to an amateur."

Kevin gave a brief laugh and said, "So you personally don't care if this goes sideways, but you'll come to protect your own hide."

Hertz replied, "You got it," as he pulled on a yellow raincoat. He turned to the officer behind the wheel. "Hudson. You stay in the car. Keep the motor running. Don't drive through any deep water. Keep an ear to the radio. If anything looks questionable, immediately call for backup. Got it?"

"Yes sir," Hudson answered.

Hertz then asked Kevin, "Does Detective Johnston have a radio?"

Kevin replied, "No, nothing."

Hertz turned back to Hudson. "Give me your personal radio. I'm going to give it to the detective in the other vehicle so we can all stay in touch." The officer unrigged the radio from his duty belt and passed it to Hertz, who closed the window and opened the door to the wind and rain. Hertz stepped into the weather and closed the car door. He muttered, "I can't believe this rookie situation." Hertz then walked up to the passenger door of the truck and grabbed the handle. He quickly opened the door and looked at Johnston in the dim glow of the cab's dome light. He said, "Just in case," and tossed the radio on the seat before slamming the door.

Hertz turned on his flashlight and said to Kevin, "Come on," and the two men trudged up the steps to the dark front door. At the top, Kevin turned on his flashlight and directed it at the door handle. He rattled it, discovering it to be unlocked. Hertz said, "Don't you think we should knock first," and then began pounding on the door with the side of his left fist. After a long moment, Hertz repeated the pounding, but there was still no response from inside the building.

Kevin suggested, "Check the back?"

Hertz said as he turned, "I'll go to the back; that way if you went in, I wouldn't know anything about it." He then trotted down the steps and rounded the corner, following the beam of his flashlight.

When Hertz was out of sight, Kevin opened the front door. With the force of the wind pushing on it, the door nearly pulled him down as it slammed into the house. Kevin stutter-stepped then regained his balance before turning to face the opening. With his shoulder into the door, he forced it closed again.

Kevin spun back to face the room, pulled the poncho hood down, and called out, "Anybody here?" There was no audible response.

When the air in the room settled from the hurricane disturbance, the smells of human body odor, rot, and mildew penetrated the darkness. Kevin began sweeping the flashlight beam around the room. Boxes and junk were piled up against the walls all the way to the ceiling. A narrow path between the stacks led to a stairway and the rear of the house.

Kevin crept toward the back room, flashlight sweeping the floor ahead of him. At the doorway, the glare from Hertz's flashlight was visible through the rear window. Kevin scanned the room quickly, then reversed course back to the stairway.

Pausing at the bottom step, Kevin called out again, "Hello?" Listening in silence for a moment, a slight creaking sound emanated from somewhere up the stairs. "Anybody here?" he called again. The only sound was the roar of the wind and rain outside. Kevin muttered, "Here we go," and began ascending the steps with his flashlight held up near his left ear. His right hand gently gripped the worn wooden banister. When his eyes came level with the upper floor, he saw more junk and boxes. Directly at the top of the stairs, the light revealed a stack of clear plastic bins filled with artificial flowers. Standing perfectly still, he called out again, "Hello?"

In the blink of an eye, a smallish human figure clothed in a white dress, flashed through the beam of light, eyes glowing red in the reflection. The figure then charged from behind the stack of bins at the top of the stairs, toppling them and scattering flowers down onto Kevin. Kevin raised his right hand to shield his face and stepped back, off balance. Falling backward when he missed the lower step, he tumbled down the stairs and collided with a pile of white folding chairs.

Extracting himself from the wreckage at the bottom of the stairs, Kevin immediately tried to regain a standing position. While pulling himself to a kneeling stance and getting the poncho out from under his feet, the white figure bounced off his head and outstretched hand, toppling him back into the chairs again. He regained his senses just as the front door slammed open from the wind pressing on it, and the figure dressed in white disappeared into the storm.

Kevin got his feet organized and stood up. Turning around, he faced the gale blowing through the doorway. He pulled his hood up, straightened out his poncho, then stepped out into the driving rain. At the bottom of the steps, he turned left and jogged around to the side of the building. Ahead, a slash of bright white light bounced from place to place while moving away from the house. It repeatedly swept across the white dress of the small figure running toward the SEPTA tracks, revealing the path of Hertz giving chase.

64

Monday, October 29

6:39 p.m.

KEVIN SPRINTED ACROSS the backyard toward where Hertz disappeared into the dark. When he arrived at the spot, trees and brush obscured a fence line bordering the elevated railroad. At ground level, weeds were trampled where Hertz pursued the figure in white. Looking through a gap in the fencing, Kevin could make out the individual footprints of heavy shoes and small bare feet leading up the muddy embankment. Matching the direction, Kevin squeezed through the gap and scrambled up the incline until he encountered a head-high concrete wall. The footprints led him to a tree that leaned against the wall. Directing his flashlight along the tree trunk, Kevin saw mud streaks on branches, and bark was torn away in places. Stuffing the flashlight in his pocket, Kevin climbed the branches and topped the wall. Dropping off the tree on the far side, he found himself standing on the stone ballast of the quadruple SEPTA tracks running north from downtown.

Kevin spotted the retreating beam from a flashlight on the far side of the tracks and began following it. He called out into the dark howling storm, "Hertz! Hertz!" but the beam continued moving south. Kevin switched on his own light and played it over the source of the retreating beam. The retro-reflective strips on Hertz's long yellow raincoat glowed silver as the light crossed over them. Kevin picked up the pace, jogging between the second and third tracks in pursuit of them.

After covering a city block, Kevin saw Hertz's yellow coat as he crossed the Fairmount Avenue overpass and disappeared into the shrubbery on the right. Kevin ran on, hopping the remaining tracks to where Hertz had turned into the foliage.

Probing with his light, Kevin found the trampled path. It led to a wide waist-deep trench lined with stones. At the bottom, muddy water flowed into a drainage pipe running north to the street level sewer entrance. Kevin carefully let himself down and stepped across the water to a low stone wall. Climbing up again, he emerged onto a section of old, rusted tracks and rotten rail ties. He looked right and left with his flashlight but couldn't see Hertz. Kevin wiped the rainwater from his face and muttered, "Come on! Come on!" When he saw Hertz's flashlight blink on again, Kevin pointed his own light toward him. The beam reflected from the raincoat and Kevin began running to catch up.

Kevin closed the distance and drew up alongside Officer Hertz. Walking in the center of the old rail line, Hertz yelled above the wind, "What took you so long?"

Kevin ignored the question and asked, "What are we chasing?"

Hertz shook his head and called back, "A girl in a wedding dress!"

Kevin said, "Okay. Let's go. It can't be far ahead."

Hertz directed, "You take the right tracks; don't forget to look over the side of the wall. I'll take the left." Hertz extended his arm toward the west and said, "Try to stay in line with me."

Kevin asked, "Where are we?"

Hertz replied, "On the old Ninth Street Viaduct. Used to take trains to the Reading Terminal downtown. It's like fifteen feet above street level for a mile. We should be able to spot her."

The two men split up and jogged near the walls, searching down the tracks. Another half a block along the viaduct, Hertz called out something unintelligible to Kevin and then began moving ahead faster. Kevin pivoted and stumbled his way across the four sets of abandoned tracks to the other side. The wide margin on the east side of the tracks was firm ground and Kevin began catching up to Hertz. Not far ahead, Kevin caught a glimpse of Hertz's flashlight illuminating a white figure gliding across the terrain.

Kevin yelled, "That's her!"

Hertz ran faster in the direction of the figure that suddenly disappeared in the rain.

Kevin yelled, "Where did it go?" but Hertz didn't reply as the yellow raincoat seemed to drop straight down out of sight. Kevin called out, "Hertz!" as he drew near the spot. Slowing up, Kevin directed his flashlight at a dark area straight ahead. "Hertz!" Kevin called as he came to a stop on the edge of a sink hole in the collapsed surface of the viaduct.

More than an arm's length below the surface, the storm water in the hole was already neck deep. Kevin watched as Hertz bear hugged the figure in white, yelling, "I got you! Hold still, or you'll drown us both!" but the figure's arms thrashed violently as run-off and rain poured down on them from above. Its feet kicked at his legs, and arching its back, its head repeatedly smashed into Hertz's face. Kevin watched as Hertz lost his footing and disappeared under the water, grappling with the figure in white.

Kevin yelled, "Hold on!" and then scrambled to look around himself. In the beam of his flashlight, he spotted a branch recently broken from a tree growing next to the viaduct. He dragged it to the hole and arrived just as a rush of bubbles flowed up from under the surface. Kevin pointed his light down the hole and could make out a hazy yellow spot rising from the bottom. Soon it grew into Hertz breaking the surface in a massive gasp for air. Kevin yelled, "Hertz! Grab the branch!"

Lying back in the water with just his face above the surface, Hertz slowly came to his senses. He looked up toward Kevin's light and his right hand grabbed hold of the tree limb.

"Are you okay?" Kevin shouted.

"Don't know," he uttered between pants. "I think so." Then Hertz brought up his left hand, wrapped in the white satin and lace fabric. "I think I lost her down there." He then repeated, "I lost her. She was flailing to beat all hell, then she disappeared in a cloud of bubbles."

Kevin smiled and said, "It's okay! You did a great job."

Hertz looked up in stunned disbelief. "What? What? She's still down there."

"She's gone," Kevin said with finality. While Hertz continued to float on his back, Kevin declared, "I got to figure out how to get you out of there. Can you reach the bottom, or are you floating?"

Lifting his head clear of the water, Hertz replied, "I'm on the bottom. I can stand up."

Kevin directed, "Work your way around the hole. See if there is a shallow spot or ledge. It'll make getting you out easier."

Hertz said, "Hold on," and draped the fabric and his raincoat over the branch before disappearing under water again.

Kevin yelled, "No, no! She's gone," as he watched a trail of bubbles roil the surface of the water. Kevin tensed as Hertz remained under water for longer and longer, until finally his head broke the surface again.

Kevin yelled, "What are you doing?"

Hertz called back holding up his gun belt, "I had to double check she's not down there, and I couldn't leave my gear behind." Wiping the water from his face and hair, he handed the belt up to Kevin. "There is a deep spot. I had to drop the belt before it pulled me down. Do you have any idea what the hell happened?"

Kevin set the flashlight down, illuminating Hertz and shouted, "Let's get you out of that hole first. I'll fill you in later."

65

Monday, October 29

7:17 p.m.

KEVIN LAY ON the ground next to the sinkhole, trying to pull Hertz up by his arms. Both men panted from the exertion, and after losing his grip for the fourth time, Hertz said, "We've got to try something else."

Kevin agreed, "Yeah, the branch isn't big enough, and we're both too slippery with whatever's in the water."

Hertz pointed out, "There's a century of coal dust, oil, creosote, and other crap washing into his hole with me. I'm probably going to need a proper hazmat decontamination. I mean, look at my hands, they're already getting white and flakey."

Kevin half laughed and said, "That's probably not from the water, but if it is, I can't imagine what it's doing to your junk."

Hertz exclaimed, "Aw, to hell with that; get me out of here!"

Kevin got up from the ground and said, "I've got an idea." He removed his poncho and rolled it along its diagonal dimension. "We'll use it as a rope tied to your gun belt." Kevin removed the pistol, handcuffs and radio from the belt and buckled it at its largest notch. He then tied the poncho end to the belt and lowered it to Hertz. "Put the belt around your chest, under your arms."

"Right on," Hertz said. "I see what you're doing. We'd better hurry up. I'm starting to lose feeling in my toes and fingers."

Kevin said, "Probably hypothermia setting in. Okay. Tell me when you've got it secured in place and I'll start walking backward."

Hertz called up, "Ready!"

Kevin said, "I'm going to count down from three, and on go, I want you to submerge and spring up, vertically as far as you can, Okay? I'm going to take up the slack when you do. Got it?"

Hertz said, "Got it!"

Kevin counted down, "Three, two, one, go." Hertz submerged for a moment and then sprung up, reaching for the top of the pit. Kevin backed up quickly and caught him at the top of his jump. Then he yelled, "Climb!" as he pushed backward with his legs and pulled on the poncho with his arms. Hertz groaned and scratched at the loose dirt and stone ballast. Most of it fell into the hole with him, but after a few tugs from Kevin, Hertz's head was visible above the edge of the pit.

Hertz yelled, "Come on, pull!" Kevin strained with his legs, arms and back, dragging Hertz up to the level of his gun belt, then in an instant, Hertz got purchase with his hands and launched halfway out of the hole onto his belly. Kevin stumbled and landed on the ground, his head bouncing off a rotten wood rail tie.

Kevin lay on his back, chest heaving, trying to catch his breath. Rain pounded his face, forcing him to shield it with his arm. When his breathing and heart rate approached normal, Kevin sat up and called out to Hertz. "Are you okay?" Hertz was sprawled on the ballast rock, feet hanging over the hole. Kevin yelled again, "Hertz! Are you with me?" but there was no response.

Kevin crawled over and rolled Hertz onto his side. He unbuckled the gun belt and cleared the poncho away. Kevin placed two fingers on the side of his neck and then said, "Your heart is still beating. Come on Hertz!" he yelled again. After shaking his shoulder and encouraging him, Hertz moaned and then vomited onto the rocks. Kevin sighed, "Oh, thank you, God."

Groans and spitting followed as Kevin sat back and collected his poncho. He unrolled it and spread it out over Hertz, who still didn't make any effort to move. Kevin said, "Come on, you'll be fine. You're okay," before crawling over to the tree branch and recovering the yellow raincoat. He slipped it on and stuffed the remains of the white dress into the coat pocket. At the edge of the pit, he picked up his flashlight and returned to Hertz.

Shielding most of the flashlight's beam with the palm of his hand, Kevin lifted the poncho and examined Hertz. His hands and face were dead white, and the skin was cracking like a dried-up desert lake. "Come on Hertz. I need you to get it together if we're going to get down from here." Hertz groaned in response, and Kevin added, "Good, you're responding to verbal cues. That's a start."

Kevin gathered the items he'd removed from Hertz's belt and reassembled it. Then he asked Hertz, "Think your radio will work? It was underwater for a little while."

Hertz grunted, "Doubt it."

Kevin said, "Well, I think it's worth a try. You want me to make a call, or would you prefer to do it?"

Hertz tried to sit up and said, "Give it to me."

Kevin helped him up and said, "Glad you're coming around."

Hertz moaned as he came to a sitting position and pulled the poncho around himself. He then said, "I don't want you saying something stupid on my radio."

Kevin laughed as he handed over the radio. "Well, that's something you and Johnston have in common."

Hertz coughed and said, "Damn right," while he examined the

radio. After turning it over and pressing a button on the side, he added. "It's dead anyway."

Kevin said, "Well, it looks like we're finding our own way out of here. Wherever we are."

"Ninth Street Viaduct. Somewhere south of Fairmont Avenue."

"You said that before, but where is that?"

Hertz grunted, "Got to walk south. Find an overpass and climb down."

Kevin asked, "You ready to try walking?"

"What choice do I have?" Hertz replied as Kevin struggled to his feet against the wind. Reaching down to Hertz, he pulled him to an upright position and braced him by putting an arm under his shoulder.

"What happened to your flashlight?" Kevin asked as he started walking forward at a slow pace, the poncho and raincoat flapping in the wind gusts.

Hertz muttered, "Don't know. Must be in the water. Of course, it is. It's brand new."

Kevin kept them moving south along the viaduct and soon came to an overpass. Pointing his light down at the ground, he said, "Looks like we're stopping here. The deck of the bridge is full of holes. We could fall through."

Hertz looked down at the area illuminated by the beam of light and then his head tipped up. Pointing ahead, he said, "That's okay. The cavalry is here."

Kevin looked to where Hertz pointed, and through the wind and rain, he saw the flashing blue lights of the police cruiser followed by the yellow strobes of the utility truck. They were approaching the overpass between a warehouse and the east wall of the railroad embankment.

66

Tuesday, October 30

7:17 a.m.

KEVIN'S EYES FLICKERED open to the fluorescent light of a hospital hallway. He was slouched on a plastic chair. To his right, Detective Johnston held a similar posture with her head leaning on his shoulder. Wiping at the corner of his mouth with his left hand, he muttered, "Johnston?"

"What?" she whispered.

"It's morning," he replied.

"So what?" was the retort from behind closed eyes.

"They will be doing something with Hertz soon," Kevin explained. "You should find out. Then maybe we can go home."

Johnston pushed off from Kevin and straightened her posture in the chair. She muttered, "Yeah, okay," and slowly stood up. She stretched her arms wide and yawned before adjusting her shirt and running her fingers through her hair. Fishing an elastic band from her purse as she stood up, she put her hair in a quick ponytail before saying, "I'll check at the desk."

Kevin said, "Meet you back here."

Johnston looked down at him and asked, "Where are you going?"

"Foraging."

Johnston smirked. "Yeah, sure. And, by the way, you look like crap."

Kevin sat up and looked at his clothes. Most of them were damp and streaked with mud and black stains of unknown origin. He shrugged, and she added, "You smell pretty bad too."

Kevin rolled his eyes and asked, "Anything else?"

Johnston leaned down and whispered, "It's kind of attractive," before kissing him briefly on the lips.

Kevin gave a slight smile as he watched her walk down the hall to an open bay of workstations surrounded on three sides by curtained-off patient beds.

Johnston approached the first chest-high desk and addressed the nurse seated on the other side, "Hey, good morning. Any update on what's going to happen with Officer Hertz?"

The attractive middle-aged woman looked up at Johnston and said, "The plan right now is to admit him. Unfortunately, with the storm out there, nobody's going home. So that means no open beds upstairs."

Johnston asked, "So he'll stay here until there's space?"

The nurse said, "You got it. We're pretty much stuck until the mayor lifts the 'remain at home order.'" The nurse added, "I doubt my relief will get here, but even if they did, I can't even go home when my shift ends. It looks like my neighborhood is underwater."

"Okay, thanks for your help, and I hope it's not as bad as it sounds," Johnston said.

Returning to the waiting area after a detour to the restroom, Johnston found Kevin carrying a cup of dark steaming liquid and two vending machine food packages. He handed the cup to Johnston who said, "Thanks," before taking a sip from the cup.

Kevin sat down and held out the two packages toward Johnston. "Chocolate Fudge Brownie with nuts or trail mix with candy coated chocolates?"

Johnston sat down next to him and took another sip. She then said, "Which one weighs more?"

Kevin flipped over the packages and read the printing. "The trail mix is two point five ounces, and the brownie is three."

Johnston held out her hand and said, "Trail mix, and thanks for the coffee."

Kevin smiled. "You're welcome, as long as I can have another sip before you kill it."

Johnston asked, "Where did you get it?"

Kevin replied, "I asked one of the nurses. She said they weren't supposed to share, but seeing as how there is a hurricane outside, she thought it would be okay."

Johnston took another sip and handed the cup back to Kevin and asked, "What's it look like out there?"

"Outside?" Kevin asked. Johnston nodded and Kevin answered, "Still only half light, so it's hard to say, but it looks like it's still windy. I think the rain has let up." After eating the vending machine snacks and finishing the cup of coffee, they headed to the exam area.

Kevin slowly pulled back the curtain and Johnston peeked in. Hertz was dozing in the bed and in the chair next to him, Officer Hudson was sound asleep, slumped forward with his head in his hands. Kevin walked quietly over to the monitors and looked at the displayed information, then gestured back toward the curtain. Once clear, Kevin drew the curtain again and said, "Best let them sleep some more."

Just as they started to move, a gruff voice called from behind the curtain, "Hey, where are you going?" Johnston and Kevin looked at each other and then back at the curtain. Johnston took a deep breath and let out a long sigh.

"Is that you, Hertz?" she asked.

The voice replied, "Who else, sweetheart?"

Kevin led the way back and opened the curtain. Hudson was now awake, rubbing his eyes. Hertz was sitting on the edge of the bed, his hospital gown open at the back, toward Kevin and Johnston.

Johnston said in disgust as she turned her head, "Oh god, cover that up."

Kevin followed by saying, "And don't call me sweetheart."

Hertz grinned, "You'll be glad to know the nurse said whatever screwed up my hands and arms didn't get to the important stuff. The gear seems to be in working order."

Johnston's face scrunched and Kevin snatched a hospital gown from the supply shelf in the room. He shook it open and handed it to Hertz saying, "Put this over the back, so your package isn't hanging out for everybody to see."

Hertz said, "I kind of think it needs some airing out, but okay."

Johnston observed, "It sounds like you're completely back to normal." Turning to Hudson, she asked, "How are you holding up?"

Hudson stood up and said, "Thanks for asking, ma'am. I am just a little stiff. A few hours of sleep in a real bed and I'll be good as new."

Johnston said, "Well, nobody's going anywhere for the rest of the day, so why don't you take a few minutes to freshen up and find something to eat. We'll keep what's-his-name company, okay?"

He replied, "Yes, ma'am."

Johnston watched Hudson walk away and then drew the curtain closed. Kevin stepped to the corner of the examination area, crossed his arms, and leaned a shoulder on the wall. When Hertz was finished tying up the second hospital gown over his backside, Johnston said, "You clear enough to talk about what happened last night?"

Hertz grinned as he sat down on the bed. "Is this official? Do I need a union rep?"

Johnston replied, "No, it's for Kevin's edification. Nothing legal."

Hertz shrugged, "Then, yeah, sure."

Johnston asked, "Were you able to sleep last night?"

Hertz replied, "Some. I was stretched out in a bed, wrapped in twenty of these cheap hospital sheets, if you can call that sleeping." After a slight pause, he asked, "Where did you two spend the night?"

Johnston replied, "We found some chairs in a hallway."

Hertz grunted and swung his legs back onto the hospital bed, then asked, "What do you want to know?"

Johnston said, "Walk me through the evening, starting from where you met Kevin at the front door of the girlfriend's rowhouse."

"Yeah, sure. So, Kevin knocked on the door but didn't get a reply. I told him to stay put while I walked around to the back of the house. There were no windows on the right side of the house and nothing remarkable until I got around to the back."

Johnston asked, "What did you find?"

Hertz said, "From about ten feet off the back right corner, I saw a dim light wavering around through the upper window and it silhouetted a person. I couldn't see any details, but it looked like that person was watching me. After a couple seconds, the person disappeared and the light dimmed to nothing. Shortly after that, I saw this tiny thing dressed in white come around from the front and charge right at me. I got my flashlight on 'em and said 'Stop!' but the person kept coming. It looked like a small female wearing a white dress. It was flouncy, like a wedding dress. So, I got in position like I was going to tackle her, and next thing I knew, she slipped past me."

Johnston asked, "What did she look like?"

Hertz said, "She was petite. I mean like five foot nothing and maybe eighty-five pounds." Johnston nodded at his description as he continued. "Her face was round, like a little kid, and she didn't have any hair." Hertz paused for a moment and added, "Then there were . . . the eyes. My flashlight made them glow like a snapshot from an old polaroid camera."

Kevin stood silently listening to the narrative, and his brows rose slightly at the description of the eyes.

Johnston encouraged Hertz to continue. "Then what happened?"

Hertz rolled his eyes and said, "Well, she ran off. I made a radio call that I was on foot and went after her. And let me tell you, for a tiny thing in a wedding dress with no shoes, she was surprisingly fast. We went up the embankment and next thing I know, I'm climbing up a fallen tree to the top of the retaining wall, then we're out on the Ninth Street Viaduct. I tell you, I'm glad the trains had already been stopped. I really didn't feel like writing that report."

Kevin asked, "How did you end up over on the old section of the viaduct?"

Hertz said, "She knew just where she was going. I can only guess she was a regular up there, because she went directly to a cut across the ditch. Hardly slowed her up at all."

Johnston asked, "Did you know where you were going when she crossed over?"

Hertz said, "Pretty much. I made a radio call when we turned south again. I never heard back from Dispatch," he said, then added, "But I guess you heard it?"

Johnston replied, "Yeah, and I didn't hear Dispatch either, so that's when I went looking for the utility truck. I knew we'd need a ladder or something."

Hertz continued. "It wasn't long after that Kevin caught up. He knows the rest."

Kevin agreed, "Yeah. I saw some of it. What happened to her when you were in the water?"

Hertz asked, "You were there; can you tell me? She must have somehow broke free and got out of the hole."

Kevin said, "I was smoked from the running and couldn't see much in the dark and rain."

Hertz grunted and resumed his explanation, "Well, I fell in on top of her, and she was already thrashing around. Somewhere,

I dropped my flashlight in the water and when I got back on my feet and upright, I got hold of her and supported her weight, so she didn't drown. Then she kept on flailing and headbutted me. I lost my footing and took both of us down for a few seconds. Next thing I know, there was a cloud of bubbles glowing in the beam of my flashlight. When I managed to get back up again, she was gone."

Kevin shrugged. "That's amazing. I'm sorry I didn't see what happened."

Johnston looked Kevin in the eye with a hard stare. "You didn't see her leave the hole?"

"I did not," he answered.

Johnston added, "So, to bring this full circle, I found two deceased in the row house. One matched the description of Ten Speed, and the other was a woman, like the person you described running away."

Hertz asked, "When was that?"

"After Hudson left with you two in the cruiser, I went back to the house."

Hertz remarked, "I guess with the ladder and truck business, she had plenty of time to go home and get dead before you got there."

Johnston exchanged glances with Kevin before saying, "Okay, Hertz. We'll send Hudson back in to keep you company. We'll be around if you think of anything else."

"Honestly, the whole thing doesn't make sense," Hertz added.

Kevin said, "That's kind of how my work goes. You should probably just forget about it."

Hertz exhaled. "That's fine by me. I'll do my job and you do yours."

Kevin said, "You got a deal."

67

Wednesday, October 31

9:10 a.m.

KEVIN AND BRIAN walked out the kitchen door of the old farmhouse into the new morning light. The cool wind in the aftermath of the storm still swayed the bare trees and plastered wet leaves on anything that didn't move. Brian looked around the yard and said, "After all that humid tropical air, it's chilly out here. I think we got off easy on this storm. Could have been much worse."

Kevin nodded as he followed Brian into the driveway. "Looks like a few trees down and a lot of general clean up. Come on, let's go see what we can do to help."

Walking up the hill to the maintenance shed, Kevin drew alongside his brother and asked, "Were you busy during your shift?"

Brian shrugged. "The ambulance crew wasn't too bad. We had to assist with fallen trees and downed utilities. I got tired of standing around in the rain wielding a chainsaw. How about you?"

Kevin smiled slightly and said, "It was pretty crappy out, but I think we got the second cat."

Brian looked at his brother and asked, "Who's we, and what do you mean by 'think'?"

Kevin responded, "Johnston and I located it, then with a little help from a patrol officer named Hertz, who ended up in the water with it, it was disposed of in the proper manner."

Brian asked, "And the uncertainty?"

"I didn't see the last victim to confirm it was actually one of my cats, but Johnston did, and I think she knows what she's looking at." After another step, he added, "A genetic test will confirm that the victim's DNA was corrupted, and that will be that."

Brian slapped his brother on the shoulder and said, "That's got to feel good, getting another W for the home team."

"I will say, not getting my face rubbed raw was an improvement, but Hertz, well, he's got a pretty good case of the peels on his hands and some on his face. Not as bad as I had it, but enough to make him question his life choices."

Brian added, "No other casualties?"

Kevin gave a short laugh and added, "No, nobody but me and Hertz, but you should have seen the look on his face when I suggested he might get the peels on his junk. He literally thought his life was over."

"That's pretty funny, and also not funny, all at the same time!" Brian laughed as they walked to the door of the building.

Kevin reached out to open the door when Mr. Warren emerged from the passageway. His eyebrows shot up at the sight of the two and said, "I trust everything's okay down at the house?"

Brian answered, "Just the power outage. I'm sure it will come on eventually, but in the meantime, we thought we'd see if there was anything we could do for you."

Mr. Warren replied, "Thank you, thank you. I have an extensive list of cleanup tasks. I've got some rake work and a tree down. Either of you skilled with a chainsaw?"

Kevin looked at Brian, who glanced back at Kevin. Brian said, "Rakes sound good. Where do you want us?"

Mr. Warren grinned at Brian's answer and said, "Take my Gator. The tools are already in it, and head over to the City Avenue side of the front hedgerow. See if you can get the area around the signs and sidewalk cleaned up."

Brian replied, "You got it," and the two walked around the side of the building to the six-wheeled vehicle parked in the garage.

As they approached, Kevin said, "Shotgun."

Brian looked at him and asked, "What are we, sixteen?"

Kevin climbed into the passenger side and said, "We just got the boss's vehicle and permission to drive it off the property and down the public sidewalks. It just seems like this could get crazy, and since you're the responsible city employee, I thought you should do the driving."

Brian laughed and said, "Way to look out for your brother," and dropped into the driver's seat. He started the engine, backed out of the garage, and motored up the main drive to the front entrance. Approaching the gatehouse, the uniformed guard raised the barricade and waved them through. Brian turned right down Wynnewood Road, and at the corner with City Avenue, he steered the vehicle up onto the sidewalk. He parked in front of the wrought iron fence topped with a large blue sign that read *Saint Charles Seminary, Archdiocese of Philadelphia*. Shutting off the engine, he said, "Let's get to work."

Wielding leaf rakes, the two worked with quiet efficiency, filling bags with leaves and debris from the grassy triangle on the street corner.

While they raked, Brian asked, "Everything good with Johnston?"

"Yeah," Kevin replied. "When I dropped her off, she was heading to her mom's place down the shore. After we saw a news report on the television at the hospital, she was worried about her."

Brian grunted and said, "I understand there was extensive flooding past the boardwalk and sea wall. I hope her mom's okay."

Kevin added, "I guess her mom's a couple blocks in from the beach, so, fingers crossed, she should be good."

Soon they had several large bags filled and stacked in the bed of the Gator. Just as Kevin paused to look over the area, a voice interrupted his inspection. "There you are."

Kevin turned and saw Father Tucker standing on the sidewalk. Kevin said, "Hey."

Father Tucker said, "I've been all over this place looking for you two. Mr. Warren said you were working near the street corner, but I guess I didn't understand that he meant outside the fence."

Kevin smiled and asked, "So you walked all the way down here on the other side of the hedge?"

Father Tucker shrugged. "Halfway from the tennis court, then I got smart and went back to the guard and asked him if he'd seen you."

Brian joined the conversation and commented, "Good thinking."

Father Tucker said, "I needed the exercise after being cooped up for the last two days."

Kevin asked, "What brings you out here?"

The priest said, "I got an update from Stepan. It looks like he got booked for a flight."

Brian asked, "When will they arrive?"

Father Tucker said, "Tomorrow at five fifty-four in the afternoon."

Kevin took a couple steps forward toward the big blue sign and looked up at the crest of the archdiocese emblazoned on it. After a moment, he turned back to Brian and Father Tucker and said, "That's November first. All Saints Day. Seems appropriate."

Brian looked at the priest and asked, "Anything we need to do?"

"The arrangements have been made. Your uncle didn't want anything elaborate. The funeral mass will be here in the chapel, probably on Saturday, and there is a plot for him in the Old Cathedral Cemetery. The headstone is already in place."

Brian looked down at the damp grass and stuffed his hands in his pockets, then after a few breaths, he said, "Okay. Didn't know about the cemetery. That's good. Do we need to tell Mom?"

"The chancellery has already contacted her."

Kevin shook his head and Brian turned to the Gator. He said to Father Tucker, "We're done out here. Can we give you a ride back?"

Father Tucker said, "I'd appreciate that."

Kevin placed the rakes in the bed and said to his brother, "I think I'll walk."

Brian nodded and slid behind the wheel. The priest took the empty seat and the Gator rumbled to life. Brian cut a U-turn and said to Kevin before motoring off, "See you at the shop, brother."

Kevin waved and watched the Gator maneuver off the sidewalk and accelerate up Wynnewood Road. Stuffing his hands in his pockets, Kevin started walking in the same direction.

68

Saturday, November 3

1:49 p.m.

THE OLD CATHEDRAL Cemetery occupied an eight-block section of a western neighborhood. The burial ground was encircled by a narrow asphalt lane, with another bisecting it along its long east-west axis. Led by a black hearse, a string of vehicles that included an unmarked police car and a red Jeep Cherokee parked along the central lane.

Exiting the cars, an irregular line of mourners followed Father Tucker and Protodeacon Micevych toward a new grave located some distance from the pavement. Dressed in shades of gray and black, the mourners clutched themselves and their coats against the gusty, cold wind. Brian and Kevin, supporting their mother, made their way out into the field of shadowless headstones, feet squelching in the rain-sodden grass as they made wandering deviations to skirt low ground.

Contrasting with the colorless gray of horizon-to-horizon mackerel clouds, a carpet of artificial grass in a jolting color of green was laid out around an opening in the earth. Rows of white folding chairs were arrayed on the carpet. A few random chairs were toppled by the blasts of wind that combed the open terrain. Picking up the fallen chairs, the mourners arranged themselves in semicircular ranks and faced the clergymen across the grave. Coming in behind them, a cluster of bearers placed a black casket on a cradle over the newly installed burial vault.

When the movement of people settled, Father Tucker made a crossing gesture and began to speak. He then raised his hands out toward the assembled mourners, causing his coat and stole to flap in the bitter wind. His words were inaudible at a distance, and soon he bowed his head, followed by the mourners doing the same. After a time, the mourners huddled closer together, sometimes sitting but mostly standing.

At a moment midway through the proceedings, and clearly a surprise to the assembly, Mark Francini led his wife Jessica away from the grave toward a waiting car. She clutched at her protruding belly. Distress was evident in their body language.

When the clergymen completed the burial rights and made a pronounced crossing gesture, the group dissolved into a moment of entropy. Brief conversations and gestures were followed by the mourners and clergymen retreating to the parked vehicles, leaving Brian and Kevin standing tall on either side of their mother.

They pulled each other into a close embrace and held it until previously unseen workmen walked up to the opposite side of the grave. The men were dressed in dark blue coveralls and carried the tools of their trade. After a brief exchange of words, the Maloney family departed Father Matthew O'Conner's burial plot.

69

Saturday, November 3

4:44 p.m.

THE FARMHOUSE ON the grounds of the St. Charles Seminary was again crowded with people. The soft hum of hushed voices filled the kitchen and living room. A collection of wet and muddy shoes was piled near the back door. Serving dishes of food were arranged on the kitchen table and a pair of coolers with iced beverages were stashed underneath.

A woman with shoulder-length brown hair and wearing a black dress printed with flowers collected dishes and added them to a pile by the sink. Next to her, a taller woman, wearing a black blouse and form-fitting gray skirt fiddled with a coffee maker. When the basket for the coffee grounds wouldn't seat correctly, she let out a huff and turned to the woman at the sink. "Pardon me, do you know how to get this thing to fit?"

"I made a pot of coffee earlier, and I had to get Brian to show me the trick. He claims to be the firehouse expert you know, but anyway, see that little latch in the back, the black comma shaped thingy? Slide that left and the basket will drop in."

Following the instructions, the device went back together, and the woman said, "You're an angel." When the coffee maker was again hissing and dripping black liquid into the carafe, the women introduced themselves. "By the way, I'm Daisy."

The woman washing dishes extended her right hand to Daisy and said, "I'm Michele."

Daisy smiled and said, "I love your dress. Do you know what kind of flowers those are?"

Michele smiled at the compliment and said, "Thank you. I think they are primroses."

Daisy said, "Very pretty," and after a pause, she asked, "How did you know Father O'Conner?"

"I didn't," Michele replied. "Brian and Kevin came over to St. Malachy three weeks ago. They helped me and my mom. Mostly Kevin did the work, but Brian and I have been chatting ever since, you know?" Michele looked back to her dishes before asking, "Did you know Father O'Conner?"

Daisy turned and leaned against the counter and said, "I'm here for moral support too. Kevin worked for me over the summer. He's a good guy and I know his uncle was important to him."

Michele looked at Daisy with wide eyes and asked, "So who was the couple who left? The pregnant lady?"

Daisy responded, "That was Mark and Jessica Francini, and it looked like today might be the day, didn't it?" Michele's head nodded repeatedly as Daisy continued. "I know him from work."

Michele said, "I said a little prayer for her. I wouldn't want my child born in a cemetery." After a brief pause, Michele then asked in a hushed voice, "So are you involved with the dead-people thing, like Kevin?"

Daisy cocked her head and replied, "Uh, no, sugar. I manage

a bar." Daisy shook her head and said, "Wow, I've got to keep up. When he worked for me, Kevin was a bartender on the *Moshulu*. Then he left for a hospital job. I guess that didn't last long."

Michele asked, "So you don't know what he does?"

Daisy smiled. "I guess I don't, but maybe you'd better fill me in."

As she said it, Brian walked up behind Michele and asked, "Fill you in about what?"

Michele turned to Brian, placed a hand on his arm, and said, "You know, family and stuff."

Brian said, "Right. *Stuff*." He extended a hand to Daisy and said, "By the way, I'm Brian."

Daisy smiled and replied, "I'm Daisy. It's nice to finally meet you. I heard a lot about you when Kevin worked for me on the ship."

Brian shook his head, and said, "Yeah, right, okay, you're *that* Daisy. Boy, that seems like a lifetime ago."

Daisy remarked, "Just a couple months, but I know what you mean."

Brian looked at the coffee maker and then at Daisy. "Is that a fresh brew?"

Daisy looked back and said, "Just started. Give it a sec and I'll pour you a cup."

Brian nodded. "Tell you what, why don't you two find a seat and I'll bring you a cup. Cream and sugar?"

Daisy said, "Neither. Just hot and black."

Brian grinned and then retrieved a pair of cups from the cabinet above the sink.

The two women made their way into the living room and were replaced in the kitchen by the bulk of Protodeacon Stepan and another man coming in from outside. Stepan shook off his coat and wiped his feet on the mat before kicking his shoes into the corner. He waved at Brian and his voice rumbled. "Hello Brian, how are you doing?"

Brian nodded and said, "Okay, but I'll be better when this

machine has finished brewing my next cup of joe."

Stepan ran his hand over his head and said, "Hmm. If you can spare a cup, I'd be most grateful." Gesturing to the other man, Stepan said, "Brian, this is Borys, my driver from the Ukrainian Cathedral."

Brian stepped forward, shook hands with Borys, then gestured to the food. "Help yourselves. There's also beer, soda, and water in the coolers underneath."

Borys hung back by the door and said, "Thanks. Maybe I can get a cup of coffee? It smells very good."

Brian pulled two more cups down and lined them up with the others. Stepan asked, "Is Kevin here?" Brian nodded and Stepan continued in a softer, deeper rumble. "After things settle down, I have the materials from La Specola. Your uncle would want them shared as soon as possible."

Kevin entered from the living room and crossed directly to Stepan saying, "I heard a familiar voice calling my name," and immediately bear-hugged the older man.

Stepan pounded on Kevin's back and then pointed him toward Borys saying, "You remember Borys?"

Kevin smiled and shook his hand. "Of course I do. I think I owe him my life."

Stepan looked at Borys and asked, "Some story I haven't heard?" to which Borys just shrugged. Turning back to Kevin and Brian, Stepan said, "He's modest."

Kevin responded, "He may be modest, but his timing is impeccable. Thank you, Borys." Then Kevin said, "We appreciate you coming; I think we have a lot to talk about."

After a brief wait, Brian pulled the carafe from the coffee maker and began pouring. When he was finished, he instructed Kevin as he walked out of the room with a cup in each hand, "Give these to the gentlemen, and I will take the rest to the ladies."

Kevin responded, "Aye aye, captain," and handed over the coffees.

Stepan held the cup up to his lips but didn't drink. "It is very hot, I think. I will hear Borys tell the tale of saving your life—then it should be ready."

Borys held the steaming cup in his hands and shrugged once without saying anything.

Stepan coaxed, "Come now, Borys, we will not think anything less of Kevin for needing your assistance."

Borys set the cup on the corner of the table and shuffled his feet before saying, "There were a couple moments, I'm not sure which you mean."

Kevin and Stepan looked at each other and back at Borys. Stepan said, "Start with the first incident."

Borys scratched his ear and rubbed his chin before beginning to speak. "It was like this. I heard about Kevin getting thumped by Johnny Square's lookouts, so after that, I made a point of knowing when Kevin was in the area. And next time he comes in to do his job, I get Yakiv to help me keep an eye on things. We made sure no trouble was looking for Kevin."

Kevin asked, "Was Yakiv with you the night I was surrounded in the truck?"

Borys nodded and said, "We followed at a distance. It wasn't too hard. That big truck could be heard for blocks. When you stopped near the park, Yakiv saw it and said we needed to move before you got hurt. We arrive just in time, I think. The windows in the cab of the truck were the next thing that they were going to break, and maybe you after that."

Stepan asked, "How did you convince them to leave Kevin alone?"

Borys replied, "Just a whisper from Uncle Mikhail."

Stepan rolled his eyes and said, "Anything else?"

Borys continued. "Kevin came back with the lady detective, so we made sure none of the gangbangers were out."

Kevin asked, "What did you do?"

Borys said, "Tipped them off that an undercover cop was in the neighborhood."

Kevin shook his head. "Johnston won't like that."

Stepan suggested, "Maybe you should keep this to yourself. It was in the interest of everybody's safety."

Kevin asked, "Were there any other times?"

Borys smirked, then said, "When you came in the orange car? You got a Ukrainian police escort."

"What? That was on purpose?"

"Another way to keep you safe," Borys said.

"That has to be it. I wasn't in the area any other times."

"Just the night of the storm."

"How's that?" Kevin asked.

Borys chuckled at Kevin's question, then said, "The utility truck that was sitting all by itself, not doing anything?"

Kevin rolled his eyes back and groaned, "Who was that?"

"Good Ukrainian man who works for the power company. Relative of Yakiv. He was out watching you and managed to keep the power on at the cathedral too. When the lady detective came to him for help, he was not un-expecting her."

Stepan said, "That is good work, Borys, but I want to know how you knew Kevin was in the area."

Borys clapped his hands together and said, "The security guard calls me when you leave."

Kevin hung his head and covered his face with his hands, mumbling, "That easy? I must be the dumbest dude in the city. I am such an idiot."

Borys then explained, "You were very brave. I look at it like this, you knew what danger you faced because you were already ass-kicked, but you kept coming back anyway. I admire your determination."

Kevin let his hands drop and he looked at Borys. "Thanks for that, and thanks for looking out for me and Johnston."

Borys said, "No problem."

Kevin then asked, "One more thing. Did you call the police with the looting report?"

Borys smiled. "No. But that's a good idea. This one, I think it was a real call."

70

Saturday, November 3

8:13 p.m.

ALL AFTERNOON, PEOPLE came and went, with a few staying longer than others. Most of the visitors were finally cleared out with the onset of darkness. Father Tucker announced his departure as the lower limb of the sun peeked beneath the clouds at sunset. Mr. Warren and the grounds crew followed soon after. When Mrs. Maloney and her neighbor were sent home with dishes of leftover food, the census dropped to eight yawning and exhausted individuals.

The kitchen was now dark, and in the living room the only light came from the lamp at the end of the couch. Its shaded glow revealed Johnston, Stepan and Daisy seated on the leather cushions. Kevin, Brian and Michele slouched by the television on kitchen chairs. Borys leaned against the kitchen door frame, and Skip sat across the bottom of the stairs, his back against the wall. Conversation ground to a halt with the departure of Mrs. Maloney, and a welcome silence blanketed the room.

The deep quiet persisted long enough to hear the wall-mounted thermostat behind the couch make a mechanical click, followed by the rumble of the furnace blower coming on in the basement. Seated next to one of the floor vents, Michele reacted to the air blowing up her back and animating her hair. She flinched and said, "Oh my!" Within a heartbeat, several of the room's occupants chuckled or gave a short laugh at Michele's reaction. "I didn't expect that," she said.

Johnston smiled from behind half-closed eyes and said, "Reminds me of a cat my mother had. It used to sit anywhere there was air movement. Registers and fans were Sonny's favorites."

Stepan chuffed and brought himself a little more upright. He looked around the room and then at Kevin. "I think it's time we have a lesson from La Specola."

Kevin sat up straight and replied, "Yeah, okay." Looking around, he asked, "Are you comfortable with a big group? I mean everybody here's connected some way or another."

Stepan rumbled, "The more ears the better."

Kevin asked, "Will I need paper and pen?"

Stepan replied, "I have Mathew's notes for you. For now, I'll tell the story of the things that are no longer hidden from us. Then we'll analyze as best we can."

By the time Stepan finished his sentence, the other seven in the room were wide-eyed and fully keyed on his voice. Stepan continued. "Matthew and I first enquired at the Vatican Library about what the church knew of these extraordinary occurrences. After describing what we were looking for, we were not able to convince any of the research librarians to assist us. We thought our trip was doomed. Then a young man from Florence, interning with the library, followed us out one evening. He told us we needed to travel to La Specola and conduct our research there."

Kevin asked, "Why Florence and La Specola?"

Stepan continued, "From the late medieval period up into the Renaissance, it was common for wealthy families to keep menageries. Traders and merchants would bring back exotic animals to be kept in the gardens of the villas and castles of Europe. These early zoos employed animal keepers, often slaves, to maintain the collection. Some of them even kept detailed records. By the beginning of the eighteenth century, it became fashionable for men of wealth to explore the natural sciences."

As Stepan spoke, the occupants of the room glanced at each other momentarily, but were drawn back into the narrative. "La Specola is one of the surviving collections from that time. There is an incredible number of preserved animals dating from over two hundred years ago. There is also a collection of written materials. It was in this library that we found our peculiar animal."

Michele looked at Stepan and asked, "Preserved animals. What does that mean?"

Stepan asked, "Stuffed? What is the word in English? Matthew used a word that sounded like taxes."

"Taxidermy," Skip chimed in from his dark corner. "Like the deer and moose hunters take for trophies."

Stepan smiled. "That's the word. Anyway, they have many, many animals. Male and female. But most important, they have a library and records from family collections." Michele nodded her understanding, and Stepan continued. "The powerful families in Italy were always trying to get one up on each other. In one case, an Egyptian slave shared a tale about the cat that can steal the soul of a dead man. And more important, once stolen, the soul never makes it to the afterlife. Very important to the Egyptians, you see. So, this slave was commissioned to get one of these cats. After an exhaustive search, he brought his catch back to the villa, where he began exhibiting the cat and its craft."

Kevin's eyes widened, and he asked, "How did they catch the cat?

Did your research tell you that? That's what we really need to know."

"It did," Stepan said. "But it is not something we can do."

Kevin asked, "What did they do? Kill people to attract them or something?"

"Precisely," Stepan said. "They used fresh bait. Mostly low-value slaves. Then they dropped a cage on the cat when it came to feed."

Kevin sank into the chair as he said, "I guess you're right. We can't do that."

Stepan continued his description. "The cat was fed a regular diet of slaves, and the keeper was able to record what happened."

Daisy, jaw hanging slack, leaned in from the end of the couch and said, "That is barbaric. And these people called themselves civilized Christians?"

Stepan nodded. "Never underestimate people's ability to make things worse."

Daisy asked, "How could it be worse?"

Stepan said, "They did it as a show for their friends and as a threat to their enemies."

The occupants of the room sat in silence, and after looking around at his listeners, Stepan continued. "The keeper found that he could control the cat by lowering its cage into a pit, where the cat, or human form would go lifeless until the cage was lifted out again. This is how the remains of the slaves were removed. Similarly, the creature de-animates when the sun transits the horizon. It is effectively dead for those two minutes. No sign of life."

Johnston chimed in, "That sounds exactly right. I wonder if the cat knows that and finds a place to shelter during that period of vulnerability?"

Stepan made a soft grunt sound and then said, "I don't recall seeing anything about that in the translations. I suspect that since these creatures were caged, they couldn't exhibit that behavior." Johnston sat back, nodding her head as Stepan continued. "Of course, in the period of observation, the keeper was unable to feed it and never saw it eat anything, aside from the soul part. Consequently, these cats became inexpensive favorites for menageries."

Brian said, "I'm sorry. I'm still back on the showing it off part. That's one hell of a party trick."

Stepan agreed, "Yes. The Mediterranean economy of the sixteenth and seventeenth centuries was not what most of us were led to believe in school. Slavery and the slave trade were the engine of the Renaissance wealth. That is shocking enough, but the most important observations are coming next."

Brian said, "Sorry. I didn't mean to interrupt. Please continue."

Stepan coughed once and then continued. "What I never could find or theorize was how these special cats were created or reproduced. How did they spread across the world?" Looking around the room, he took in a breath and said, "Now I know, and you shall understand as well. It is that these creatures are spread through the attempt to fight them. You see, in a battle with an edged weapon, when a creature is dismembered, its flesh is sweeter than mother's milk for the offspring of natural felines. When a juvenile cat consumes the creature's severed tissue, it undergoes a conversion, becoming a new creature."

Skip's voice came in softly from the corner. "I hate to think of how they figured that out."

Stepan made a deep "Hmmm," before continuing. "I recall reading about how one of the creatures was accidentally turned loose, and the noble men of the household downed it with swords. They severed the limbs and rendered it immobile, but it could not be killed as such. Then, before the household servants could recover the body parts, they had created another brace of creatures when kittens from a nearby litter came across some flesh."

Skip let escape from under his breath, "That figures."

Stepan added, "The writer of this document recognized that when the creature returned to the cat form, it was unharmed. He also pointed out the hazard of edged weapons near the enclosure."

Brian's hand came up to his forehead and he let out a sigh. "So that's what happened."

Kevin looked at his brother and said, "The third hand."

Brian's head bobbed up and down, then said, "Yes."

Stepan said, "I think we've answered an old question."

Brian replied, "Yes, we have. When the first creature was in human form and got hit by the train, it lost some body parts. For sure a hand, maybe other parts, but then it transformed back to a complete cat."

Kevin added, "And a juvenile black-and-white cat got a taste of what was leftover from the train wreck."

Borys, still standing in the doorway, was silent until this moment. "If I may?"

Stepan said, "Go ahead."

Borys continued. "I didn't understand this mission until now, but tell us, is there a natural end to these creatures, or must they all be destroyed to finally be rid of them?"

Stepan looked at Borys, smiled, and said to the rest of the room, "Borys is a master of the 'bottom line.'" Borys smiled back at Stepan and crossed his arms on his chest. Stepan then explained, "I will get to that."

Stepan settled himself again and resumed his narration. "Now, if the creature does not feed, it can survive in cat form for a long time. The writer didn't say how long. He did write that it naturally wanted to refresh itself at least once a lunar cycle, but more often if bodies were present." Stepan took a breath and made a drinking gesture to Borys. Borys disappeared into the darkened kitchen while Stepan resumed. "The feeding process is interesting to me. I might have witnessed it many years ago, but I didn't know what I was seeing. The writer observed that the cat would take human form to feed. It would place its mouth over the nose and lips of the recently dead and inhale strongly. It then fell asleep for an hour or more and slowly transformed into the image of the new victim. The victims," he paused as Borys handed him a cup of water, "well, we know pretty well what becomes of them."

Stepan took a long pause, draining the cup of water before resuming the narration. "Now, to answer the question Borys asked. The bottom line, as it were. Yes, in theory, the cats can become extinct without someone or something hunting down each and every one of them." Borys smiled at the answer, and Kevin blew out a long breath.

Stepan continued. "The natural enemy is water. It will run away or seek shelter from rain or similar splashing. Getting wet may impair it. The translation implied it would assume a fetal position, but that is not enough to destroy it. To properly dispose of it, the creature must be submerged for a period of time, where it will eventually dissolve."

Brian spoke up, "We kind of already knew that. Is there something else that will take them out?"

Stepan smiled and said, "This last part, I think you will find reassuring. The creatures can die of old age."

Brian said, "Finally, some good news."

The gathered people in the room chuckled briefly before Stepan concluded, "After consuming the materials of enough humans, the creature becomes lethargic and immobile, basically old age. If it hasn't reverted to cat form, it dies within weeks."

Michele interrupted Stepan by tapping him on the shoulder and then asked, "How many people are we talking about?"

Stepan cocked his head and said, "Di nove."

Michele asked, "But what does that mean?"

"It means nine of something," replied a new voice in the kitchen. Every head spun toward the kitchen door and Borys, startled by the sound close behind him, spun around and took a staggered stance with his hand dropping to his waistband.

Kevin called out, "Mark! Why are you here?"

Mark stepped into the light of the doorway and said, "They

kicked me out of the hospital and suggested I go home and get some rest."

Johnston asked, "Is everything okay?"

Mark replied, "Yes, it is. Jessica is resting after delivering a healthy baby boy."

"Holy crap!" Kevin said as everybody stood up.

"Congratulations!" was heard from every voice in the room, and Mark was hugged and pulled into the center of the space.

The jostling slowly died down, and everybody returned to where they'd been seated. Johnston broke in by asking more questions. "What are the stats? Who does he look like?"

Mark replied, "Six and a half pounds, with a head of jet-black hair, and if he looks like anybody, I'd have to say he looks like his father."

Brian piped up, "Who's that?" and the room devolved into a round of groans and laughs.

Mark laughed and said, "I love you guys!"

When the noise returned to the more somber level, Kevin said, "We were getting the download from Stepan, and there is a lot to tell. I'll catch you up after I see the notes."

Mark said, "I heard some of it, and all I want to know is what happens to the old cats?"

Everybody looked at Stepan, and he said, "As a cat, it might survive up to a year, but it becomes bloated, lethargic, then crawls off to die in some hidden location."

Mark groaned, "Speaking as a person that lives with them, that could be just about any cat, but I can say it is good to know they don't live forever."

Acknowledgments

Like the previous work, this story relied heavily on the support of my wife Angela and son Brendan. I am also indebted to my group of test readers, including Janet Rupert, Jarod Gray, Eric Baker, Mike Kirk and Jan Savage. They provided helpful feedback and kept me on track. Thank you for your time and ideas.

www.ingramcontent.com/pod-product-compliance
Lightning Source LLC
LaVergne TN
LVHW091708070526
838199LV00050B/2315